Michael Shew, a former London headteacher, began writing fiction after retiring from a successful career in education. His debut novel, *Lessons in Lying* (2019), was followed by *Backlash* (2021). *Betrayal in Berlin*, a shift into historical fiction, spans the period from 1925 to 1945 in London and Berlin. Michael lives in Hackney, London, with his wife and adult daughter.

BETRAYAL IN BERLIN

MICHAEL SHEW

The
Book
Guild

First published in Great Britain in 2025 by
The Book Guild Ltd
Unit E2 Airfield Business Park,
Harrison Road, Market Harborough,
Leicestershire. LE16 7UL
Tel: 0116 2792299
www.bookguild.co.uk
Email: info@bookguild.co.uk
X: @bookguild

The manufacturer's authorised representative in the EU
for product safety is Authorised Rep Compliance Ltd,
71 Lower Baggot Street, Dublin D02 P593 Ireland (www.arccompliance.com)

This work is entirely fictitious and bears no resemblance to any persons living or dead.

Typeset in 11pt Minion Pro

Printed and bound in Great Britain by 4edge Limited

ISBN 978 1835742 358

British Library Cataloguing in Publication Data.
A catalogue record for this book is available from the British Library.

1
—

APRIL 1925, CAMDEN TOWN, LONDON

"Careful how you go there, friend, there's some dodgy characters hanging around the towpath this time of an evening."

John glanced at the barge making its way down the canal towards the Thames as it slowly drew level. Dark-orange rust on the hull, scrap metal stacked haphazardly on deck and frayed curtains hanging out of the cabin's broken window didn't inspire confidence in its seaworthiness. The deckhand grinned at him, making a throat-slitting gesture with his hand. He returned a forced smile. It was true, the Lee Navigation had a bad reputation for robberies and worse. Far worse. But he'd needed to get out of the house and think, away from the brooding presence of his father, to be certain about the decisions he had to make by the end of tomorrow. Decisions that could determine the direction his life would take. He smiled to himself as he remembered the reaction of Sam McKay, his good friend and fellow post-graduate Physicist at Imperial College, when he'd shared his doubts about taking up the offer he'd received from Friedrich Wilhelm University in Berlin.

"*Are you mad? How many opportunities for British scientists at one of Berlin's top universities do you think there are? Of course you must go, you'll be working in the same area as Niels Bohr!*"

Objectively, Sam was right. Most of his colleagues in the physics faculty would be insanely jealous if they knew.

Thinking about his fellow academics brought home another truth. He lived for his research, but from the start of his PhD he'd found it difficult to socialise and develop friendships at the university. Most of his colleagues seemed to live on a different planet, taking Daddy's sports car down to Brighton and partying all weekend in a pal's country house with a stacked wine cellar. Light years away from the rented terraced house in Kentish Town with an outside toilet that he shared with his haunted father and younger sister, May. The house hosted many sad memories; reminders of his brother, Jack, who'd been blown to pieces in the Great War and his mother who, grief-stricken by her son's death, succumbed during the influenza epidemic a year later.

Six years ago, eighteen years old and in his first year studying physics at Imperial College, he'd suddenly found himself supporting his father and sister as they struggled to deal with his mother's death. His father, a skilled toolmaker in a small light engineering company in Gospel Oak, couldn't accept the loss of his wife for a long time. Now, after six years, he was just coping, thanks mostly to the companionship he'd found in the company of workmates in the Admiral pub after work. But May, his seventeen-year-old sister, remained fragile. Could he leave her with only her father for company?

As he continued along the towpath, his mind went to the other decision he'd have to make by the end of tomorrow.

A week ago, one of the university technicians had approached him and said that there was a gentleman in the admin office asking to see him "*on a matter of some importance.*" Intrigued, he'd gone to the office where an immaculately dressed man in his early forties was waiting. Judging by the way he held himself, John guessed he was either in, or had been in the army, and immediately felt intimidated. The man introduced himself simply as a friend of the Dean and suggested they went for a cup of tea *"in a little place I know nearby"* and proceeded to walk out. As he'd got to the door, he'd turned around and looked at John, who hadn't moved.

"Are you coming, Mr Samson? I rather think you should."

John had followed him out of the door, annoyed with himself for succumbing to the man's presumption.

As they'd sat at a discreet table in the 'little place' – it was clearly a gentlemen's club – John wondered if this was really happening, and why. The man had introduced himself immediately they'd sat down.

"My name is Lawlor. I must apologise for my abrupt behaviour in the office back there. I only hope that when you hear what I'm about to say that you'll see that we couldn't have this conversation in public. I'm aware that you've been offered a postdoctorate position at Friedrich Wilhelm University in Berlin to research applications of the photoelectric effect."

Taken aback that Lawlor knew this – it hadn't been announced – John began to interrupt, but Lawlor waved him away and carried on.

"My department insisted on screening the shortlist of applications that were made to Friedrich Wilhelm and other top German universities. I can see you're surprised, but please remember that it's less than seven years since we were at war with Germany. Her Majesty's Government is very keen to be kept informed about the latest breakthroughs in physics research being made by German scientists. Some of their physicists are pre-eminent in their fields, as I'm sure you know. Ever since Einstein's paper in 1905 proposing the equivalence between mass and energy, research into subatomic particles has taken off."

Lawlor was looking pleased with himself, clearly thinking that John would be impressed.

"We'd like you to keep a lookout and let us know about any research in your area that the Germans are keeping under wraps."

Hardly believing what he'd just heard, this time John interrupted Lawlor before he could carry on.

"If I understand you correctly, you're telling me that I got this offer from Friedrich Wilhelm because I was considered to be the most potentially useful informant, not because of the quality of my research. If my department is aware of this and sanctioned it behind my back, that's a disgraceful way to treat one of their postdocs."

"Please calm down until you've heard all that I've got to say. My Service has been looking out for intelligent young men with spotless credentials who are about to take up legitimate positions in Berlin. People like yourself; a young research scientist without a history of political involvement which might arouse suspicion. Imperial only agreed to go along with this on the cast-iron assurance that you must be allowed to continue with your research unimpeded.

"We're not asking you to become a spy; you've no experience in espionage and would probably be spotted immediately, which would be counterproductive. Essentially, it's about keeping your ears and eyes open and asking questions. Not only at the university, but socialising with your fellow scientists. Don't be too obvious, and you'll be fine. I'm going to be frank with you. Many of us believe that some Generals in the Wehrmacht – that's the German Army – who've never accepted defeat are determined that Germany rearms. If German scientists are on the verge of discovering something big, we need to know. You'd be playing a small but significant role in helping your country prepare. What do you think?"

John had been listening with rising incredulity.

"Before I reply, you've produced no proof of who you are or represent. You could be anybody; how do I know you haven't just walked in off the street."

"Well done, you've passed the first test. Here's a letter from the Chiefs of Staff Committee introducing me as Major Lawlor. You may recognise some of the names of the Committee at the top of the page. The phone number for the Clerk to the Committee is underneath that. I suggest you memorise it and contact him if you're interested in taking this further."

John glanced over the letter for appearances sake. He was still trying to comprehend the implications of what he'd been told. If true, he was being asked to take on a role that could compromise his position at the university and divert him from the thing that he most cared about – making a scientific breakthrough that got him noticed. And for what purpose? Judging by his conversations so far with Berlin academics, the Weimar Republic was coming out of the inflationary crisis and doing okay. There was no evidence of an imminent army coup.

But he was excited by the idea. If he went ahead, he'd make crystal clear that his research would come first; any intelligence gathering would come a distant second. Before that, he needed to confront the major about the apparent carelessness with his background check. He memorised the phone number, looked up and said,

"I would have more confidence in your organisation if they hadn't made such a basic error in checking me out. You say I've got impeccable credentials, but I've been a member of the Labour Party for the last three years, and campaigned for them at the 1924 election. I'm not politically neutral."

"My dear chap, we're not talking about the dear old Labour Party here. Of course we know about your membership and occasional forays leafletting on the streets. Until recently, your Party leader was the head of a minority government. One of the establishment, almost one of us."

"What if I can't agree to do this?"

Lawlor looked at him.

"Then you'll take up the position at Friedrich Wilhelm as if this conversation had never taken place. The offer of a place came through the university and it obviously wasn't conditional on the government supporting your application. But I very much hope you consider this carefully before turning down the opportunity to serve your country. So many young men just two years older than you did that and paid the ultimate price, like your brother. Please take time to think about what I've said for a day or two. If you're willing to go ahead, I'll arrange for you to meet a chap in the British Embassy in Berlin. Here's my card."

"If I do decide to go ahead, it must be on the understanding that my research will always come first. If I feel that spending time on this is affecting my work adversely, I'll have to stop. That's fair, surely?"

"If you're interested, give this chap a ring by Friday. He'll answer all your questions."

That conversation had taken place six days ago. Friday was tomorrow.

He left the canal, took the footbridge over the railway tracks carrying the LMS express trains to the North, walked past the Somers Town Goods Yard then decided to stop for a pint in the Trafalgar. It was surprisingly quiet – the railway workers had been on strike and money was scarce – and as he sat alone at his regular corner table, he made his decision. He'd speak to his father after tea tonight and confirm that he was going to Berlin; he couldn't let this opportunity at Friedrich Wilhelm slip through his fingers. He'd call the Major's 'chap' tomorrow.

"Dad, I understand you'd rather I didn't take up this post and I realise there are consequences for you and May. I'm being selfish, I know. But I'll be back in England soon enough, and working alongside brilliant physicists like Niels Bohr is an amazing opportunity. It could change my life, but I don't want to go ahead without your blessing."

His father looked at him, smiling ruefully.

"You've been a wonderful support to me and May since your mum died. I don't want to stand in your way, John, but I'm worried. It's not just the anti-German feeling here in England, though I understand where that's coming from. Haven't you been reading about the political unrest that's been going on over there? Just when it seems the German Government have steadied things, we start hearing about thugs roaming the streets and communists fighting with right-wing mobs. As an Englishman, surely you'll be a target?"

"If I'm honest, I have been concerned about the level of violence on the streets between some of the opposing political parties. They seem to take things to another level compared to Britain, so I asked some academics at Friedrich Wilhelm University if I'm likely to encounter hostility as an Englishman; they've reassured me I won't. They said, '*We Germans are too busy fighting each other to worry about the English!*' There's something else, too. When I speak with them, I don't pick up the snobbery and disdain towards working-class people that I've experienced at Imperial. Berlin could be a more welcoming environment for a bloke like me than Imperial has been; some of my fellow students talk openly about breaking any future strikes."

"You've got a point, son, right enough. After the war, I was hoping we'd see a change in the way that the upper classes in England assume they had a God-given right to keep their land, wealth and power forever. How gullible could I be? The divisions are just as wide as before, and the ruling class is cock-a-hoop.

"You should go, John. I'm so proud of what you've achieved, and May has told me that she'll never forgive me if I try to stop you!"

The following morning, John walked half a mile to one of the new public phone boxes, dialled the number on the card in his pocket and arranged to meet Captain Grey in three days' time. He had an opportunity to use his last six years of scientific research to benefit his country; given his brother's sacrifice, it was the least he should do.

2

AUGUST 1925, THE ENGLISH CHANNEL

Delays in acquiring one of the recently introduced British passports had almost ended his new job before it started, as one barrier after another was put in front of him. Feelings from the war were still running high with some clerks at the Passport Office, many of whom appeared to be disabled war veterans. Just as he'd decided to throw in the towel, the obstacles in his path had melted away one after another; visa approved, accommodation in Berlin sorted, passport ready to collect. He'd realised that high-ups in the Foreign Office had read the Riot Act to the jobsworths in Petty France as soon as they'd heard from Major Lawlor that their little scheme was about to collapse.

Because of all the last-minute problems, he'd deliberately reined in his excitement at the incredible opportunities that the next two years might bring. Now, as it sunk in that he was going to spend the next two years as a research physicist at one of Europe's top universities, he could finally feel elated as he anticipated the future.

He even mastered some basic German words and phrases.

John stood lost in thought at the guard rail of the Dover to Oostende ferry, looking back at the stained white cliffs slowly receding in the ship's wake. He'd become increasingly aware about the challenges he'd be facing in the next two years as he'd prepared for his journey over the past week. Several academic colleagues had tried to dissuade him. No doubt some of that was jealousy, but the strength of feeling against *'helping the Hun to get ahead of us in science'* was real enough.

He made his way down to the bar, getting the feel of the slow roll of the ship beneath him, then settled into an armchair in a quiet area with a double malt whisky. Feeling Helen's letter in his jacket pocket, he took it out. He'd almost thrown it away when he'd discovered it at the back of his desk drawer two days ago, then changed his mind.

Dearest John,

Malcolm and I got married yesterday in a quiet ceremony at a little church in Gerrards Cross. I'm very happy and looking forward to our future together, but I want you to know that those months we were together were my happiest times since I lost Robert and they helped me realise I could fall in love again. I will never forget you. You're a special man, and I wish you the happiness that you so deserve.

All my love, Helen

A year ago, two years after starting his PhD, he'd begun a relationship with a woman in her late twenties who'd worked as the Dean's personal assistant. Like many young women her age, she'd lost her husband during the war and when it was over, at the age of twenty-four, she'd found that she had to work to live.

She had shoulder-length chestnut hair, piercing hazel eyes and a smile for John whenever he visited the Dean's office. One afternoon, when there was no one else around, she'd asked for his help deciphering the text in a physics paper she was typing up.

Unravelling badly written scientific papers for her became a habit and on a warm July evening he'd taken the plunge and asked her out for a drink. They'd walked up Exhibition Road, past the Albert Hall to the Queen's Arms, one of an increasing number of pubs that had started to allow women drinkers. Relaxed in each other's company, they both sensed that the other wanted more than friendship but were equally unsure of making the first move. He'd only had two girlfriends and remained a virgin; Helen had fended off unwanted advances from much older, dubious men and hadn't had a relationship since her husband died.

John had initially lacked the confidence to take the initiative, but after their third visit to the Queen's Arms, he'd kissed her as they'd said goodbye outside South Kensington Tube station. She'd enjoyed a passionate relationship with her husband when he was on leave and now missed that sexual intimacy, like many other young women who'd lost husbands in the war. After three weeks of increasingly ardent kisses, she'd turned to him one evening as they'd left the college and said,

"Would you like to come back to my flat instead of going to the pub this evening? I've got some sherry, or gin if you'd prefer that?"

He was caught off guard by the unambiguous, carnal intention behind her question and hesitated. She'd mistaken this for disinclination.

"I'm sorry if I misread things, I thought you'd want to. I hope I haven't embarrassed you."

"Of course not, Helen! I would love to come back to your flat for a sherry."

She'd taken the lead the first time. Feeling conscious of her creaking iron bed as they'd begun to move, she'd calmed his apprehension.

"Don't worry, John, there's no one underneath. Except me!"

11

The second time, clutching him fiercely against her, she'd shed bittersweet tears for the past. And glimpsed, finally, what might be possible in the future.

"Is everything okay, Helen?"

"Yes, that was lovely. You're a really sensitive man, you know."

They'd carried on seeing each other for several months, and he'd sometimes stay the night, enthusiastically taking Helen's lead on what worked for her. They made each other happy; looking back he couldn't remember them ever having a serious argument. But the differences in their situations eventually became too big to ignore.

He was approaching the end of his PhD and looking for an academic post, wherever he could find one. She was nearly twenty-nine, and wanted to marry a man who was ready to start a family. They both understood that if such a person came into her life, she would have to grasp the opportunity, even though ending their affair would break their hearts.

So it wasn't a surprise, just horribly sad, when she'd taken him out to lunch on a mild but overcast day at the end of October, held his hand as she'd looked at him across the table with moistening eyes and told him that she'd met a caring man in his thirties, a widower, no children, with a secure job in the Ministry of Public Works. He was going to ask her to marry him, and she wanted to say yes.

They'd gone back to her flat, made love for the last time on her creaking bed and said goodbye.

As he sat in the bar thinking about what might have been, his thoughts turned to the implications of his new role as an informal spy for His Majesty's Secret Service. Captain Grey had been subtly and surprisingly persuasive, and once he'd agreed to John's condition that the assignment would be reviewed after six months, the deal was done. He could stop after that if he wanted to.

"You won't have to do anything at first. Your contact at the British Embassy will be in touch after a couple of weeks."

3

—

AUGUST 1925, BERLIN

Ilse Lipsky left the family flat in Prenzlauer Berg feeling elated, skipping along the pavement. This morning she'd received a letter confirming that she'd got the job of production assistant at the Funkstade Berlin radio station that she'd applied for a month ago. She knew her father would try to persuade her not to take it, but she was twenty-four, and he couldn't stop her this time.

She'd intended to go to university when she left her gymnasium grammar school in 1920, but her father had coerced her into taking a dreary job as a part-time clerk in a law practice near the family flat.

"I know you've set your heart on taking a degree in English, Ilse, but with your mother's nerves the way they are at the moment, she won't be able to cope with you and your twin sister on her own. You'll have to stay in Berlin and support the family."

That was five years ago, and the twins were now fourteen. Enough was enough. When she'd seen the advert for a production assistant at the radio station two months ago – specifically asking for applicants who could speak good English, type fast and cope with a frenzied working environment – she'd told her father she was applying and resisted all his cajoling to change her mind.

Intending to walk on past the bakery in Oderburger Strasse as usual, today she stopped. *Stuff the anti-Semites,* she thought, *I'm not going to give them the satisfaction of intimidating me. Not today, not again.* The bell clanged as she pushed the door open, causing the women in the queue at the counter to turn around. She recognised most of them, neighbours from her block of flats. The looks on their faces ranged from friendly recognition to openly hostile. Several immediately turned around to look at the baker and his wife behind the counter, trying to judge their reaction.

She smiled politely and took her place in the queue, behind a middle-aged woman dressed in black. *So you've taken a stand and walked into one of the openly anti-Jewish shops in Prenzlauer. Don't congratulate yourself yet; what are you going to do if they refuse to serve you?*

"What do you want, fräulein?"

"Two rye-wheat loaves and two slices of apple strudel, bitte."

I suppose this is progress, Ilse thought, as the scowling woman grudgingly wrapped her bread. But she was premature.

"Sorry, fräulein, there's no apple strudel left."

"But I can see two slices on the middle shelf."

"I'm afraid they're reserved for our regular customers."

"I look forward to becoming one, then."

The chaotic and violent years that followed the first-ever elections for a German National Assembly in 1919 – a communist uprising, right-wing assassinations, an army putsch, soaring inflation – had been a precarious and uncertain time for all Germans. For Ilse's family, as German Jews, it was even worse. After the surrender of the army in 1918, nationalists immediately started looking for scapegoats to explain their country's defeat. The big lie that fifth columnists and Jews had conspired to bring about defeat spread rapidly, and led to a rise in anti-Semitism. Some shops refused to serve Jews, including the bakers, and some Jewish businesses were boycotted.

It made Ilse furious rather than frightened. Her father had joined the army and fought throughout the war, alongside many other Jews. *He's given more to this country than many others who've turned against us, including the baker and his wife. He's even received insulting comments from some of his pupils.*

That hostility had begun to diminish when the country's runaway inflation had been brought under control last year, but resentment against the huge reparations and loss of the Rhineland imposed on Germany after the war was still causing bitterness across all classes in society. Adolf Hitler's National Socialists were starting to find a small, receptive audience.

Ilse paid for her bread and left. This was a good day and she was determined not to let people like the baker's wife get to her. She'd got a new job, and the first thing she was going to do this morning was to tell Herr Gunter she was giving in her notice. She'd already met people who worked at the radio station, and they were far more tolerant, cheerful and broad-minded than the baker and his wife.

But there was a darker reason she couldn't wait to leave Gunter and Sons. Just over a year ago, one of the junior partners in the law practice had asked her out for coffee and cake at lunchtime. That was followed by invitations to the theatre and dinners at expensive restaurants. She was flattered; he was good-looking, ten years older and paid her compliments with sufficient sincerity to be believable. But she'd made it clear that she had no intention of having an intimate relationship with him.

"I'm only twenty-three, Leopold. I just want us to be friends; one day I hope to fall in love and I think we both know that's not going to happen with us. I don't wish to cause offence."

His response was one of exemplary reassurance:

"You sweet girl, I understand completely, I don't see us in

that way either. I enjoy being with you very much; you make me laugh, bring light into my dreary existence and don't seem to mind listening to my boring anecdotes. I also must admit that being seen with an attractive young woman boosts my ego."

At the end of their next dinner date at a classy hotel a week later, he'd added a sleeping draught to her wine, half carried her to his previously booked hotel room, tossed her on the bed and assaulted her. When she'd come to alone the following morning, groggy and in pain, the bloody sheets were all the evidence she'd needed to realise he'd raped her after she'd passed out. She'd sobbed uncontrollably for almost half an hour, initially from shame but then with growing fury. Once she'd got herself under control, the tears slowly stopped. *I trusted him, how could he defile me? I thought he was a friend. I'll never trust a man again.*

She'd had a bath, taken two aspirin and then ordered coffee and breakfast to the room. Sitting at the desk trying to eat her eggs and sausage, she'd begun to plan her retribution. There was no point informing the police; he was a junior partner in the practice and it would be her word against his. But before she'd checked out of the hotel she'd insisted on paying for the soiled sheets, settling the bill for breakfast, getting receipts for both payments and a copy of the invoice for the room and dinner.

When she'd got back to her parents' house at 10am, her father had angrily confronted her.

"Your mother and I were up most of the night worrying what had happened to you, imagining the worst. You could have let us know you'd be out all night, at the very least." She managed to calm him down by explaining that she'd run into some of her old friends from the gymnasium. One of them was now working in a nightclub that had just opened in Friedrichstrasse and got them in. They'd all had too much to drink, gone back to her friend's flat and passed out, drunk. She didn't have a telephone so she couldn't ring them but she'd got back as soon as she could and was very sorry she'd caused them so much worry. Her father had wanted to believe it, but when they were alone her mother had taken her to one side.

"I'm not fooled for one minute, Ilse. You're looking pale and are clearly in pain. I know your period isn't due, so what's wrong?"

"You've got to swear you won't tell Father."

"I can't promise, Ilse. He's my husband."

"If you do, I'll leave home. I mean it." Ilse paused, then carried on.

"I think you know I'd become friendly with one of the lawyers at work. We'd go out for a coffee at lunchtimes, to the theatre occasionally, that's all. Yesterday evening he took me out to dinner. We shared a bottle of wine between us, no more than I've had before and always stayed completely sober. This time, I started to feel really drowsy before we'd even finished the main course. I remember him taking me up to a hotel room, then nothing else until I woke up this morning alone, feeling drowsy, bleeding and very sore.

Ilse paused, bit her lip and carried on.

"I realised that he'd forced himself on me when I was unconscious. Clearly, he'd put a sleeping draught in my wine. He raped me, Mama."

Her mother sat looking at her daughter as her eyes filled with tears. She began to say something, then stopped herself and put her arms around her.

"Go to the bathroom now and use my douche to wash that bastard's filth out of you. When you come back, we'll think about what to do. Don't worry, I'm not going to tell your father. Some things he doesn't need to know, and it would only make this worse if we told him. But this man should pay for what he's done to you."

When she'd returned, they'd sat talking for over an hour about how to deal with her rapist when she went back to work. Ilse didn't share her plan with her mother – she knew she wouldn't approve.

Working in the same office as him for the last twelve months had led to extended periods of self-doubt. *Was I complicit in some way?* Leopold had taken a callous delight in making suggestive comments and innuendos about that night, leading to rumours about her sexual experience spreading around the office. It was awful, but in a way it helped her overcome the self-doubt; his behaviour proved what a vile human being he was. The thought that this was her last day felt liberating. Before she left at the end of the day, she went to Herr Gunter, told him of Leopold's assault and presented him with the receipts and invoice she'd gathered from the hotel.

"I realise it's my word against his, and when you speak to him he will probably insist that it was consensual. But I didn't want to leave without telling you what he did to me. He's a danger to women and I felt you should know. Thank you for the kindness you've shown me over the last few years."

4
—
MEETING THE SPIES

19th September 1925

Dear May,

I'm sorry not to have written sooner, but life has been hectic since I left England two weeks ago. The journey was interesting and uneventful, apart from one fellow traveller. A calm Channel crossing, then a train to Paris and the sleeper train to Berlin. I'd been looking forward to travelling on the sleeper, but unfortunately I shared my compartment with a middle-aged Austrian who insisted on smoking, then complained when I opened the window. We had a heated argument, as he wouldn't compromise. I'm pleased to say that every German I've met has been quite the opposite – well-mannered, friendly and helpful.

I'm staying in a cosy little flat reserved for postdoctorate fellows, which will be mine for as long as I stay. It's small, but the rent is very low, so that suits me. There's a landlady, Frau Hessler, who seems a good sort and doesn't bother us. It's about two kilometres to my laboratory in the university (about a mile and a quarter, but I'm trying to get used to the metric distances here). My physics laboratory is impressive – at least as well equipped as Imperial College. I share the space with three other postdocs. They're all very friendly, and I don't think the language barrier is going to be a problem. They've agreed to speak English when talking to me, but my German is improving all the time and they're happy for me to try my German on them. They may change their minds when they hear more of it!

Berlin seems to be much livelier than London, which has surprised me. There are lots of bars, clubs and theatres, crowded with young people determined to enjoy themselves. Many young women have adopted the 'modern look' with simple dresses that barely come down to their knees, while many men dress well too, in casual suits. I feel very dowdy in my heavy woollen suit! I'm really looking forward to exploring the city when I've settled in at the university; two of my fellow scientists are taking me on a tour of Berlin nightlife in a few days. They seem sensible blokes, so you don't have to worry, we won't be getting drunk. Not much, anyway!

Please pass this letter on to Dad. I miss you and think about you both a lot. I would love to get a letter from you and hear your news.

All my love,

John

As he walked the two kilometres from his flat to the university, John idly wondered whether there'd be a letter from the British Embassy waiting for him. Lawlor had undertaken to give the Embassy John's contact address and said that his contact there would get in touch within the first two weeks of his arrival. He'd arrived in Berlin nearly three weeks ago, and there'd been no word so far.

Everything about his new life in Berlin reinforced his feeling that moving here had been the right decision; the stimulating, open discussions he was already having with his fellow physicists, his well-equipped experimental laboratory, the welcome party that Doctor Grosserman, his Head of Faculty, organised for him and his comfortable flat in a lively part of the city. He'd begun to wonder whether the powers that be had poured cold water on Major Lawlor's idea, leaving him to concentrate on his research. It wasn't as if his work on photon scattering would leave him with time to spare.

Such thoughts evaporated when he was handed a letter from the Embassy as he passed reception on the way to the physics faculty. He walked quickly to his desk and opened it.

> Dear Mr Samson,
> I understand from an old colleague whom you met in London that you would be interested in establishing a joint liaison group with scientists in the Weimar Republic.
> Can you please come to the Embassy at 09:00 on Monday 21st September? I will explain exactly what we're looking for and what's involved. Please ring the Embassy on Berlin 847655 and ask for me if you cannot make the appointment.
> Sincerely,
> Mark Chastain

Reading the letter, which deliberately obscured the real purpose of the meeting, John felt a sense of disquiet. He'd told himself that what he was doing was different – it was about Britain's security – but he couldn't help but feel guilty towards those whose research he was intending to 'steal'.

He put the letter back in its envelope and filed it in the document tray on his desk.

Mark Chastain was a breath of fresh air after the arrogant superiority of Major Lawlor when he met him two days later. John had been waiting outside Chastain's office for over ten minutes when a short, slightly overweight man in his late forties, with greying, straggly hair and crumpled shirt, came hurrying along the corridor.

"So sorry to keep you waiting, John, I had to brief the first officer about the latest developments at the Reichstag. Parliamentary democracy in Germany is a million miles away from ours. Many political parties, from the far left to the far right, but no Party with a majority, so there's always a coalition. The coalition partners are always finding ways to disagree among themselves. Come in and sit down, please.

"Tea or coffee before we start."

"Coffee, please, Mark."

"Right choice. The coffee is excellent in Germany. The less said about their tea the better. So, how have your first few weeks in Berlin been? Have you settled in?"

John was warming to Mark Chastain. He seemed almost a regular human being after Lawlor.

"I couldn't have wished for a better start, Mark. Everyone in my lab seems friendly, my boss has given me a very clear steer on my line of research, I've got a comfortable flat twenty minutes from the university and Berlin feels like an exciting place to be for the next two years. But I'm keen to know more about this role I've agreed to. What exactly am I? Major Lawlor rather dodged that question, and I'm hoping you're going to enlighten me."

Mark looked at him quizzically.

"As you'll be reporting to me and not Major Lawlor, it doesn't really matter what he told you. I'll explain the role as I see it, John.

"It's a sobering thought that almost every government in the world spies on its own citizens. In some countries, it may just be a loose network of informants who are paid by the police to report on their neighbours. The powerful countries in the world – all of the European ones, certainly – go much further than that. Britain set up MI5 and MI6 before the First World War; roughly speaking, MI5's role is to identify and stop spies from other countries spying on us, while our agents in MI6 spy on other countries. MI5 was very successful in helping to capture a number of German spies during the war. Many agents in MI6 are based in foreign embassies, with cover roles. Formally, I'm a diplomat here at the Embassy; in reality, I oversee a number of German citizens with bona fide jobs who report back to me. We're all spies."

Every time Mark mentioned spies and spying, John became increasingly concerned.

"No one has implied before that I would be doing anything that could be called spying. To be honest, Mark, I'm now a little concerned."

Mark hesitated. Had Lawlor misled Samson about his role? Now was the time to find out – there was no point carrying on otherwise.

"I'm sorry you're feeling that, hopefully I can clear things up. I assume it's normal for scientists to read and interrogate the research of others in their area?"

John nodded, and he carried on.

"On top of doing that, we're asking you to be vigilant about new research outside your area as well. Developments with possible military applications that the German Government might wish to keep secret. I understand your area of research concerns the interactions between atomic particles and electromagnetic radiation, so it would mean being inquisitive about developments outside of that area."

"What if I find something that I think you'd be interested in?"

"Bring it to me before you do too much ferreting around. We'll discuss it, and if I think we need to know more, then find out as much as you can. That's why we need a research scientist, and can't just rely on one of us – you'll have a feel for what the applications could be. You won't be assuming a false identity or breaking into places you have no right to go. Keep your wits about you and back off if you sense you're arousing suspicion."

John pondered this new information. Rationally, Mark Chastain wasn't telling him anything he didn't already know. But he'd always thought of himself as someone with a strong moral code, a sense of what's right and wrong. If *he* made a breakthrough in future then found out that someone had managed to steal and publish it, he would be incandescent. Accusations of plagiarising others' research could end his career before it had begun. But Lawlor had been right about one thing; many young men only months older than him at grammar school went to the front and never came back. In an odd way, he felt he owed it to their memory to even things up a little.

He became aware that Mark had begun speaking again.

"There's little risk involved, providing that you don't start looking in places you've no right to be. If in doubt, ask me. Compared to the risks that some of us in the Service take when on active duty, it's nothing."

"Thank you for being straight with me, Mark."

"Carry on as normal at Friedrich Wilhelm; it's important that you have the chance to establish yourself with your new colleagues and get to know Berlin in the next few weeks. I'll be in touch again before Christmas; until then, keep your eyes and ears open and contact me here if you do see anything of interest to us. Until then, goodbye and good luck."

***

"Fräulein, where's the script for the six o'clock news bulletin that I asked for? We're fifteen minutes from broadcast."

"I'm on the last sentence of the final item, Herr Weiss. You'll have it in one minute."

"It takes you a minute to type a sentence?"

"No, but I want to check it first."

"Don't bother with that, girl, just bring it over."

"Okay, Herr Weiss, but don't blame me for any typos."

Weiss looked at her disapprovingly. *Shit, have I crossed a line?*

God, I hope not; we've been getting on well so far. All the same, he is my boss, I need to be careful with my quips.

"My apologies. I'll bring it over now, Herr Weiss."

Crossing the studio to give him the bulletin, she noticed his faint smile and relaxed. The environment at the station couldn't be more different than her previous experience. There was a hierarchy between the producers, editors, newsreaders, technicians and production assistants like her, but it existed within an office culture that encouraged the junior staff to speak up and contribute their ideas. Everyone's role was respected, as long as they did their job. She felt liberated after the humourless culture in the law practice.

"Thank you, Ilse."

He seemed to hesitate, think about something for a moment, then said,

"Pull up a chair, please. Something's come up I think you may be interested in."

Intrigued, she moved one of his modern Bauhaus chairs – too expensive to be used anywhere else in the station – over to his desk.

"We've been asked by the head of the physics department at Friedrich Wilhelm University if a group of their young research physicists could visit the station when we're broadcasting to see first hand how discoveries in their area are being applied in radio technology. Something to do with thermionic emission. Obviously they'd like us to be on air to create a sense of drama, so I can't spare many people to take care of them. I was hoping you might like to liaise with them, make the arrangements and organise the visit. What do you think?"

"I'd be delighted, Herr Weiss, that sounds interesting. But won't they want to ask lots of scientific questions? I could get out my old physics textbook and revise, but I think Einstein has moved things on a bit since then!"

He smiled at the joke.

"I'll free up Fritz for twenty minutes at the end of their

visit to answer any questions they may have, but you're pretty knowledgeable now about the process of putting a radio broadcast together and I'm sure they'll be hanging on your every word when you take them through that."

His mouth turned up to show he wasn't teasing her.

"In fact, I've been meaning to tell you that everyone here has been saying how well you've settled in. And I agree. How long have you been with us?"

Feeling her face grow warm as she blushed, she said, "Two months. I'm really enjoying the work, Herr Weiss. Everyone has been friendly and helpful, even when I've slipped up. Not that I'll make any mistakes with this visit!"

He handed her a small file.

"I know you won't. Here's the information you'll need to set things up. Please make this a priority, Ilse."

5
—

OCTOBER 1925

"Where are we, Karl? There's nothing like this place in London. There are pubs where men go to drink, occasionally with their wives or girlfriends. Then there are dance halls, but the atmosphere is nothing like this. They're more sedate, although older folk are getting agitated about the immoral goings on between male and female dancers these days. They'd have a heart attack if they saw this."

He laughed at the thought of the reaction of the regulars back in the Admiral if they ever came in here. He was sitting at a small table far away from the stage and the bar, which was the only one available by the time Karl had managed to persuade him to leave the lab and go out for a beer. John had guarded the table while Karl got their drinks, repeatedly refusing requests to join the frenetic dancing.

"This is cabaret, John. There are now many clubs like this in Berlin, and what you see wouldn't be considered out of place in any of them. I didn't think you'd be so easily shocked. You're not prudish, are you?"

John looked around. The scantily costumed dancers on the stage were cavorting and twisting their bodies into increasingly suggestive positions; the people on the dance floor seemed to be forever changing partners, or not bothering to partner anyone in particular, simply gyrating against anyone who took their eye. At a table in a corner nearby a man and woman were unashamedly pushing their hands inside each other's clothing. *Maybe I am a prude, as far as Berlin goes.*

"I didn't think I was prudish until I came here. What was the compère's last act about? My German isn't good enough to understand all of it, but I gathered it was political from the parts I did understand."

"You're right, John, well done – your German's really improving. Welcome to Berlin in 1925. The old ways of doing things are being constantly challenged in the arts, science, and politics – even the way people are expected to behave in public – as you can see from looking around."

"As a physicist, it's inspiring to be around at such a revolutionary time. Einstein, Heisenberg, Schrödinger – quantum mechanics has turned Newtonian physics on its head. But I'd like to know more about German politics. I'd call myself a socialist, a member of the British Labour Party. But the socialists here seem more radical than the Labour Party, and you've got the Communist Party to the left of them. We haven't got any communist Members of Parliament, and I'd be surprised if there ever will be. And what about the National Socialist Party, who are actually on the extreme right, which sounds like a contradiction to me. Has democracy led to more extremist politics?"

"I'm not that interested in politics, John, I like to leave that to the politicians. Getting to grips with the implications of Schrödinger's wave equation is all my brain can deal with. But you're right to say that politics has become more radical and divisive since Germany became a democracy in 1919."

"*Prost.*"

John stood up to go to the bar to refill their glasses, but before he'd taken a step two women came up to their table and told them they had to dance. When it was clear John hadn't understood, Karl explained that he was English and didn't speak much German. He'd just begun to translate when he was interrupted by one of the women.

"I said you two guys must dance," said the taller of the two women in passable English, pulling him onto the dance floor as her friend dragged Karl along behind.

Up to this point, the only dances John had attended were the end-of-year balls at Imperial College. Because of the war, there was a lack of good-looking single men of his age with their limbs and faces intact. Much to his surprise, he'd found himself in demand from middle-class young women who wanted the chance to go to a ball and potentially meet someone of their own class. There was no pretence about the nature of the arrangement on either side – the girls were even prepared to go Dutch on the tickets.

He gradually relaxed as Eva led him onto the heaving, sweating dance floor, losing the apprehension that had gripped him since she'd accosted him. He grinned at Eva vigorously swinging her arms up and down and her hips from side to side. Trying to mirror the movement of her body as best he could, he noticed how her short, loose-fitting dress exposed several inches of thigh and revealed the outline of her breasts under the thin fabric. Catching him looking, she burst out laughing.

He lost track of time and Karl. Suddenly, Eva stopped gyrating, draped her arms around his neck and shouted in his ear, "I need a rest, John, and if you're offering, I would love a martini as well. You should try one, and don't let the barman cheat you as you're English. Give him ten marks maximum."

One of the confident, liberated Berlin women I've heard about, he thought, as he grabbed his jacket from the back of the chair and went to the bar.

He was half expecting to see Eva on the floor again with a new partner when he returned, but she was sat at their table, smiling as he weaved his way back through the dancers.

"Thank you. Here's to improving Anglo-German relations."

She smiled and raised the martini glass to her lips; as she looked at him over the rim without taking her eyes off of his, he wondered if they'd sleep together tonight.

"So what brings you to Germany, John?"

He gave Eva an edited version of the last six months of his life, trying to make it as light as possible. As he finished, he asked her where she'd learnt to speak such good English.

"We have to learn English at school, and I also took it as part of my degree. I'm a kindergarten teacher, and I enjoy teaching the children basic English. I hope to travel to England in the next year or so, my mother's got family in Manchester. What other places should I visit?"

"London, definitely, then perhaps Oxford, or a seaside resort, and some beautiful countryside like the Peak District."

John paused, aware that he'd lost Eva's attention.

She finished her cocktail, looked at him and said, "I think I'd like to leave now, and go somewhere more comfortable."

There was little chance of mistaking her double meaning. As they walked into the surprisingly chilly air outside, they stopped, turned towards each other and kissed. The last time he'd kissed a woman, he was saying goodbye to Helen over six months ago, and the sensation of their lips pressing together immediately aroused him. As they broke away, Eva said, "We'll have to go back to your place, as my landlord is a monster, but I need to drop by my flat on the way. I hope you don't live too far."

"It's just fifteen minutes' walk from here, in Rosenthaler Strasse. Luckily, my landlady doesn't mind visitors, and everyone minds their own business. But why do you need to go to your place first?"

"A gentleman should know not to ask such things, John. Use

your scientific brain to work it out. It's on the way, so just be patient."

Later, listening to Eva breathing deeply beside him, he contrasted the thrilling, spontaneous sex of the last hour to his only previous experience. The second they'd walked into his room, she'd kissed him, tugged off his coat and jacket and pulled him onto the bed. It had undoubtedly been exciting, yet not as fulfilling as making love with Helen; he wondered if it was possible to have both.

Eva had gone when he woke in the morning, and he immediately noticed that his wallet was no longer on his desk; luckily, his passport was still in the drawer. *I was obviously set up from the minute she approached us. Was everything we talked about last night a fiction? Being a teacher, travelling to England to see her mum? Maybe she was unemployed,, desperate for money.* He felt let down rather than angry. There was only fifty marks in his wallet as he'd spent the rest last night in the cabaret, and he'd get by for the rest of this month.

He had a bath, dressed and decided to go into the lab, even though it was Saturday. His initial motivation to bury himself in his research had cooled somewhat since he arrived, and he needed to rekindle that earlier passion. In particular, he had to satisfy his concerns that the work of the American physicist Arthur Compton didn't invalidate any of his work.

As he walked into the physics faculty, he saw his Head of Department about to leave.

"Good morning, John, I'm glad I caught you. I've asked an old friend who's Head of Programmes at the Funkstade Berlin radio station if a group of our researchers could visit it and look at the application of our work to theirs. He's given me the name of someone at the station who'll be responsible for making the arrangements. I'd like you to contact her and agree a date. Her name is Ilse Lipsky. I'll give you her number on Monday."

John hid his irritation. Being robbed by someone he'd trusted had unsettled him, and now his Head of Department had landed him with an additional time-consuming task that could further disrupt his research. He'd like to tell his boss on Monday that he couldn't take it on, but it wouldn't look good to be saying 'no' to his Head of Department so soon after arriving. *If only I hadn't gone drinking with Karl last night, I wouldn't have been robbed and I may not have ended up bumping into him today.*

John spent the rest of the day reading and re-reading Compton's paper on *'the change in wavelength of X-rays following collisions with electrons'*, but he was finding it difficult to concentrate and fully grasp Compton's argument.

He went to bed that night feeling somewhat despondent.

Two days later, he grudgingly rang Ilse Lipsky's number.

"Ilse, there's a scientist on the phone from Friedrich Wilhelm University asking to speak to you. He says you will know what it's about."

"Thanks, Fritz, I'm coming."

"Hello. This is Ilse Lipsky."

"Hello, I'm John Samson. I understand you and I are to discuss arrangements for some of our scientists to visit Funkstade Berlin during a broadcast."

As she listened, Ilse quickly realised that her English was far better than his German. But how to tell him without causing offence?

"Hello, Herr Samson. I was expecting your call. We can speak English if you'd find that easier?"

He pushed aside his vain annoyance at the implication that his German wasn't good enough. *Don't be churlish, she's clearly more fluent than me and it will speed things up. The less time I spend on this ridiculous idea the better.*

"I expect that you regard this visit as an annoying diversion from your real work just as I do, Fräulein Lipsky, so if you're okay to speak English, then I'm happy if that makes our jobs easier."

Her heart sank at Herr Samson's grudging response. *I was really looking forward to making a success of this and showing Herr Weiss what I'm capable of. That's going to be impossible if I'm working with someone who resents every minute he spends on it.*

"I'm sorry, Herr Samson, but for me this isn't an unwelcome diversion at all. In fact, I was excited by this idea when my boss asked me to set it up. Surely it can only be a good thing if scientists and engineers exchange ideas?"

John groaned inwardly at her well-meaning naivety. *A good thing for who, exactly? Every hour I'm taken away from my research is bad for science, and every hour their engineers are taken away from running the station is bad for the quality of the radio broadcast.*

"I apologise, Fräulein Lipsky. I've had a frustrating day and it's not a true reflection of my feelings. Of course I want to do all I can to make sure this visit is successful. Should we meet to discuss and agree the arrangements?"

Ilse was relieved, but not entirely convinced by his sudden change of heart, suspecting that he wouldn't want word to get back that he was unenthusiastic. For now, she must be positive.

"As soon as possible, please. I can suggest a café that's halfway between the university and the radio station. It's large enough for us to find a quiet table at the end of the day. Which day would suit you, Herr Samson?"

She's really keen to get going, he thought. *Are all young women in Berlin as efficient as this?*

"Wednesday at five o'clock would be good for me, Fräulein Lipsky. Is that okay for you?"

"That's good for me, too. It's called the Schumann and its opposite the theatre. I'll get there a few minutes early, wear a bright-yellow scarf and sit right at the back. I look forward to meeting you, Herr Samson."

"Likewise, Fräulein."

Two days later, he double-checked as he approached the place he assumed to be the café. *This can't be the right place, surely?* Looking through the huge plate glass windows at the noisy crowds milling inside, he couldn't imagine they'd be able to have any conversation, let alone a serious one. But this was the Café Schumann. Going through the swing doors he was engulfed by the noisy, smoke-filled atmosphere and slowly began to negotiate his way through the crowds, across a floor made slippery by spillages of beer. The place was vast, but as he got nearer the back he began to see empty booths and tables. It was quieter, too. He looked around, searching for a woman with a yellow scarf, surprised by his nervous anticipation. He suddenly saw her waving at him from one of the booths. Had she been studying him? The thought made him self-conscious.

She stood to greet him with her hand outstretched. She was almost as tall as him, her face smiling and open, dressed casually but smartly in trousers, a white blouse and tailored jacket. They held eye contact a second longer than would be usual for two strangers.

"Herr Samson, it's good to meet you. You found this place without problems, then?"

Her English was excellent. He realised he was already feeling at ease in her presence.

"Yes, thank you, Fräulein Lipsky. Although I did wonder if I was at the right place as I approached – the atmosphere inside didn't seem appropriate for our discussion. I should have had more faith in your judgement," he said.

A waitress approached their table and asked him what he'd like.

"I'd love a coffee with milk, please," he said, turning to Ilse and asking her if she wanted another.

"The same for me, please, thank you. Before we go any further, I think that our discussion will be more relaxing if we use our first names and drop the 'Herr' and 'Fräulein'. Mine is Ilse."

John laughed. "I'm very glad you suggested that, Ilse. I was beginning to wonder at what point it would be acceptable to use first names, but didn't want to put my foot in it, if you know what that expression means. I'm John, which I believe is Johannes in German."

"Your German is coming along well, John, to use another English expression," she said, with a twinkle in her eye.

"I think you're teasing me, Ilse. I'll watch out for that in future. Before we get into the details, would it be a good idea if we shared what we want to get out of the visit?"

"Yes, particularly as I got the impression from our earlier conversation that you weren't very enthusiastic. I do understand why you want to focus on your research, but as I will be doing most of the work – the visit is happening on our premises – there shouldn't be much for you to do."

"I apologise for my tone on the phone, Ilse. It wasn't acceptable, and won't happen again. I can't say that this visit would normally be my top priority, but I give you my word that I'm fully committed."

He was studying her face, looking for any sign of scepticism. Her eyes met his gaze frankly and remained on his. For a moment, he felt she was reading his mind, searching for evidence of pretence. Then came relief as her mouth formed a reassuring smile. She nodded.

"I know you are, and thank you for saying that. Before we go any further, do you think it might help our working relationship if we knew a little more about each other?"

"That makes sense. Why don't you go first?"

Ilse spoke animatedly about her family, her mother's anxieties, her thwarted desire to go to university and the reasons behind the decision, and her dissatisfaction with her previous job compared to working at the radio station. After hesitating briefly, she explained that she was Jewish and that this was a problem for some of her countrymen and women, even though her ancestors had lived in Germany for hundreds of years.

"There's a minority who blame Jews for Germany's defeat. They can make life unpleasant but I choose to ignore them. But it upsets my father; he fought in the war and lost many comrades, and yet he suffers slurs from others who sat safely behind a desk throughout the war."

She saw the look on his face and paused.

"I'm sorry, that was tactless of me to mention the war. Just seven years ago you and I were being indoctrinated to hate each other. Did your family lose anyone? Did you have to fight?"

John's thoughts were a maelstrom of confusions and contradictions. Ilse seemed like a warm, thoughtful human being. They'd met less than thirty minutes ago but he'd already got a strong sense that she was a fundamentally decent person. *But her father could have been the soldier that blew my brother's brains out. And yet, so what? Ilse isn't responsible for her father and anyway, he was just doing what Jack had volunteered to do. With a different twist of fate, Jack could have killed her father.* He felt his eyes welling up at the thought of his brother, and fought back his tears. He composed himself, but before he could answer her question, she reached across the zinc table and put her hand on his arm.

"I'm an idiot for coming out with a question like that. I apologise."

"There's really no need for apologies, Ilse. I was too young to be called up, although some boys I knew lied about their age and went to fight. I got a scholarship to study physics at Imperial College in London in 1919 and finished my PhD three months ago. My brother Jack, two years older than me, was killed in September 1918, just two months before the end of the war. When I heard, I won't pretend that I didn't hate the German soldier who killed him. But that emotion was short-lived; my hatred's for the pointless war itself, and the horrible jingoism that encouraged us to hate all Germans. I now feel that my generation have a duty to make sure there's never a war like that again. I think it was one reason that I applied for the position at Friedrich Wilhelm; I wanted to make a point to my fellow scientists, some of whom are still going on about the horrible Hun. I wish they could speak to some of the Germans I've met since I arrived here; it might change their minds."

He looked up, saw her looking at him intently and smiled. At that moment she became aware that her hand was still on his arm, and withdrew it, to his regret.

"I didn't realise there is such dislike of Jews in Germany. Where does that come from?"

Ilse laughed.

"If you've got another day to spare I can begin to help you understand. It's a very long story."

"I'd like to hear that story sometime, if you could bear it."

"Only if you promise to stop me if I go on too long. Now, I think we should probably spend time discussing numbers, dates and the things your colleagues would like to see during your visit."

"Yes, I suppose we should." *That's a shame, I'm enjoying this conversation.*

They spent the next hour finalising the details for the visit in four weeks' time.

"I'll let you know if my boss suggests any changes; do you have a phone number at the university that you can give me, just in case? I'm not expecting any problems, though."

"I'll ring Funkstade and leave the number for you of the faculty office – we don't have a phone in the laboratory yet. I've enjoyed this afternoon, Ilse; we make a good team. I'm looking forward to this visit now."

Ilse beamed at him. "I agree, and I think we should toast our success!"

She beckoned a waiter over and ordered two glasses of Sekt.

"This is on me, John. Women are becoming liberated in Germany now – in Berlin, anyway!"

"What a marvellous idea, thank you, Ilse. The drinks are on me the next time."

Their drinks arrived and they toasted the future success of the visit, their eyes meeting again. She was attractive, strikingly so when the light caught her cheekbones, and it was difficult to look away. Trying not to lose the moment, he said, "I've been in Berlin for nearly two months now and have only seen the inside of several bars, one cabaret and well-known attractions like the Brandenburg Gate. I was wondering if, as a Berliner, you could suggest more interesting places to visit."

Where's he going with this? He seems nice, but I'm not ready for anything serious.

"I'll think about it and have some ideas for you when you come to the station."

6
—

UNDERCOVER

In the week after he'd met Ilse, he became increasingly frustrated about the lack of progress with his research. Friedrich Wilhelm had offered him a two-year fellowship on the basis of his research proposal:

'Identifying the implications of the Compton effect for collisions between photons and electrons in fixed, bound orbits.'

Presumably they'd thought it was a worthwhile proposal. But everything he'd uncovered so far suggested that there were few implications. *This could be the shortest piece of original research in the history of physics.*

His thoughts were interrupted by Karl telling him there was a call for him from Herr Chastain.

"He says that you'll know what it's about."

"Hello, this is John Samson."

"Hello, John. Mark Chastain here. I hope we've given you enough time to settle in. I'd like to set up that meeting we discussed between you and one of my colleagues. How does this Friday at eleven at the Embassy sound? Your mentor is Andrew

Russell; he's looking forward to meeting you."

John found that he was looking forward to getting out of the laboratory and spending a day discussing his role as a part-time informant with Andrew Russell.

"I think I can rearrange my work around that, Mark. Do I need to bring anything?"

"Marvellous, I'm glad you can make it. Just bring your passport as ID when you present yourself at the gate. I look forward to seeing you, John."

The British Embassy at 70, Wilhelmstrasse was much grander than John was expecting, with an ornate portico supported on four enormous pillars above the entrance. The two policemen on duty outside waved him through after a cursory glance at his passport. Once inside, he was ushered over to a long dark wooden counter in the reception area, where a young man in a suit and wing-collar shirt looked at his passport and asked him to wait while he contacted Chastain.

Mark appeared after less than a minute.

"Excellent to see you again, John. Sorry about the short notice but Andrew had a sudden cancellation. Please follow me."

Mark set off up the main staircase, John imagining various dramatic scenarios to explain Andrew's last-minute cancellation. As they entered a grand-looking meeting room with two huge windows on the first floor, a tall man in his early thirties rose out of a chair to greet him.

"Good morning, John, pleased to meet you. I'm Andrew Russell. Please have a seat. Will you be joining us, Mark?"

"I'm going to leave you two to it. I'll arrange coffee for you both."

The two men looked at each other, sizing one another up, although that little game was an unequal one. Andrew was a professional on his home turf whose life could sometimes depend upon getting such judgements right, looking at John with an expression that said, *'tell me something that will surprise me.'*

Andrew leant forwards, smiling, and said, "Mark has briefed me, of course, but I'd like to hear from you how you've got yourself into this – whatever 'this' actually is."

"You could say that it was a combination of altruism and personal gain – like many decisions in life, I suspect." He could see that he'd got Russell's attention.

"I was coming to the end of my PhD at Imperial and had applied for a number of postdoctorate research positions. One was at Friedrich Wilhelm University in Berlin, which I didn't think I stood much chance of getting, frankly. To my surprise, I was offered the post. Shortly after I accepted, I had a visit from a Major Lawlor," – Russell rolled his eyes – "who took me out to lunch and asked if I'd be willing to help Her Majesty's Government by feeding back information about advances in my area that might help Germany create powerful new weapons.

"Although Major Lawlor made it clear that my place at Friedrich Wilhelm wasn't conditional on me agreeing to his request, I obviously wanted to do what I could for my country, so here I am."

Russell had been listening with increasing amazement.

"My God, these people at the centre. Someone at the top thinks up a hare-brained scheme, no one dares to shoot it down, fearing for their own career, and people like you and me get lumbered with it."

Russell paused, considering his next words more carefully.

"Okay, there's no point fighting this now, it's a fait accompli. As I see it, John, my role is to make sure that a complete amateur such as yourself – no offence – doesn't make our work here in Berlin more difficult by blundering into a situation that puts you – and others – at risk."

"I appreciate your directness, Andrew."

"Can you enlighten me – in layman's language – about the sort of research in your area that our chaps back in England might be concerned about? I mean, aren't significant advances in scientific research always published in papers that are publicly available? That's the whole point isn't it? Scientists rely on their hypotheses being tested out by other scientists and either proven or disproven?"

"That was exactly my reaction when Major Lawlor proposed this idea. You don't need me to do this, I said, just get German-speaking scientists in England to read all the scientific papers written on particle physics. His point seemed to be that the German Army still occupies a controlling role in the Weimar Republic. He believes that there could be discoveries that have potential military use that the army ensures don't actually get published. They're the ones he wants to know about."

For the second time in a matter of minutes, Andrew looked askance.

"This is more serious than I'd realised. If the German Army wants something to remain secret, they'll try very hard to make sure it does. You could be putting yourself in greater danger than I initially thought. Where would you begin?"

"Trial and error at the beginning. I thought I'd look for research papers in the obvious areas that had been making good progress but then disappeared for no apparent reason."

"What are the relevant areas, do you think?"

"Particle physics, ballistics, uses for electromagnetic radiation outside the visible spectrum."

He could see Andrew glazing over.

"Okay. Don't wait, bring me anything you think might be interesting."

"Where will we meet?"

"I suggest you come here. You'll need a cover story for why you're visiting the Embassy occasionally, but it will be safer than a café."

"What if I hear of something that seems urgent?"

"In that unlikely event, phone Mark. Otherwise, let's meet here in one month's time."

They continued talking over their coffees. Much to John's surprise, Andrew was keen to get his views on the current political mood in Britain. John, in turn, probed Andrew (unsuccessfully) about how he'd ended up working for the Secret Service. Andrew abruptly ended their conversation after half an hour.

"I'm afraid that I must go, John. It's been good to meet you. Stay safe."

John walked out of the Embassy into the weak afternoon sunshine. *I mustn't let this interesting nonsense distract me. I need to make a breakthrough with my own research by Christmas.*

7

THE VISIT TO FUNKSTADE

"Ilse Lipsky on the telephone for you, John. Is there something you're not telling us?"

"Thank you, Karl. These calls are just about arrangements for the visit tomorrow."

"If you say so, John."

"Hello, Ilse. How are you? I'm sorry if you overheard any of that. Karl thinks he's hilarious."

"Don't worry, I'm not offended. We've got a similar character here in the station. So, have you got the final numbers for tomorrow?"

"There will be six of us, as Karl has decided he wants to come after all. I think he wants to see who my mysterious phone caller is."

"He's going to have to be disappointed, then," she said, laughing. "Six will be okay, as I've split them into two groups. I'll meet you at the main entrance at ten forty-five and take you up, so please make sure you're all there on time. If anyone is late they won't be allowed in. The station will be playing classical music for half an hour non-stop, so my boss can give you a short speech about our work during that time. Each group will then spend time in the studio and interrogate Fritz, our engineer, about the technical aspects. Is that the kind of visit you were expecting?"

"That sounds perfect, thank you, Ilse. I'm looking forward to seeing you tomorrow."

Although the weather had turned much colder since he'd arrived at the end of August, the late autumn sun was taking the edge off the chill as he walked to the radio station the following morning. The streets were bustling with young, well-dressed working men and women. The German economy was picking up quickly after the disastrous hyperinflation caused by the government printing money to pay war reparations to France and Belgium.

Funkstade Berlin was easy to find; based in a relatively nondescript, early twentieth-century building with a grey-white stone façade, it had a tall steel aerial rising from the roof, visible from several streets away. He got there early, hoping that Ilse might do the same. As he turned a corner, he saw her standing in the entrance wearing a long dark-yellow coat, a bell-shaped hat and trousers. Her dark, wavy hair spilt out under the hat and her face was set in fierce concentration as she read her notes and began to write in her notebook. He watched her until he suddenly felt guilty about observing her like this and began to walk towards her.

She turned in his direction and gave him a warm smile.

"Good morning, John, I hope your colleagues are looking forward to their visit. We're all prepared here, I think!"

His colleagues turned up almost immediately. As soon as he'd introduced them, she led them upstairs.

"Herr Weiss, the manager of the station, would like to talk to you all first."

Fifteen minutes later, John looked towards Ilse and caught her eye. She raised her eyebrows, sharing his frustration that Herr

Weiss was going on so long and showing no sign of winding up. *There won't be any time for questions at this rate.*

At that moment, as Herr Weiss paused for breath, Ilse jumped in.

"I'm sorry to interrupt, Herr Weiss, but I'm sure that our guests may have a number of questions after hearing that fascinating history about the station. Do you think we should take questions now?"

Her boss stared at her, just managing to hide his annoyance. *I should have stood up to my Head of Department like that when he asked me to set this visit up. Although that would have meant that I wouldn't have met Ilse...*

"You're right, Fräulein Lipsky, thank you for reminding me that our guests have much more to see. Does anyone have a question?"

Ilse began to look increasingly anxious as the seconds ticked by without a hand going up. John raised his hand without thinking – he didn't have a question. Herr Weiss looked towards him, smiling.

"Yes, Herr Samson."

John looked over at Ilse, who mouthed, "Thank you" and a question popped into his head.

"A friend of mine who works for the BBC told me that the major obstacles they'd faced developing a national radio broadcast service weren't technical but social and political. What obstacles have you encountered here in Berlin?"

John realised that all eyes in the room were on him; he'd put Herr Weiss in the difficult position of criticising politicians, station executives or both.

"That's a very good question, John. The problems were overwhelmingly technical, and we're still trying to solve some of them. For example, sometimes our broadcast frequency can drift a little, which is very frustrating for our listeners. But the mayor and his team have been very supportive of our project.

"I suspect Fräulein Lipsky is getting anxious that we're running over time, so let's move on. I'll be very happy to answer any further questions after you've completed the rest of your visit. Will you explain the arrangements for the next hour to our guests, please, Fräulein?"

She confidently organised John's colleagues into two groups, patiently sorting out those wanting to swap and reminding them of the need to stick to the schedule. The more she revealed of herself, the more attracted he became to this warm, self-assured yet guarded young woman.

"Well, do you think your colleagues found their visit worthwhile?"

They were sitting in the staff canteen; he'd asked Ilse if she'd be free for a 'debrief' after the others had left.

"They were fascinated to see how programmes are put together, with changes still being made up to the very last minute. Your colleagues really need the music intervals to recover!"

"Yes, it does get very *hektisch* – I think it's almost the same word in English. But I love the energy, the adrenaline that flows when we're rushing to get a broadcast ready in time. We almost always do, though. I'm glad they found it interesting. What happened towards the end – I couldn't find you?"

"I suddenly noticed that some of my group were missing. Then I realised they might have gone to study the transmitter and the rest of the electronics. Sure enough, that's where I found them – behind the door marked with '*Achtung! Hochspannung*' and a skull and crossbones. I hauled them out immediately."

"Oh my God! They could have been electrocuted. Thank goodness Herr Weiss didn't find out, I'd have been in serious trouble."

"He doesn't seem much of a tyrant."

"He's not most of the time, but he makes it very clear if he's annoyed with you."

Ilse paused, looked at John, and seemed to decide something.

"Remember I said that I would try to think of unusual places in Berlin that you could visit? You could go to Treptower Park. It's in the east of the city, on the bank of the Spree, and it's got a charming lake in the middle with rowing boats for hire. You'd need to go in the next two weeks because the boats are moored up over the winter. There's a footpath beside the Spree that goes most of the way there, or you could catch a train. Either way, I can give you directions."

"Thank you, that sounds interesting. I was about to ask you if you'd thought of anywhere and wondered if we could go together."

She'd been assuming John would be going on his own, even though part of her was hoping he might ask her. She didn't want to presume, or appear too eager.

"I'd like to, it's a long time since I've been out on the lake. We could go next Saturday afternoon. I can't take time off from Monday to Friday and I've got to help Herr Weiss with next month's schedules on Saturday morning."

"Marvellous! Where shall we meet?"

"Let's meet at that tram stop over there. We can walk to the Spree, then along the bank to the park."

8

TREPTOWER PARK

"This place is lovely, Ilse, I'm so glad you suggested it. Do you come here a lot?"

"I used to, but my new job is much busier and I have less free time now. Rowing a boat isn't as much fun on your own, of course."

They'd met at the tram stop as arranged then walked along the bank of the Spree, the water an uninviting rusty brown. He'd been surprised at the speed of the current, carrying huge barges towards the Elbe and onto the sea at an astonishing pace. He thought of the barges that chugged slowly along the Lee Navigation, tiny in comparison.

"I hope there's a boat to take out. It should be fun."

"As long as we take turns on the oars. I hate it when men assume that the woman just wants to be rowed and then take over without asking."

He gave a mock salute, smiled and said, "Understood, Captain. You have the oars."

She looked at him, disappointed.

"Please don't patronise me, John. I hate it when men mock

women like that. I experienced it so much in my old job in the law practice, I began to lose confidence in myself."

"I meant it as a joke; I'm sorry it came across like that."

"I realise you didn't intend to offend me, unlike those lawyers I mentioned. But this dismissive attitude that many men have towards women's opinions never seems to change. I think it must stem from the way they're brought up, ingrained in them by their parents, who probably don't realise they're doing it. It's depressing, as each generation seems to pass it on to the next. Sorry, I'm going on."

They walked on in silence until they came to the place where the rowing boats were moored, ready for hire. John looked at Ilse, knowing that if he wanted to see her again, he had to regain the mood they'd had at the beginning of the afternoon.

"Do you mind if we don't go rowing, John? I think the moment has passed; can we just walk back?"

His stomach lurched.

"I'm sorry I upset you, I feel awful. What you said about men dismissing women's opinions has made me think. But can we still take a boat out? I don't want there to be any tension between us, even if we don't see each other again."

"I can't take back the point I was making, but perhaps I should have been less abrupt in the way I said it. I don't like leaving on a bad note, either, so let's get on the water. We'll need to be quick, there's only one boat left and that couple look as if they've got the same idea."

John watched as she pulled confidently away from the jetty, blades cleaving the water cleanly as her slim, supple frame established a rhythm. Strands of long dark hair had escaped from under her beret and were falling over her face. As she tried unsuccessfully to blow them out of her eyes, he leant forwards, moved the wisps of hair aside and tucked them back under her hat.

"Thank you. I'm really enjoying this, I'd forgotten how good it feels. The exercise is warming me up, but you must be cold, it's getting chilly. Do you want to take over?"

"No thanks, I'm enjoying being a passenger. You're an impressive rower – if you're okay to carry on, let's do another two circuits of the lake, then moor up. I'd like to buy us coffee and cake in the café in the park we passed on the way. Think of it as a 'thank you' for organising the visit."

"That's a lovely idea, thank you, John."

They returned to the jetty and strolled to the café, making small talk about the weather – "It will get much colder in the next few weeks, the winters can be very harsh in Berlin" – and missing London – "I do a little, but there's still so much to learn about Berlin and my research is only just beginning." A sense that there were more portentous topics to discuss hung in the air.

Once they'd found a table and given the waitress their order, John finally found the nerve to ask Ilse the question he'd been working up to all afternoon.

"Would you like to go out for dinner one evening next week?"

I sensed this was coming, it's been obvious all afternoon he'd like to take things further. There's much to admire, he's sensitive, a strong character with a reflective mind. A handsome face, a warm genuine smile and an underlying gentleness. But I can't say yes, I'm not ready to start a relationship. Oh God, this is going to be awkward.

The rape had left Ilse with demons that surfaced merely at the prospect of intimacy with a man. In her darker moments, they caused her to question whether she'd somehow colluded and encouraged her rapist, undermining her sense of who she was. And she knew little about this young Englishman, who came from a different class and culture.

She took a deep breath and looked at him across the table.

"I'm flattered, John. I've really enjoyed your company today, but my work is frantic these days, my parents and sister need my support and I'm afraid I really don't have the space in my life for a commitment at the moment. I'm sorry."

He felt crushed, which he knew made little sense. He'd only met Ilse four weeks ago and had spent less than three hours in her company. Before this moment he'd felt his life might be going on a different course – which was ridiculous. Struggling to hide his feelings, he said, "I can't pretend I'm not disappointed, but of course, I understand. We hardly know each other, after all. I hope I didn't embarrass you by asking?"

To her surprise she felt a pang of regret that he hadn't tried harder to persuade her.

"Of course not, John. As I said, it's very flattering to be asked out to dinner. I hope you don't feel that I've misled you in any way?"

"Certainly not, Ilse."

The mood between them turned flat; twenty minutes later, after quickly finishing their coffee and cakes, John paid the bill. They said polite but cool goodbyes to each other and went separate ways, both feeling miserable.

He hadn't felt this low since he'd arrived in Berlin. The prospect of a relationship with Ilse, however slight, had been lifting his spirits. Putting his hands in his pockets against the cold, he started to walk aimlessly. Hearing a tram, he turned to see one approaching that was going past his university. Determined to achieve something by the end of the weekend, he ran to the next stop and jumped on. *I'll recheck my results from the last experiment, I might have missed something.*

Walking back to her parent's house, Ilse felt oddly ambivalent; pleased for having the confidence to say no, yet frustrated at not giving herself time to reflect. *Why didn't I say I'd like time to think about it; he's an interesting man and I enjoy his company. Does everything between men and women have to be about sex?*

The following Monday morning John was lost in his experiment when he heard his name being shouted.

"Herr Samson, there's a call for you in the office. It's from Fräulein Lipsky. Again."

"Hello, is that you Ilse?"

"Hello, John. I want to apologise for spoiling the end of a lovely afternoon on Saturday. I should have explained myself."

"Please, it was my fault for asking you at an inappropriate time. I respect your honesty."

"Thank you. I would like to explain my response, but it's personal and I assume that you can't talk openly at the moment. Can we meet for a coffee, somewhere near the university?"

"I'd like that, but you don't have to give me a reason why you didn't want to go out for dinner."

"I know, but I want to. Wednesday afternoon, in the place we went to a month ago to discuss your visit to the station?"

"That's good for me. I'll see you there at three."

Ilse had arrived early at the café and swiftly downed two glasses of schnapps at the bar before going to their table. She needed to calm her nerves before she could explain her reasons for declining his invitation. Why was she doing this? She had no cause to feel guilty or owe this relative stranger an explanation. Women turn down invitations to dinner all the time.

She thought she understood what lay behind her impetuous phone call. Her belief in the importance of treating her fellow human beings as she would wish to be treated and her need for reassurance that he didn't think badly of her. That was all, wasn't it?

She'd judge how much personal detail to reveal about her rape as their meeting progressed, depending how sensitively he responded.

She watched him approach their table. He had the build and open face that she'd always found attractive; but it was his outward confidence along with a sense of vulnerability underneath that had aroused her interest right from the start.

"Hello, Ilse, it's lovely to see you. Before we begin, I want to say that you don't owe me any apologies for declining my presumptuous invitation last Saturday."

"Thank you, John, but I don't want there to be any misunderstandings between us. Let's order – I'm having coffee and a slice of strudel."

"I'll have the same."

She waited to start *the* conversation until their coffee had arrived, then began.

"I understand why you tried to move our friendship on to something deeper on Saturday. There was a rapport between us, we'd enjoyed each other's company, a physical attraction, perhaps." She blushed. "But I've never had… an intimate relationship with a man."

She paused, surprised that she was able to speak to him so freely.

"Before I worked for Funkstade, I was a solicitors' clerk in a small local practice. One of the partners and I went out for coffee and cake at lunchtime occasionally, but I'd made it clear to him that I wasn't interested in a romantic relationship, which I thought he'd accepted. Against my better judgement, I then accepted his invitation to dinner at a nice hotel.

"Sorry, I need to pause for a moment."

John looked at her, concerned. *She doesn't need to do this.*

"Ilse, please don't put yourself through this for my sake."

"I want to do this for my sake. I'm okay, really.

"So this man, full of a sense of his entitlement to take whatever he wants from his inferior female colleague, drugged me, half carried me to his hotel room and raped me. When I woke in the morning, alone, I knew immediately what he'd done. I also understood that there was no point reporting him to the police."

As she paused and steadied herself again, he reached over and held her hand. He felt it trembling.

"He's a lawyer, a partner in a respectable practice. Even if the police took my accusation seriously and prosecuted him – which was unlikely – I would be dragged through a trial, counter-accusations would be made against me, my reputation would be sullied and my family shamed. The worst thing was that I had to remain working there for another year, seeing him every day, smirking and gloating. My family depend on my wages; I couldn't just leave. Up to now, I've only told one other person, my mother.

"I recovered quickly from my injuries, but the psychological scars are taking longer to heal. I can't stop blaming myself for what happened; did I lead him on, could I have tried harder to alert the hotel staff? Worst of all, I no longer trust men. Are they capable of having a close friendship with a woman without expecting it to become sexual? When you asked me out for dinner that was all I could think about. I'm sorry. You seem a good man, John, so it's very unfair. But now you know."

John was struggling to find the right words; he was surprised, yet humbled, that Ilse trusted him to reveal such an intimate experience.

"I'm so sorry, Ilse, that must have been horrific. I can't imagine what it was like facing him every day for a year afterwards. You're right, I was trying to move our relationship on to a deeper level, and I understand you're not ready for that. I'd still like us to continue as friends, if you would? We get on so well."

"Wouldn't you find it… frustrating?"

Of course I would.

"Only time will tell, Ilse. I really enjoy your company, and don't want to lose you as a friend."

9
—

WINTER ARRIVES

Winter arrived swiftly in Berlin. As December wore on, John was caught out as the temperature regularly plunged to near zero. He'd been expecting it to be similar to London, but had started to feel miserably cold without a proper winter coat, so leapt at the chance when Ilse offered to take him shopping. Casual observers in the Wertheim department store in Leipziger Strasse probably assumed they were romantically attached, like most of the other browsing couples.

As they spent more time together, they sometimes found themselves about to touch the other in an affectionate way, then holding back. So they carried on with their deepening friendship, deceiving themselves as their desire to take things further grew.

Two days later, ten days before Christmas Day, he saw a letter from Ilse on the table in the hallway as he left for work. He took it back up to his room and opened it.

It was beautifully written in English, with several phrases and sentences in German (*to make sure she's not doing all the work?*)

Dear John,

I've decided to spend this next week leading up to Christmas with my father, mother and sister. I'm not looking forward to it, but it's the right thing to do, as I'm going to start looking for a room to rent. I won't tell my parents until I've found somewhere. Many of my friends are now living on their own or sharing, and they tell me there are lots of places available at a reasonable rent these days. Not as cheap as living at home, of course, but a small price to pay. Would you like to meet in the next few days? I was thinking of the Christmas market at Potsdamer Platz for a glass of glühwein and cake? What do you think? It would be lovely to see you – better to phone me at work rather than write to me at my parents' home,
Love, Ilse

As he re-read her letter, his buoyant mood at receiving such a clear sign of her growing feelings for him suddenly clouded. Ilse was about to spend several days around Christmas with her family, and yet it hadn't crossed his mind to even send his father and sister a card. Ashamed, he hurriedly wrote them a loving letter, ran to the nearest post office and sent it via airmail.

Two days later, Karl, John and colleagues from work were jostling their way through crowds of revellers, looking for somewhere to get a drink. Karl had invited him to join them for a Christmas celebration after work, but finding a bar that wasn't packed with revellers was near impossible. Suddenly spotting one that looked relatively empty, he shouted at Karl, "Come on, this one's less crowded," and set off towards it, ignoring Karl's shouts.

"Come back, John, we can't go in there."

As he approached the entrance two men wearing brown uniforms with dark-brown belts appeared out of nowhere, stood in front of him and demanded to know his name and which Party he supported.

He took in the situation and looked at the men's faces. Adrenaline-fuelled fear told him to run, but he stood little chance of getting away in this street packed with people. Keeping the sentence as simple as possible, he said in German, "I can't vote, I'm in Berlin to study science."

The two men smiled at each other.

"Are you from England?" said the smaller man. John noticed that he had a glass eye. Probably a war injury. *This isn't going well.*

"London."

"You English swine have brought misery to the fatherland, but you dare come here and take a place at our university? I lost my eye in the war, you *scheise* Englishman. I should kill you, get out of here."

As John turned to go, two more Brownshirts came out of the bar and joined the two that had confronted him. He walked away, then ran as he heard the new arrivals shouting after him. Weaving and pushing his way through the crowd, people swearing as he barged into them, he looked in vain for Karl and the others. After fifty metres he chanced a glance back and saw Glass Eye and one of the others about twenty metres behind. He kept running and weaving until his lungs were burning and looked behind again. There was no sign of them, but he kept walking until he was sure he'd lost them.

The crowd thinned out as he approached a main road ahead; as a sense of relief surged through him, two Brownshirts turned into his path from the main road. He prepared to defend himself.

Bleeding from a cut to his mouth and gasping for breath, adrenaline slowly wearing off, John finally felt safe. He only had a vague idea where he was – the police hadn't wanted to spend time explaining how he could get back home. He was in a wide street with numerous bars and clubs, thronged with crowds of young Berliners enjoying a night out. Some glanced distractedly at the young man with a bloody face and torn coat, slumped on a bench with a policeman standing nearby, but most ignored him. To them, he was just another victim of the vicious fighting between rival political factions.

He assessed the damage; one tooth loose in its socket; a sore ribcage on his left side and a sharp pain where he'd been punched, probably a minor fracture, but he'd had one at university playing rugby and it healed on its own; his cheekbone was sore and starting to swell, he'd have a black eye in the morning unless he iced it quickly. Considering what might have happened, he'd got off lightly.

His assailants, the Brownshirts, were members of the Nazi paramilitary group, identifiable by their swastika armbands. Shorter but stockier than him, it had been obvious that trying to talk his way out of a fight would have been useless. *Get back against the wall, shout for help and fight dirty.*

"You don't look so confident now, English. We're going to give you such a lesson, you'll never want to come back to Berlin."

He'd screamed, "Someone call the *polizei*" at the top of his voice and reached into his coat pocket, clutching the laboratory keys he'd luckily forgotten to remove last night. They'd come at him together, one aiming a kick at his groin, the other swinging a well-telegraphed punch to his head. He'd parried the kick with a counter-kick to the assailant's kneecap, which had connected accurately judging by the scream. The punch to his head had also connected, but with less force than he feared as he'd ducked away at the last minute. When the same man had swung at his head again, this time he'd managed to block it with the fist holding the keys. The Brownshirt yelled as his knuckles hit the pointed end of his keys.

Another punch, this time to his ribs, had taken his breath away, and then a punch he hadn't seen coming hit him hard on his cheekbone. He realised that he couldn't sustain much more punishment and knew he had to seriously hurt one of them. Seeing an opening, he put his full weight behind an uppercut to the man who'd kicked him, jolting his head back with a snapping sound before he went down in a heap. John had taken one more punch to his mouth just as a cacophony of police whistles sounded nearby. Revellers carried on, ignoring him.

As the Brownshirts hobbled away as quickly as their injuries allowed, he slumped back against the wall. Two policemen stayed with him long enough to make sure he wasn't seriously injured, then helped him walk one hundred metres to a bench in the main street near the police station.

He didn't think the fascists had done serious damage, but needed someone to look at his injuries. There was really only one person he wanted to do that and only one way to contact her at this hour – if there was anyone still working at the police station. He got up and walked painfully over to the policeman. His ribs felt worse.

"Can I use the telephone in the police station to call a friend, *bitte*?"

He was given permission to do so and dialled the number.

"Hello? Is that Funkstade Berlin?"

"Yes. Who is this?"

"John Samson. I brought a group of scientists to the station a month ago, you may have been there."

"I was. I remember, you're Ilse's friend."

That's interesting, he thought, then carried on.

"I know it's late, but is she still there?"

"No, she left an hour ago. It's nearly nine o'clock."

"I know, I'm sorry to telephone at this hour, but it's important. Do you have her number?"

"We keep a list of numbers for all the staff. Your voice sounds strange – are you okay?"

"I've just been assaulted in the street. Would you mind dialling her number and asking her to ring me back on this number, please? It's a police station, but they've let me use their phone, I haven't been arrested. If her father or mother answers, please don't tell them why you're calling, just ask for her."

There was a long silence on the other end of the line.

"Why do you want to speak to her?"

"I'd like someone to accompany me to my flat, in case I'm more seriously injured than I think. There's no one else I can call."

"Give me the number you're using and I will call her now. If she's not in, I'll call you back."

10

REPAIR

Ilse handed a five-mark note to the driver as the taxi pulled up outside John's address.

"Thank you for coming to get me, Ilse, I'm so grateful. What story did you give your parents to explain why you were going out?"

"I told them I was going to help a friend who'd been beaten up by Nazi thugs."

"Did they ask who?"

"Yes. I told them it was you. They just asked me to be careful, hoped you weren't badly hurt and didn't say anything further. I think the driver wants to go, we should get out."

"I'm okay now. If you help me out of the cab you can take it back to your house. Your parents will be worried."

"Don't be a martyr. I'm coming up to check there's nothing broken. Please don't argue, John. You asked for my help, and I'm going to make sure you're all right."

She assisted him onto the car's running board and down to the pavement, then followed him into the house and up the stairs to his room. She noticed him wince as he reached up to put the key in the lock.

His room was clean and tidy except for an unmade bed; more civilised than she'd expected. Pictures of his family were on the mantelpiece, but no evidence of a girlfriend.

She helped him take off his torn coat. He looked a mess; pale, cut mouth, left eye already swelling. She was confused and disconcerted by her feelings for him, which went beyond care and compassion.

"What's in your bag, Ilse? It's enormous."

"You're about to find out. I'm going to clean up the cuts on your face first and then have a look at the rest of the damage. If you light the gas fire and take off your shirt and vest, I'll get everything I need from the bag."

He did as he was told, watching her as she assembled lotions, ointments, iodine, scissors and rolls of bandages, then scrubbed her hands thoroughly and filled the sink with hot water.

"Blimey, Ilse, did you rob a hospital?"

"All the girls in my year at school were encouraged to volunteer in 1918 to help nurse the huge number of wounded soldiers overwhelming the hospitals. I saw horrific injuries and watched men die from infections they could have survived with better hygiene. So I've gradually built up a stock of disinfectants and dressings at home, to use if we ever needed them. Lucky for you, eh? Come over to the sink, I'll clean you up."

His whole body ached, his wounds now becoming more painful. They stood in front of the sink together as she examined and cleaned his lacerations, then dabbed them with iodine. Finally, she applied a thick paste to the swollen eye.

"I think the damage to your handsome face will heal itself, but I want to feel your ribcage. I'm going to put my hands on both sides of your chest and I want you to take deep breaths."

John winced as she held his ribs.

"Does it hurt when you breathe in?"

"No worse than when I cracked a rib playing rugby. I remember the feeling."

"Carry on breathing in and out."

As they faced each other, Ilse was caught unawares by the sensation of her hands pressing tightly against his skin, surprised by an urge to move her fingers over his chest muscles. She forced herself to concentrate.

"I'm sure it's only a fracture in one rib and not a break. You were lucky."

"Well, I wouldn't say that, exactly."

He smiled, showing he'd understood what she'd really meant.

"I think you're teasing me, John. No matter, I'll bandage your ribs, but not too tightly. Are you in pain anywhere else?"

"The top of my left leg is very sore, I must have been kicked there. But it's in an intimate area, so I think I should look at it."

"I saw naked men every day when I was working in the hospital. It's up to you."

He stood up, wincing again, then took his shoes and trousers off. At least he'd changed his underwear two days ago. He pulled up the left leg of his underpants, feeling exposed and embarrassed as Ilse peered closely at his groin.

"There's going to be a nasty bruise where the skin is broken. Lie on the bed and let your leg go limp, I'm going to check if anything's damaged."

She held his lower leg in both arms and moved his knee in a circle.

"Is that painful?"

"Sore, not painful."

"Then I think the hip socket is okay. I'll leave you a bottle of iodine to clean the area regularly, but the kick may have damaged a blood vessel. You must go to a doctor if a lump develops. Here's a bottle of aspirin. Take two before you go to bed, and rest as much as possible in the next few days – that will help the ribs to heal."

"I can't stay cooped up in this room over Christmas, Ilse. What about our visit to the Christmas market?"

"Let's see how you're feeling in two days. There would be a lot of walking around, but I'll come and see you first and we could decide then?"

"That gives me something to look forward to. I'm sure I could go for a short walk."

"Have you got enough food?"

"I'm fine. There's a grocers and café around the corner. Now you should go. How will you get back?"

"There's a taxi stand nearby. I'm so sorry you got caught up in our horrible German politics, John. Several of my Jewish friends have been attacked for no other reason than being Jewish, some of them very badly. There's always been anti-Semitism in Germany, but it's getting much worse since Hitler formed the Nazi Party. They're vile people with hate in their hearts; many of my friends think we should ignore them and keep our heads down, but they're wrong. The only way they'll be defeated is if we fight back. I'm very proud of you. Please rest – I'll call round in two days' time, around five o'clock."

She picked up her bag, started to leave, then returned and kissed him on the cheek.

John suddenly felt very tired. He turned the fire off, took two aspirin tablets, started to brush his teeth until his lip began bleeding then collapsed into bed with his socks and underpants on. He fell asleep thinking about the smell of her perfume and the sensation of her lips brushing his cheek.

There were no taxis on the rank, but she knew the way back and decided to walk rather than wait for a tram; it would help her to unscramble her thoughts. Her feelings had gone beyond the bounds of friendship this evening and she needed to know if he felt the same way. After what he'd said a month ago in the Treptower café, she had every reason to believe he did. And she was the one he'd come to this evening when he'd needed help. The intimacy of touching him and feeling for damage to his body had aroused her. And, she'd noticed, aroused him.

As she walked along the frost-covered streets, she made a decision. *I'm not going to allow that degrading experience with one man eighteen months ago continue to define me. I won't let that bastard blight my life; if I'm sure of my feelings, then I should act on them.*

She spent so much time worrying how to make the first move that Herr Weiss had to frequently remind her to stop daydreaming. *Stop complicating things; if we go to the open market, just pick the right moment and ask him if he still feels the same way about me as he did at Treptower. If he says yes, I'll make clear that's what I want too. I won't think about him saying no.*

"Herr Samson, there's a young woman to see you. She says that you're expecting her."

"Can you please ask her to come up, Frau Hessler? Thank you."

As she went up, Ilsa imagined how things could be different between them the next time she climbed these stairs.

"Hello John, how are you feeling? That's quite a black eye you've got."

"It's good to see you, Ilse, even with one eye. I've made an amazing recovery thanks to your nursing and I feel much better. I hope we're still going to the market – I'm looking forward to it."

"So am I. How are the ribs feeling? And your leg?"

"Both doing well, thank you. How far is it?"

"I thought we'd go to the nearest one, as it will be your first long walk. It's smaller than most, but they've got good gift stalls and I know of a lovely café there."

Ilse noticed he was limping slightly as they walked to the market. But compared to two days ago, he'd recovered remarkably quickly. She'd wondered if he'd be anxious in public, as this was the first time he'd been in crowds since he was beaten up. But he seemed to have lost none of his confident aura. It was one of the things she found attractive about him.

Ilse was wrong; this wasn't the first time John had been in a crowd since he was attacked. He'd forced himself to leave the flat yesterday afternoon to visit an ironmongers three streets away. As he was browsing there a month ago, he'd noticed a display of knuckle-dusters; at the time, he'd just registered it as something interesting. When he remembered the shop after Ilse had left his flat two nights ago, he decided he needed to swing the odds in his favour if there was a next time. He felt its weight now, in his coat pocket.

As soon as they arrived at the market, he was captivated by the smells, the stunning decorations and the warm, festive mood of the crowd. He would have been happy to browse, taking everything in at a relaxed pace, but Ilse seemed distracted.

"Let's find an available table, sit down and order some *glühwein* and stollen. You can't say you've been to Berlin until you've done that. Look, there's an empty table, I'm going to grab it."

John limped in her wake as she virtually pushed another couple out of the way to claim the table.

"Remind me not to get in your way when you're determined. Are you okay? You seem a little on edge."

"I'm fine. There's a waiter, let's order. 'Two *glühwein* and two pieces of stollen, bitte.' Is that okay with you?"

"That sounds wonderful."

Something was wrong. He hadn't seen her like this before. Was it something he'd said or done? He decided not to push the question further for the moment. She was looking lovely and he didn't want to spoil their time together.

Their stollen and *glühwein* arrived quickly – he'd noticed before that the service was much faster here than in London – and he raised his glass of the hot, spicy, aromatic wine towards Ilse for a toast. Surprised that she'd already started to drink hers, he kept his glass raised and waited for her to pause.

"I was going to make a toast to the guardian angel who came to my rescue two nights ago, but I see she's beaten me to it. *Prost!*"

"*Prost!* And thank you, that's a lovely toast. I've been looking forward to this all day. So what do you think of your first Berlin Christmas market?"

"I love the mix of street stalls, food, wine, music and decorations. Thank you for bringing me. Are you going to buy something?"

"Maybe, but first I'm going to have a second glass. I hope you're going to join me!"

Something definitely wasn't right. She'd almost finished her wine already – he'd never seen her drink like this before. The *glühwein* was strong, too.

"Ilse, is everything okay? You just seem a little... distracted this evening."

About to protest that she didn't know what he could mean, she stopped. *This is your opportunity, seize it!* Taking another gulp of wine, she looked at him and said, "Do you remember when you asked me out for dinner after we went rowing on the lake in Treptower?"

"Of course – I'm sorry I jumped the gun. And I remember our conversation in the café four days later when you explained the consequences of your assault to me. Is that what it is? Has that bastard been bothering you again?"

"No, nothing like that. Since last week, I've been wondering if you still feel the way you did that afternoon in the park? You wanted us to be more than friends, more like... lovers. I would understand if your feelings aren't the same now, after I said I wasn't ready to trust a man. But after what happened two days ago, my feelings towards you have changed, so I had to find out if..."

She stopped, waiting for John to say something. He reached across the table and took her hand in his.

"I've never stopped having those feelings for you. And never stopped hoping yours might change."

She blushed, trying to find the right words.

"Oh, I see. Well…"

One of us has to move this forwards, he thought.

"Ilse, I would be delighted if you could join me for dinner tomorrow evening?"

She roared with laughter and said, "I'd love to."

Catching the waiter's eye, Ilse beckoned him over and ordered two glasses of Sekt, but John interrupted her, saying to the waiter, "Can we change that and have a bottle of Sekt with two glasses, please?"

"John, I've got work tomorrow morning. I'll be drunk!"

"If we're going to celebrate, Ilse, let's do it properly. More stollen, please, waiter."

Feeling uncomplicated joy in each other's obvious happiness, both swept along in the moment, they embraced. Holding her gaze, John cautiously moved closer until his lips touched hers. She sensed his reserve and knew what lay behind it. Deciding that the conversation about boundaries could wait, Ilse placed her hand behind his head, pulled him towards her and crushed her lips against his.

11

1925-1926, A NEW YEAR

Concerned that John was going to be on his own at Christmas, Ilse had suggested they meet at his flat on Christmas Eve.

"In Germany, we give each other presents and celebrate on Christmas Eve as much as Christmas Day, so I'll come round then with some snacks from the market."

As he opened the door, she embraced him with a long, exploratory kiss neither felt like ending. Sitting on his bed with a glass of schnapps, Ilse felt an underlying sense of things to come for both of them; she realised that she had to take responsibility for how fast their relationship moved on. *After everything I've told him about my rape, I can't expect him to take the lead. I need to send out unambiguous signals.* She was excited to feel that the prospect of intimacy between them stirred longing, not anxiety.

"*Prost!* Happy Christmas."

They raised their glasses to each other and downed the fruity liquid. Pulling a small package out of her bag, she said, "I'm afraid this won't be the most imaginative present you've ever received, but I promise it will be one of the most useful!"

"Wow, thank you so much. I have something for you, too. Happy Christmas, Ilse."

He'd spent hours searching for her present yesterday. She looked genuinely surprised that he'd bought her something, given he was still recovering from his injuries.

"Thank you! I wasn't expecting you to get me anything. Do you mind if I open mine now? It will mean much more opening it with you."

"I'd love you to. I was going to buy you one of those corsets the cabaret dancers wear, but I thought better of it in case you opened it in front of your parents."

She looked at him with incomprehension. How could he get it so wrong? Seeing the grin spread across his face, she realised.

"You're teasing me again, I hate you!"

She unwrapped her present, tearing at the paper.

"I love them, John! They must have cost you a fortune. Now, please open mine."

He could finally relax; she clearly genuinely liked the art nouveau earrings. But after he'd carefully undone the paper around her beautifully wrapped gift, he frowned. What had she bought him? It was a polished metal case with holes at one end and a removable top, slightly larger than a packet of cigarettes. Seeing his confusion, Ilse put him out of his misery.

"It's a hand warmer! I don't understand the science behind it, but it can keep your hands warm all day, apparently."

"What a brilliant present, Ilse. I love it, thank you."

"There's something else. Helga, a friend of mine, is having a New Year's Eve party, and you're invited. I didn't have to persuade her, she's dying to meet my new English boyfriend, so I hope you can come."

John had been dreading New Year's Eve. The thought of staying in his flat nursing a bottle of beer or joining the celebrating crowds was utterly depressing. He hadn't wanted to ask Ilse what she was doing, for fear of putting her in an awkward position if she'd made other arrangements.

"I'd love to come. Sounds scary being paraded as your new boyfriend; I hope your friends will go easy with me."

"You've got to dress up, it's the tradition here in Berlin."

"I don't have any dressing-up clothes. My wardrobe's very basic, as you've noticed."

"Aren't there any work clothes in your laboratory you could borrow for the night?"

"There's lots of white coats, that's about it. I'm going in for a few days after Christmas Day to try and get some work done in peace and quiet. I'll have a look."

"You're working between Christmas and New Year! Are all Englishmen so dedicated to their work?"

"I desperately need a breakthrough, Ilse. My review's coming up in two months, and frankly, I haven't got much to show from my research so far."

"Where will we meet on New Year's Eve?"

She thought about the options.

"If you're okay to walk to the taxi rank, I'll give you Helga's address and you can meet me there. Come around eight o'clock."

"Good idea, my leg is feeling much better. I hope you manage to enjoy Christmas with your parents and sister."

"I'm not looking forward to it, to be honest. There's an agreement between us to try and make the day a happy one, but I doubt if my father will be able to keep to it. Happy Christmas, John."

He put his arms around her and kissed her, excited by the way she kissed him back, then reined himself back. *Just take things slowly.*

"That was nice. Very nice. Happy Christmas, Ilse."

She felt lucky growing up celebrating both Hanukkah and Christmas with her family every year.

In less than two months John would have to account to his Head of Department for the meagre progress he'd made so far. If his boss wasn't satisfied, he'd have six months to turn things around or his place at the university could be in doubt.

But that wasn't the only reason he'd volunteered to work at the university over Christmas. The opportunity to search the shelves unobserved for weapons research of interest to Mark Chastain was too good to miss. Presenting him with such evidence wouldn't solve his research problems, but at least he'd feel he was achieving something.

It also went down well with the Dean.

"It's good that there'll be someone around in the laboratories over the Christmas and New Year holidays, Herr Samson. I'm most grateful. You say that you'll need the keys to the library as well?"

"Yes, please. I want to go through all the papers we've got on the Compton Effect and make sure I haven't missed anything."

He got lucky. After three days in the library he'd identified three research projects with a potential military application which had apparently been abandoned just as they were producing promising results – which was almost unheard of.

He made little progress with his own work.

***

"Hello, you must be John, Ilse's boyfriend. I'm Helga, please come in."

The young woman who'd greeted him looked dazzling; short satin dress adorned with sequins, kohl-black eyes and vermillion lipstick that wouldn't be out of place on a cabaret stage. He was relieved to see she wasn't wearing fancy dress, as he'd decided he looked too ridiculous in a white coat, large round glasses and a glue-on Einstein moustache. A glittery bow tie was his only contribution.

"Thank you for inviting me, Helga. Has Ilse arrived yet?"

She kissed him on both cheeks and took his coat as he handed her the bottle of wine he'd brought.

"Yes, she's here. But you may be waylaid by some of my friends before you get to her. Everyone is dying to meet this new man in her life. I can see why she likes you!"

He followed Helga towards the sound of the party, feeling increasingly apprehensive.

Guests had already started dancing enthusiastically in the large living room, some more co-ordinated than others. He was reassured that Ilse wasn't one of them.

"She must be in the kitchen, John," said Helga, as two young women who'd been dancing together stopped and walked over. Helga smiled and introduced them.

"I did warn you, John. Allow me to introduce Ingrid and Anita. Good luck! I'll let Ilse know you're here when I see her." Helga gave both women a look as she mentioned Ilse's name.

"You must dance with us, John. It wouldn't be fair for Ilse to have you all night. There are so few good-looking young men in Germany since the war, we have to share them."

He knew their teasing was in good fun, but his German wasn't good enough to extricate himself and he felt uncomfortable.

"You're here!"

Ignoring Ingrid and Anita, Ilse rushed over and kissed him on the mouth.

"All right, Ilse, we get it. 'Keep off, he's mine'. You don't have to be so obvious."

Ingrid and Anita laughed as Ilse took him into the kitchen to get drinks.

They were both drunk as midnight approached, Ilse more so than John as she wasn't used to drinking heavily. He stayed close to her, making sure that none of the other men jumped in for a kiss. She realised what he was up to.

"Are you making sure no one else grabs me for a kiss before you? That's very wise, I've seen a few men here this evening I wouldn't mind being kissed by."

"Just let them try!"

As the near-hysterical newscaster counted down on the radio, they looked lovingly at each other, absorbed in the moment. John felt joyously, childishly happy.

"*Vier… Drei… Zwei… Eins… Prosit Neujahr!*"

He held Ilse in his arms and kissed her, feeling aroused as she clutched him against her.

"You're a very sexy man."

"And you're a very desirable woman."

"*Prosit Neujahr*, John."

"Happy New Year, Ilse! What a wonderful party, I'm so happy being here with you."

She pulled him closer and said quietly, "Let's leave and go back to your flat."

He looked at her.

"Is that what you want?"

"I wouldn't say it if I didn't mean it. I'll say goodbye to Helga, you get your coat and I'll meet you outside."

It was below freezing, but trams were running and one came along after five minutes. They sat together, holding each other close for warmth as the tram wheels screeched around bends and over points. The journey gave John time to reflect on what they were planning to do, allowing doubts to creep in. Ilse was clearly much drunker than he'd thought she was. If they slept together tonight, this would be the first time that she'd willingly gone to bed with a man. He was excited about the thought of making love to her, and she clearly wanted him. But would she regret giving herself to him when she was drunk? He needed to think for both of them.

He had to keep her upright as they walked from the tram stop to his flat; however much she wanted to, he couldn't have sex with her in this state. She was in no condition to go home, either, so she could have his bed and he'd sleep on the floor under a rug.

His plan fell apart as soon as they were in his room. Swiftly removing her coat, she kissed him lustfully then started to remove her blouse.

"Let's get into bed. What's the matter, don't you want to?"

He wanted to more than anything, but this wasn't right.

"Of course I do! You're a beautiful woman and I'm aching to make love to you. But you're so drunk I can't be sure you'd be wanting this if you were sober. I don't want to wake up in the morning with you feeling regretful and me ashamed."

She was furious to be told by a man what she really wanted and began to speak.

"I'll decide what I want! If you've changed your mind and no longer want to make love to me, then why don't you…"

She stopped abruptly, her face suddenly ghostly pale with beads of sweat appearing on her forehead.

"Oh God, I think I'm going to be sick, John. Where's the toilet? Quickly, please, I can feel it coming up."

He'd seen what was happening and helped her out of the door and down the corridor to the bathroom. He held her hair back as she knelt over the toilet and vomited copiously into the bowl. The smell almost made him throw up, but her retching slowly subsided.

"Thank you, I'm so sorry, can you stay with me until the worst is over?"

"Of course I will. You'll feel better once you've emptied your stomach."

Back in his room, he helped her sit in the only chair.

"How are you feeling now, Ilse? You're looking less like a ghost."

"Awful. Ashamed. I just want to lie down. Can I stay here tonight, I'm happy to sleep on the floor if you've got a blanket?"

"Of course you must stay here, and you'll have the bed. Why

don't you undress to your underwear, drink some water and get into bed while I clean up in the bathroom? Please don't argue with me, I'll sleep in the chair. Will you do that, please?"

Ilse looked at him lovingly.

"Thank you, you're my hero."

She was fast asleep when John came back. After an hour trying to sleep in the chair with a blanket – cold, cramped and uncomfortable – he went to the toilet and checked Ilse hadn't been sick in her sleep. When he saw that she'd moved in the night, leaving him just enough space, he carefully slipped in under the eiderdown and went to sleep.

When he woke in the morning, she'd rolled over and was lying snuggled alongside, one arm draped across his chest, breasts pressed against him. The warm sensation of her body shaped around his felt wonderful. He lay still, looking at her face and waited for her to wake up.

She surfaced gradually, eyes slowly focussing on his and taking in that, self-evidentially, they'd slept together. He was anxious she might assume they'd had sex, given her previous experience. But she just lifted her arm off of his chest, slowly moved her body away and gave him a pained smile.

"Good morning, Ilse, how do you feel? Or is that a stupid question?"

She looked at him, brow furrowed, corners of her lips turned down.

"I feel ashamed. Who was I last night? I've never been that drunk before, and don't ever want to be again. You were so caring, thank you; I'm glad you got into bed, it's freezing in this room. I've got an awful headache; have you got any aspirin left?"

"Yes. I'll find them, put the fire on and make us some coffee."

"Wonderful, thank you. Could I lie here for a while until I feel half human again?"

"Stay as long as you need and let me take care of you."

She watched him get up, pull on trousers and a shirt over his vest and underpants and begin to make the coffee.

"John, I have hardly any memory of last night after we'd got off the tram. What happened after that?"

"The truth? We walked back here, with me supporting you most of the way. As soon as we got upstairs, you started to undress, kissed me and proposed that we go to bed. Before anything could happen, you suddenly felt sick so I took you to the toilet and stayed with you to make sure you were okay. I put you to bed and tried to sleep in the chair, but when I got up in the night and saw there was room to get in beside you, I climbed in. It was freezing cold in the chair. Nothing happened, you don't have to worry. But I did appreciate being warm at last."

Ilse studied his face with bleary eyes and a throbbing headache.

"I know nothing happened. But hearing that, I feel even more disgusted with myself. What must you think of me? Being liberated and having the right to drink alcohol in public shouldn't mean having a licence to get insensibly drunk. I wouldn't blame you if you wanted time to reconsider our relationship – but please don't! I won't ever get into that state again."

"My feelings for you haven't changed one iota, Ilse. One night of excessive drinking doesn't change anything, you must know that. Don't scold yourself."

They spent the rest of the day together; she had a bath, brushed her teeth with John's toothbrush – "Do you mind, my mouth feels like the bottom of a bird cage" – and drank several cups of coffee. He had enough bread and cheese to keep them from going hungry; they sat on cushions in front of the gas fire, kissing, talking about the party and her plans to move into a flat in two weeks' time. At three o'clock in the afternoon, she said, "I would love to stay here longer with you, but my family will be worrying by now in spite of my earlier phone call, so I should be going. I had a wonderful time last night until I disgraced myself. Thank you for taking such care of me, John."

They walked to the tram stop among the crowds of Berliners enjoying the New Year's Day holiday, holding each other close until the tram came.

12

BREAKTHROUGH

As a result of his enforced convalescence, John began to worry even more about the lack of progress with his own research. He'd never found science a struggle intellectually, always assuming that he would progress through higher school certificates, on to a science degree, a postgraduate position and then a postdoctorate position. Up to now, scientific research had been rewarding and inspiring; he couldn't remember a time when he'd seriously doubted his abilities, so the current lack of progress had begun to undermine his confidence.

Don't get this out of proportion. You'd previously gone up blind alleys with your doctorate research, yet the breakthroughs always came. Take some days away from the lab, that usually worked before. You've got nearly two months before your review.

While he'd begun to realise the potential military value of the papers he'd identified in the university library, any time spent following up this lead would further reduce the chances of making a breakthrough with his own research.

There was, perhaps, one way of buying time: going off on a tangent.

Soon after arriving at Friedrich Wilhelm he'd made interesting observations about the effect of applying high voltages to krypton gas held in a glass tube at low pressure. At a particular voltage, the gas would emit a green-yellow glow. While it didn't seem to have an immediate relationship to his core research, he could probably develop a believable hypothesis and write it up for his review.

He'd set up the experiment again when the department opened up officially in two days.

It was several days before John and Ilse could meet again; she was overwhelmed pulling together the changes to the programme schedule and the preparations for moving into her flat. Bad timing. She could hardly ask her boss to hold back the new schedules for a week so that she could move in. The changes seemed to be taking the station in the wrong direction, as the time for news had been reduced and replaced by features about life in the city. To Ilse, this downplaying of serious news wasn't coincidental; the station had been criticised by politicians for carrying too many stories about the number of strikes and violent confrontations between the communists and Nazis. But it was her job and she'd do it professionally.

There'd been angry, emotional scenes with her father and mother after Christmas when she'd told them that she'd finally found a flat and would be moving out of the family home in two weeks. She'd reminded them of the times she'd told them she'd be moving out, but they refused to accept it. They'd obviously never believed that she was serious, so when she stuck to her decision, they stopped talking to her. A year ago, that would have hurt her deeply, but not now. Her father's attitude to her relationship with John had built a wall of misunderstanding and hurt on both sides, and she was in no hurry to rebuild it.

She was sad for Greta, but hoped this might eventually give her sister the confidence to stand up to their parents too.

If ever the arguments threatened to upset her, she reminded herself of the opportunity that her own flat would bring. She wanted an intimate, physical relationship with John, and they could now explore that at their own pace, in their own way. Reading an illustrated book for newlywed brides by the sex reform movement that explained the ways couples could achieve a pleasurable sex life, Ilse felt her pulse quicken as she imagined them making love like the couples in the illustrations.

She'd been afraid that her shameful New Year's Eve behaviour might change John's feelings towards her. He'd been so lovely that night, giving up his bed, looking after her throughout the day. Although it was a surprise to find herself lying closely against him when she woke, she'd felt completely safe.

They'd arranged to meet outside her new flat in two days' time, on the morning she collected the keys. She couldn't wait to see him.

John knew he was going to be working flat out over the next six weeks. He was at his bench by seven thirty, spending the rest of the morning attempting to replicate the results from his early experiments with krypton gas. After half an hour for lunch he spent another four hours trying to track down where the three suspiciously vanished research papers had ended up. Both tasks were consuming time that he wanted to spend with Ilse, but he knew he had no choice if he was going to keep MI6 and Friedrich Wilhelm University happy.

Three days after going back to work, he had a breakthrough. One of the three suspiciously abandoned papers – *On the practical implications of combining two liquids under pressure and igniting them* – had ended up in the hands of a German aeronautical research company called Flussig Dynamisch. Any competent scientist would know immediately where this was leading; the development of liquid-fuelled rocket propulsion. He became increasingly excited as he realised this could be exactly the sort of research the Germans wanted to keep hidden. *Don't get too excited, the difficult part is still to come – finding out if they'd had any promising results.*

That had to wait for after this weekend, as he'd promised to help Ilse move into her flat. Which is how he found himself stamping his boots on the pavement trying to keep warm with Ilse's hand warmer at nine o'clock on Saturday morning, patiently waiting outside her new address. He'd never been to the area before, but he'd enjoyed taking in the new neighbourhoods on the thirty-minute walk from his flat as dawn was breaking. Her flat was on the third floor of a typical 1880s Berlin block.

He saw her crossing the road two hundred metres away. Smiling broadly, she gave a little wave and picked up her pace. Her lips felt warm against his as they kissed.

"Thank you for coming out on such a cold morning, John. I've missed you."

"I've missed you too. The place looks interesting from the outside, Ilse. Can we go in, I'm freezing."

"Sorry to be late. My father had another go at me just as I was leaving, and I wasn't prepared to walk away this time before I'd explained once again why I was moving out. My life is going to change enormously once I'm out of his house. In more ways than one!"

She looked at him knowingly and opened the front door to the block.

"The landlord has assured me that the place has been cleaned, but you can never be sure, so I don't know what state it's in. Be prepared for a shock."

He followed her up the stairwell, which seemed clean enough, admiring her calf muscles flexing under her silk stockings as she took the stairs two at a time. As they stopped on the third floor to the sound of jazz coming from the neighbour's flat, Ilse nervously unlocked the door, walked in and gave a shriek of delight.

It was basically one very large room, but each different area – sleeping, cooking and living – had plenty of space. The previous tenant had even sectioned off the 'bedroom area' with a floor-to-ceiling curtain. The living area had a sofa, two armchairs and a small dining table. Although dawn was less than half an hour ago, the flat was light enough for John to see that the furniture and décor seemed in good condition.

Ilse had been standing in the middle of the room, taking her time to scrutinise everything. She turned to John, a look of delight on her face.

"It's wonderful, John, better than I ever imagined it would be. I'm going to be very happy here."

She came over and kissed him, and this time she didn't break away.

As she checked that everything in the kitchen was working, John quietly got out the bottle of Sekt from his satchel.

"I think we should toast your new home! Why don't you see if there are any glasses in the cupboards while I get the cork out of the bottle?"

"What a wonderful idea! You're always surprising me, come here."

They toasted the health of the flat and its new occupant and kissed again, mouths awash with fizzing Sekt. After breakfast at a local café they went shopping at the nearest department store with the list Ilse had made of the essentials she'd need.

While Ilse unpacked, John bought food for their evening meal at the local shops. He still felt apprehensive about the reception he might get whenever he went into a shop for the first time. While his German was much improved, it was immediately obvious he was English when he asked people to speak more slowly. Men of a certain age who'd been in the war gave him the hardest time.

That evening, eating sausages, garlic mashed potatoes and red cabbage together, they shared her joy at being in her new flat. There was no sexual tension – they both knew that nothing was going to happen tonight. It would come in the future, and that was all that mattered. They opened a bottle of red wine and sat talking, taking it in turns to ask the inquisitive questions they'd been holding back up to now, making discoveries about each other's hopes, dreams and lives. *What did you think of me the first time we met? Tell me about your affair with Helen – who made the first move, were you in love with her, what did you feel when she met someone else? What benefit to mankind will your research bring? Will your community disapprove of you having a non-Jewish boyfriend?*

It was midnight by the time John left. They kissed each other goodbye and agreed not to meet again until the following Friday; they both had lots of work to do. She was still behind with the new schedules; he had to track down the research on rocket propulsion and start creating 'promising' results from his own experiments.

13

FOLLOWING THE EVIDENCE

He'd only intended to spend three days investigating Flussig Dynamisch, the company that now owned the research paper on compressed liquids, but it took twice that. He began by arranging to meet the young scientist responsible for the original research, on the basis of discussing shared areas of scientific interest.

The meeting with David Finkelstein went well. Once he'd deftly moved their conversation about light-emitting gases on to other areas of research they'd been involved in, Finkelstein brought up his research on igniting compressed liquids. He was furious that his small university department had been told to hand over all his work to Flussig Dynamisch. What's more, he'd been instructed to have nothing more to do with 'his' research. "Because I'm Jewish, probably." The name of Finkelstein's successor at Flussig Dynamisch was Hans Meyer.

John now had the name of the scientist who was potentially leading the German military's research into liquid-fuelled rocket propulsion. He spent the whole of Friday in the Library for Physical Sciences, going through physics scientific journals searching for recent articles citing work by Hans Meyer. By the end of the day he'd only scratched the surface, although any feelings of frustration were swept away by the prospect of spending the evening with Ilse. She'd promised to cook him a meal.

He went back to his flat, had a bath and a shave, changed his shirt and underwear then bought flowers and a bottle of Sekt on the way to her flat.

"Come in, John, welcome! Flowers and wine, thank you! Just what a woman appreciates from her boyfriend. Tonight it's your privilege to eat the first home cooking that *kochin* Lipsky has prepared in her new home. You are my honoured guest. Please take your coat off, pour us both a glass of wine and make yourself comfortable while I carry on. It should be ready in about fifteen minutes."

John did as instructed, sat down and looked around the room. It looked different. There were several posters from Berlin theatres on the wall behind the table, a picture in the Art Deco style of four women bathing, three new cushions on the bed, a table lamp and a bedside light. She'd replaced the grubby-looking curtain around the basin with a new floral print.

"You've made the room look really welcoming, Ilse. You've got a talent, but I'm surprised you had the time after the work you had to do on the new schedules."

"My other lover helped me, we did it in no time."

She half turned and grinned at him as he walked over to her. Standing behind her, he put his arms around her and bent his head next to hers. Her hair smelt of lavender soap. He kissed her neck, then said, "So I'm sharing you, am I? What's he like, this other lover?"

"He's a very serious, upright Prussian officer who demands that I cater to his every need. He says that if he ever meets you he'll demand a duel. I'm afraid to tell you he's a top marksman and swordsman."

"So how can I win you over?"

"I think you already have. Now sit down and be patient, it won't be long."

He did as he was told. Watching her as she stirred the stew and shifted pans from the hob to the oven, he realised that his fascination with everything about her came from much more than physical desire. She was beautiful and he found her sexually attractive, but his feelings went beyond that. He wanted to protect her from the evil in the world, to know what she thought about every conceivable subject, big and small, to share plans for the future together.

He was in love with her.

At the end of the evening, both of them slightly drunk, John said, "I think I should be going back as I need to go to the university early tomorrow morning."

"You don't have to go back, John. It's a big bed and I'm sure we could share it, as long as you understand that I don't yet feel ready to have sex. Of course, I won't be offended if you don't want to stay."

He thought about it, then said, "I'd love to, but I've got to get up early tomorrow. If I'm honest, I'm worried that I haven't yet produced enough convincing results for my review in four weeks' time. I need to focus on several of my experiments until I've got a believable set of results to present. If I don't, there's even a chance I won't get funding next year."

"I understand. Why don't I get us tickets to see a play next Friday? We could have a meal somewhere beforehand too."

"That a wonderful idea, I'd love to."

Walking back to his flat, hunched down into his scarf and coat against the freezing air, he felt slightly guilty. It was true, he would have to spend most of the coming weekend and the following week producing more results from his research so far – embellished or not – and continue to search scientific research journals for articles from Hans Meyer. But the real reason he'd declined to stay was that he wanted the first time they truly slept together to be the first time they made love, and he was prepared to wait for that moment.

His life suddenly seemed influenced by big risks and amazing opportunities, any of which could suddenly change. He could fail his review and be asked to quit his position at Friedrich Wilhelm; if he was stealing the research on liquid-powered rockets he could be arrested; Ilse might decide that she wasn't ready for sex and end their relationship, breaking his heart. He felt more alive than he could ever remember.

Ilse lay in bed, unable to sleep, tormented by her confused feelings. She knew that when she'd suggested to John that he could sleep with her, her risk-taking side had taken charge in the knowledge that sex might result. Which was crazy; apart from anything else, she didn't have any contraception and assumed he didn't either. But given their mutual physical attraction and the trust between them, what, exactly, was she waiting for? Aroused by the possibilities, she consulted the appropriate pages of her book for newlywed brides and relieved her tension.

When she woke in the morning her mind was clear; she would visit a sympathetic female doctor who she'd heard about from a colleague at work and have a cap fitted.

Doctor Hans Meyer would need to publish his results somewhere in order to have his work peer-reviewed. Without standing it up to critical interrogation by his fellow scientists, the research would lack credibility. But as Flussig Dynamisch didn't want the world to know about this work, they would have to bury it somehow in the middle of another piece of research.

Four days later, mentally fatigued after scouring through volumes of research with apparently irrelevant titles, John had the breakthrough he was looking for:

Pressures needed to achieve combustion between a liquid fuel and an oxidiser. Theoretical maximum energy released by burning ethylene and kerosene in oxygen.
Doctor Hans Meyer

Removing Meyer's research paper from the science library was out of the question. Security was strict; everyone's bags and coats were searched entering and leaving, and his career would be over if he was found removing papers. But he'd noticed that people wearing indoor clothing weren't personally searched; if Mark Chastain would cough up for a Kodak vest-pocket camera, he should be able to bring it into the library, take pictures of the document and leave again without being detected. They cost the equivalent of three pounds, so it shouldn't be beyond MI6's budget.

He phoned Mark early the next morning.

"Hello, John, I was talking to Andrew yesterday and we wondered how you were getting on?"

In other words, what the hell have you been doing for the last five weeks?

He didn't want to reveal too much over the phone, so he simply said, "I think I may have found something of interest that I should only tell you face to face, but I'll need a small camera. Can you get me one?"

"That sounds interesting. A little worrying, too. Come round to the usual entrance on Monday and ask for me. I'll have a little Kodak for you. Good man, well done!"

He felt elated by Mark's response. He'd only just put the office phone down when it rang. It was Ilse, sounding happy but rushed.

"I hope you've remembered our date tonight, my darling man. The theatre's in Friedrichstadt, and I've booked us into Café Marlene, two hundred metres away. Let's meet there at six o'clock. I must go, sorry, they want me in the studio. Goodbye, my love."

He'd barely had time to respond with "Hello" and "Goodbye"

before she put the phone down, but he couldn't feel annoyed. The call had been so warm and loving – *my darling man* and *my love*. The thought of being with her this evening raised his spirits even further; he didn't even begrudge having to spend the rest of the day setting up his apparatus and massaging some results for his review in three weeks' time.

By the end of the afternoon he'd managed to produce two sets of observations that could form the basis for a presentation at his review that might cover up his lack of progress.

Ilse was standing outside as John approached the café three minutes early, smiling broadly. There was something different about her, but he couldn't name it. As he went to embrace her she put her hand behind his head and kissed him hard on the mouth. Her perfume was different. More earthy.

"Has anyone ever told you what a sexy man you are? I'm a lucky woman. Let's eat, I'm starving."

Intrigued, he followed her inside.

After the play – a little too avant-garde for him – they went back to her flat for a nightcap. She knew what she wanted, had thought it through and taken precautions, but worried that her lack of experience might mess things up. *You can only get so much information from a book, Ilse.*

Pouring them both a brandy as soon as they'd walked in, thinking that she'd need one to take the next step, she found she didn't. Chinking her glass against his, she said, "*Prost.* Shall we get into bed?"

Caught off guard, he seemed to hesitate.

"In case I'm not making myself clear, I want you to make love to me."

She took off her jacket and kicked off her shoes.

"I'd like to take this slowly," he said, as they undressed down to their underwear.

"Here, let me help," she said, as he struggled to take off her camisole, arching her back and leaning forwards so he could pull it over her head.

He looked at her, transfixed.

"God, you're so beautiful."

As his lips lingered over her breasts, she could feel her heart beating fiercely against her chest.

"Is this real?"

"Very real, John."

"But is this, you know, safe?"

"I've taken care of that, so why don't you take these off."

Ilse slowly opened her eyes to the sound of running water in the corner of the room. She'd slept deeply ever since they'd gone to sleep in each other's arms. John was standing at the sink, cleaning his teeth. He stopped and turned to look at her.

"Good morning, my love. Can I make you a coffee?"

"That would be lovely. But I'd like you to kiss me first."

He did as he was told, then went to the stove to make their coffee. She pulled her underwear and dressing gown on, took a tube from the bedside cabinet and went to the bathroom. When she returned, he took her the coffee and got into bed next to her.

"That was so intense, John. You were very passionate and considerate. If I'd known what I'd been missing, I would have started earlier." She laughed, then kissed him.

"It was incredible for me, Ilse. I felt such a connection between us."

"I felt that too. I didn't want it to end."

She saw the look on his face.

"I'm sorry. It won't always be over that fast, I promise."

She weighed up her response.

"I think I can help. Can I show you?"

Afterwards, they lay in bed talking, asking each other big careless questions when everything is new and nothing is off-limits. When they finally got up, they spent the rest of the day walking along the Spree, making plans, telling each other "I love you."

14

GETTING SERIOUS

Early the following Monday morning, John skipped light-headedly up the steps to the front of the British Embassy. He gave the sentry his name, informed him that Mark Chastain is expecting him and waited at the imposing reception desk. The young man he finally sees approaching is definitely not Mark.

"Good morning, Mr Samson. Please come with me, Mr Chastain is expecting you."

As he was shown into Chastain's office he was surprised to see Andrew Russell and another man, as well as Mark. They all stood and shook his hand. Giving him a camera doesn't need three diplomats; John realised that his information must have stirred up considerable interest.

"It's good to see you, John. I believe you know Andrew. This is Charles Drummond, who I've asked to join us. He'll explain how to get the best pictures from the camera we've got for you. To start with, though, could you please take us through what you believe you've discovered and how you came upon it."

John went methodically through the laborious steps he'd taken to finally narrow his search down to three promising research projects, the reason he'd chosen this particular one to start with, the problems he'd overcome tracking it down and his need for a camera to photograph the research document in situ.

"I've discovered research into liquid-fuelled rockets that the Germans are trying to keep out of the public eye. Possibly with army involvement. Given the search procedures entering and leaving the library, it would be far too risky to try and remove the document itself."

"We understand that, but I didn't think that liquid-fuelled rockets existed – they're solid-fuelled, aren't they?"

John turned to Charles.

"They are at the moment. They've been around in China for hundreds of years, if not longer. But amateur scientists in America and Europe are beginning to experiment with liquid-fuelled rockets. There's a gentleman in America that's built one. No successful launches so far, but he's getting somewhere, I believe."

"What's the advantage of liquid fuels?" asked Andrew.

"There are two. The energy delivered per pound of fuel is much higher with liquids like petrol or ethanol, compared to solid alternatives. Plus, as the liquid-fuelled rocket gets oxygen from a tank in the rocket, not from the atmosphere, it can fly much higher and further, into the stratosphere where there's little oxygen."

"What's the point of that? Solid-fuelled rockets can already fly long distances, can't they?"

"That really depends what you mean by a long distance. Going to the moon, for example." He saw the astonished and dismissive looks on their faces. John was enjoying himself.

"I agree that's a science-fiction fantasy at the moment. But think of the implications for a country of being able to launch an armed rocket high into the stratosphere at another country thousands of miles away, far greater than the range of the largest gun."

He watched the implications sink in. Mark looked at Andrew

and Charles, then said, "I'm convinced this is worth pursuing. Charles will show you the Kodak vest-pocket camera, which MI6 have adapted for taking close-up photographs of documents. If at any time you think there's a risk you'll be discovered, expose the film and ditch the camera. Contact us as soon as you've got the pictures. From now on, don't talk about this to anyone. Well done, John. And good luck."

He almost ran down the steps outside the Embassy after he'd signed out at the desk, charged with adrenaline after the meeting. Once he'd left Mark's office, Drummond had taken him through the basic controls on the tiny Kodak camera and explained how it had been adapted to take close-up pictures indoors. He'd then asked John to explain everything back to him and only let him go when he was satisfied John had done it perfectly.

Although Mark had made it clear he wanted the pictures as soon as possible, John wasn't going to be rushed. He'd noticed that the library staff had less time to search bags and coats when lots of people were leaving and had worked out the best day and time to leave. He practised taking pictures of pages from his own research in his flat then took them to a chemist to be developed. When they came out well, everything was set to go ahead.

Today was Wednesday. He would visit the library tomorrow, photograph the research paper and leave with the crowd at the end of the day. What could go wrong?

He arrived the next day at 2.30, went straight to the shelves with Meyer's research then stood staring at the space where he'd last seen it, aghast. Panicking, he patrolled the aisles, looking at every desk, hoping someone had taken it out to read. No luck. He sat down at an empty desk to think and calm his nerves. There were only two options; either the paper had been put back in the wrong section or shelf accidentally, or it had been deliberately moved to stop someone else reading it. He went back to the shelf where the paper should have been and looked at the surrounding shelves, drawing a blank. *Think. If someone hides something like this deliberately, where's the likeliest place they'd put it to find it quickly the next time?*

He moved to the corresponding shelf on the two adjacent aisles, with no luck, then moved to the next two adjacent aisles. And there it was, hidden in plain sight. Taking the document to a secluded desk he'd seen earlier, he took out the camera and began to photograph the pages on liquid propellants, framing each page exactly within the simple viewfinder. The camera was small, but the shutter made an alarmingly loud metallic sound each time he took a picture; he had to look around after each shot and ensure no one had come to check. The document was twenty-two pages long and as each film held twelve exposures, he had to rewind the first film into the lightproof canister and load a second film.

Once finished, he put the document back where he'd found it – if it had been deliberately misplaced, he didn't want whoever was responsible to get suspicious – put both film canisters in one trouser pocket and the camera in the other. Picking up his briefcase, he walked towards the exit booth where there was an even longer queue than usual. As he peered towards the front, he saw the reason. To his horror, there were extra librarians on duty and they were giving everyone a thorough search, instructing them to turn out their pockets. Anything he tried to conceal today would certainly be found.

Slipping away from the back of the queue, he considered his options. He could hide the film canisters behind the cisterns in the men's toilets and return another day when security had returned to normal. Although it was small, trying to hide the Kodak camera was too big a risk. If they found it in the building there would be a painstakingly thorough search for the film. There was only one option; walk out holding the camera in full view, claiming that he'd walked in carrying it and no one had stopped him. Why was he walking around with a camera with no film? Because he was taking it to be repaired as the shutter kept sticking. He'd need to smear something onto the delicate shutter blades.

Ten minutes later, having carefully placed the two film canisters behind the cistern in cubicle three, he rejoined the queue, brazenly holding the camera. As he got to the front, one of the librarians looked askance and angrily told him it was forbidden to bring cameras into the library.

"Give me your camera immediately!"

John handed it over.

"I'm very sorry, I didn't know. I brought it in like this and nobody said anything. I'm taking it to be mended, it's broken."

He opened the camera, disappointed to find there was no film.

"What's wrong with it?"

"The shutter sticks open sometimes."

The librarian pressed the shutter lever several times. It stuck the third time.

The second librarian spoke to his colleague. "No harm's been done, Albert. Let him keep it."

Grudgingly he handed it back to John.

"You must never bring a camera into this library again, broken or not."

"Of course, thank you."

He couldn't risk going back the next day to get the film; if the same librarians were on duty, they'd search him thoroughly. He'd go back again in the middle of next week and retrieve the films. As he walked back to his flat, still shaken, his thoughts turned to the weekend ahead.

He'd arranged to meet Ilse at a café for lunch on Saturday and spend the weekend together, relaxing, talking and exploring each other's hopes for the future. The memory of their lovemaking last Friday had stayed with him all week; her passion and growing confidence had fuelled his. He didn't realise books like the one Ilse had existed; some pictures had already given him ideas. The way she'd sorted out her contraception! What an amazing woman.

Ilse had other things on her mind at that moment. The radio station management had called a meeting with the staff to discuss a letter they'd received from the Funkstade Board. The Nazi Party had complained to the Board about the station's lack of balance, of under-reporting their support and of focussing on the violence that accompanied their meetings. The Board had caved in and were demanding that Funkstade managers change their editorial line, but staff were furious and insisted the station shouldn't give in to threats from fascists.

Their strength of feeling persuaded managers to draw up a joint letter to the Board, refuting the Nazi Party's claims and providing supporting evidence. Ilse had agreed to be on the group drafting the letter on Friday evening, but disagreements over the wording meant she didn't leave the office until almost midnight.

As she left the building and turned to walk to the tram stop, her pulse quickened as she saw four Nazi Brownshirts standing on the opposite pavement.

Their obscene calls followed her down the street:

"Treacherous whore, you'll get what's coming to you."

"Keep telling lies about us and you'll regret it."

Their threats convinced Ilse that Funkstade had to play its part and keep broadcasting the truth about the Nazis. Unsettled, she heard a tram approaching and decided to catch it rather than walk home. If they followed her, they'd find out where she lived.

Saturday dawned with clear skies and a bitterly cold north-east wind coming all the way from Siberia. John was pleased with the outcome of his eight hours' work in the lab on Friday. He'd generated enough results from his krypton gas experiments to be confident of presenting a sufficiently robust case to the Head of

Department. He might be concerned about the change in direction of John's research compared to his original question, but John felt he had to take the chance.

None of these thoughts were troubling him as he sat in their usual corner window table in the Café Schumann, where they'd met for the first time several months ago. He looked around at the other customers and felt sorry for them. They didn't have a beautiful girlfriend they were falling in love with, the status of a postdoctorate position at one of the world's top universities or a secret mission to uncover German research. He'd experienced enough setbacks in his life to know that glittering opportunities like this came along through luck as much as talent, and could change at any time. Happenstance, serendipity, fate – call it what you like, he wasn't going to take good fortune like this for granted.

He sensed her presence before he saw her enter the café; it was weird, particularly for someone whose adult life up to now had been framed by reason and facts. He wasn't supposed to believe in anything extra-sensory – totally unscientific. But here was the evidence, walking quickly towards him with a huge smile on her face. They flung themselves into each other's arms, overjoyed at seeing each other. Their embrace turned into a passionate kiss that had other customers staring. As they broke apart, Ilse looked at him and said, "Do you really want a coffee, John? Or is there something else you would prefer to be doing right now?"

Their route from her flat door to the bed was marked out as clearly as Gretel's breadcrumbs; coats and jackets in a heap inside the door, her dress and his shirt hanging over a chair, his trousers and her stockings at the bottom of the bed, his underpants and her drawers on top of the eiderdown. She was still wearing her camisole as she climbed on top of him.

Hours later, feeling a little sore and hungry, they walked arm in arm to the nearest café. Several diners turned to look as they walked in and sat down. The waiter gave them a knowing look as Ilse ordered two glasses of Sekt and a plate of sausages with cabbage and potato pancakes. When the wine arrived John raised his glass and made a toast:

"To my beautiful girlfriend, long may I be able to satisfy her insatiable needs."

"You'd better, or I'll be looking elsewhere."

They laughed, then John said, "I love you, Ilse. You are the most amazing person I've ever met. I don't ever want to lose you."

"There's no chance that you'll be losing me; I love you too."

The following day was bright and cold, but the increasing height of the February sun on their backs warmed them as they walked around Treptower Park. Ilse wanted to tell him about the Nazis' threats to the station's independence and the heated disagreements between the staff and the managers about how to respond to the Board.

"We've just reported the facts about their membership and the violence that erupts on the streets after their meetings, backed up with evidence. The Nazis intimidated the Board and they tried in turn to intimidate the management, but the staff succeeded in persuading the managers to sign a joint letter to the Board. I was in the office until nearly midnight on Friday as I'd volunteered to draft it. It's good, so I hope the managers don't amend it when they read it on Monday."

"I'd like to see it. Didn't you say yesterday that a group of Nazis had shouted at you in the street? Was that as you left the building at midnight?"

"Yes, but there were other people around and I wasn't worried."

"Ilse, promise me if you ever find yourself in that situation again you'll go back inside the building and call me, or call a cab to the door if I don't answer. I've had some experience of these people, remember? I know what they're capable of."

"I can't promise that, but I will be more careful. They're trying to stir up hatred against anyone they blame for Germany losing the war – socialist politicians, the press, liberals, artists, Jews. Mostly the Jews. At the moment they don't pose a danger to the Republic because so few people vote for them, but we have to be vigilant. Is there much reporting about the Nazis in Britain?"

"Very little. But then Britain's got its own problems at the moment, so I don't expect many people are paying attention to what's going on in Germany. My father thinks there's a good chance that the mine owners are going to try and cut miners' wages, and there'll be a strike if they do."

"Cut miners' wages! There would be a revolution here if they tried to do that! It's so depressing sometimes; politicians promised that the last war would be the war to end all wars, but signs of nationalist feeling are rising again all over Europe. I just hope these anti-Jewish sentiments don't escalate. Do you ever think about the fact I'm Jewish? Does it matter to you?"

John looked at Ilse, hurt that she could ask him such a thing.

"Of course it doesn't matter, Ilse, how can you ask that? Many of Germany's best physicists are Jewish and they've inspired me. I'll always be there for you, and your family, if they're threatened."

"You can't begin to understand what it means for me to hear you say that."

"I mean it, Ilse. I will never turn away if you're ever in trouble."

Ilse looked at him and felt a fleeting concern. Their relationship had developed so swiftly over the last few weeks; she'd been swept along by her rapidly deepening emotions. He'd just said something of huge importance to her – but how much did she really know about this English, Christian man? How could he really be sure that he'd always be there for Ilse and her family? They came from such different worlds.

15

HELD TO ACCOUNT

John hadn't given much thought to the hidden spools of film during his weekend with Ilse. He'd decided to wait until Wednesday because the same librarians shouldn't be on duty then, but the possibility that the films might be discovered by chance was suddenly all he could think about. He couldn't wait any longer – he'd go to the library later this afternoon.

As he walked in he was relieved to see different librarians on duty. He waited ages for 'his' cubicle to become free and was finally surprised to see two men step out, looking startled as they saw him. They probably assumed he was a plain-clothes policeman as there were vacant cubicles, and hurried out.

There was a strong smell of eau de cologne in the cubicle. Reaching down behind the cistern his fingers quickly found and retrieved one of the spools, but he couldn't find the second one. His heart rate quickened as a sense of panic rose in his chest. *Calm yourself, it's got to be here somewhere.* He pressed his head up against the wall and looked behind the cistern and saw the second spool lying on the tiled floor behind the pedestal. God knows how it had remained unnoticed. Hurrying now, he took his shoes off and pushed each spool down to the front; there was just enough room to get his feet inside.

As he walked towards the exit he was dismayed to see that the previously suspicious librarian was now on duty again. At least they weren't searching people – everyone was just filing out. But as he went to follow the woman in front of him, the librarian put out his arm and stopped him.

"Back so soon?" He smiled. "Have you fixed your camera yet?"

"Thank you for asking, I'm going to collect it now. They said the shutter needed a good clean, that's all."

As John went to go through, the librarian held his hand out again.

"Please take off your coat. Just a routine check."

John took it off and passed it over, noticing the man's Nazi lapel badge. One or two people behind him started to complain about being held up as the librarian went through every pocket.

"Now your jacket."

John decided to take a risk. He turned round to the rest of the queue, shrugged his shoulders and said, "I don't think this National Socialist gentleman likes me. He seems to be singling me out."

Several people in the queue were now shouting, "disgraceful," "fascist" or "let him through" at the librarian, who began to look uncomfortable. Two heavy-set men came to the front of the queue, squared up to the librarian and said to John, "You go through, comrade, we'll deal with this little fascist."

The librarian looked along the queue for support, but found none.

"This is outrageous, I won't forget it. However, I've seen all I need, you can proceed."

Putting his coat back on, John said, "Neither will I. I'll be reporting your behaviour to the Dean at Friedrich Wilhelm tomorrow morning. I understand he knows the chief administrator here. Good day."

Turning to thank his two interlocutors, he put his coat back on and left. Initially pleased with his quick thinking, the feeling of the films in his shoes began to make him very vulnerable. He decided to take them straight to the Embassy.

Thirty minutes later he was sitting in Mark's office.

"So you think that once the Wehrmacht got wind of this research they made sure it was moved away from the prying eyes of the wider science community?"

"Given its potential importance, I can't see another explanation."

"Could you explain to a non-scientist why you think this research might be so important? From what I've managed to find out, there hasn't yet been a successful flight by one of these things."

John felt irritated by the question. He'd been in Mark's company for over ten minutes and he hadn't uttered a word of congratulations, or showed any understanding of the risks he'd taken.

"That's true, but the problems are slowly being overcome by a few amateurs working in isolation. If the German Army put's money into this, I think there could soon be successful longer-range flights. I agree the experiments are at an early stage, and it's not my field, so let's see what your experts think of the research paper I've taken considerable risks to obtain."

Mark picked up John's irritation and realised he hadn't thanked him.

"Of course, John, I didn't mean to suggest that this isn't exactly the type of research that we were asking you to track down. My apologies. I'll get the pictures developed and printed then send them to the Ministry of Defence for analysis. We should get their response in a week or so. Do you have any further ideas for us?"

"I need to concentrate on my own research as I've got my six-month review coming up in three weeks. It would be wise not to pay any more visits to the science library for a while, as I had an argument with one of the librarians the last time I was there. He was wearing a Nazi Party badge, and he'll certainly remember me."

"What's the significance of being a member of the Nazi Party in Germany at the moment? Does it get you some influence with the police?" John queried.

"That's a good question. At the moment the Nazis are a small Party that relies on rallies and street violence to get their message across. At present, any employee of the state is forbidden to join, so I'm surprised this man was wearing a badge. But there are many disgruntled ex-soldiers who are attracted to the Party. There are probably groups in the police force who are sympathetic, too. But I wouldn't worry, I don't think this librarian will cause you much of a problem."

"That's reassuring. Will you let me know what your experts think of the film when they've studied it? I'd be very interested."

"Of course, I'll be in touch."

It was nearer two weeks before John heard from Mark again, which suited him as he needed time to finish his submission. He knew his Head of Department would be displeased; he hadn't sought his approval for changing the focus of his research and his results so far with Krypton gas tubes were inconclusive, so he'd had to make a convincing case to justify both the changes and the lack of progress.

Ilse and John had agreed that they'd see each other every weekend and once in the week, but she'd phoned him at work to say she was overwhelmed trying to resolve issues with the new schedules and the continuing row with the Board. He was secretly relieved, as he needed more time to finesse his report. For the next two weeks they only saw each other on weekends, asking each other questions they'd stored up during the week.

"Do you think there will ever be another war in Europe?"

"What did you imagine you'd be doing at this age when you were ten years old?"

"Will your parents ever accept me as a non-Jew?"

"Do you know any lesbians? I was shocked to see women kissing in a club when I first came to Berlin."

"I do. Do you know any homosexuals?"

"Of course not – but then I wouldn't know."

"Do I detect disapproval, John? I think most people are born with an attraction towards one sex or the other. Of course, many of them hide their feelings for fear of being persecuted, even in Berlin."

John became increasingly anxious as the day of his review drew near, rehearsing answers endlessly to the obvious questions. He thought he could make a convincing case, but every time he reassured himself, the threat of being kicked off the programme brought back his anxiety. Ilse now had a telephone in her flat so on the morning of his review he'd phoned her and went over his answers. She didn't understand the science but she understood the importance of not crossing the line between embellishing and lying.

He sat stony-faced as his Head of Department summed up. It wasn't good, but could have been worse.

"Frankly, John, your results so far from your original research have been disappointing. Your decision to pause that and pursue a separate line of enquiry was premature and I'm not convinced it's a productive path to go down. I'll give you two months to carry on with it, but if you haven't made a breakthrough by then you must return to your original research. My decision to approve funding for your second year will depend on the progress you've made by September."

He'd had a reprieve; he could now relax a little and give time to things he'd neglected during the last couple of months. Such as giving Ilse more support with the problems she was facing at Funkstade Berlin. He continued to be amazed that such a wonderful woman had entered his life. To think he'd nearly lost her on their first date in Treptower Park over a thoughtless remark; some of the issues she cared deeply for were too important to make stupid jokes about.

Which is why he could never tell her about his work for the Secret Service; he knew that she'd be outraged. More than outraged.

Mark Chastain rang him the day after his review.

"Can you return the item we loaned you to the Embassy, please, John? We've just had the report we requested back and I can update you at the same time."

Initially puzzled by Mark's oblique language until he realised the need for secrecy over the telephone, John went in that afternoon and was taken straight up to Mark's office.

"The chaps at Defence Research were surprised to see that the German Army is taking an interest in this research, as they don't see the potential of liquid-fuelled rockets for military use. To be frank, they believe solid-fuelled rockets are the future for battlefield use. However, they were impressed that you'd managed to get hold of this stuff, and wanted me to pass on their thanks for your work. They also said they'd like you to continue to monitor any further developments in this area. Well done."

He felt deflated. The outcome hardly seemed to justify the risk he'd taken and effort he'd put in. He didn't try to hide his frustration.

"Thank you, Mark. At least they know that the German Army feels that liquid-fuelled rockets are worth exploring."

Mark changed the subject.

"I think you said that you'd seen two other promising research papers that seemed to have vanished into thin air. Do you fancy having a crack at one of those for us?"

He was expecting this.

"As you know, Mark, I took on this espionage role on the

understanding that it can't interfere with my research, but I'm afraid that it has. So I'm going to stop for a while."

"I completely understand. I hope things look up for you."

As he left the Embassy, he noticed a man on the other side of the road taking pictures of the Embassy entrance with a small, expensive-looking camera. John assumed he was from the German Secret Service and was checking on people entering and leaving. He wasn't worried; as a British citizen, there were valid reasons for him to be visiting his Embassy. He decided to go back to his flat and write to his father and sister – spending his weekends at Ilse's flat meant he hadn't written since Christmas. It was a bright sunny day, signs of spring were approaching and people in the streets were looking more cheerful.

As he turned into his street, he saw Ilse standing outside his flat, clearly upset. She'd been crying.

"Ilse, what's the matter? Have you been here long? I'm sorry, I should have given you a spare key."

He hugged her, feeling her damp cheek against his.

"It's nothing, really. I'm now annoyed with myself for getting upset and bothering you. I was just about to leave when I saw you, but I'm glad I didn't."

"So what's happened?"

"I'll tell you if you make us a coffee."

Once they were inside his flat he took her coat and hugged her.

"I feel better having you to talk to. Do you remember that after the Board of Governors told our managers to moderate our reporting of the Nazi Party we wrote a joint response to them explaining why we opposed that?"

John nodded, worried to see her this upset. He brought their coffee over and sat next to her.

"The Board has now instructed our managers to impose the new policy, so they called everyone together this morning and told us they weren't prepared to fight this any longer. They said that the future of all our jobs would be at stake if we didn't drop our opposition. Gradually the managers persuaded most of the staff that the station would close if we didn't accept the Board's terms until there were only three of us holding out – me and two other junior staff. I'm afraid that I got too emotional and started haranguing them, bringing up the fact that I'm Jewish, saying, 'You don't need to read *Mein Kampf* to understand that Hitler wants to eradicate every Jew from Europe'. That only seemed to make things worse, so I gave up."

She was shaking with anger and frustration. He felt helpless, out of his depth, unable to think of the right words. But he had to try.

"I'm so proud of you, Ilse, it can't have been easy doing what you did. I will always be there for you, I hope you know that."

"Thank you, my love, I know you understand. I worry that there's more anti-Jewish sentiment under the surface among German people than my friends and colleagues realise. We have to stay vigilant, but it's stressful."

"What are you going to do now?"

"Can I stay here for a while, if that's okay? I'll go back to the station later and make peace with my boss. What were you planning to do this afternoon?"

"I was going to take the afternoon off and write to my sister and father – I haven't done that since Christmas. I'd love you to stay as long as you need."

"Thank you. I realise that we often talk about my work but I never ask you about yours. Didn't you have a review coming up? How did that go?"

She was right, she rarely asked him about his work – and that suited him very well. She must never know about 'that' side of his 'work'. While it touched him that she'd remembered his review, he decided not to tell her about the Head of Department's criticisms.

"Thank you for asking, I think it went pretty well. My boss seemed pleased with my results so far and encouraged me to carry on with my current line of research, so things are looking good for the year ahead. Can I get you anything to eat? How about some cheese and pickle on rye bread?"

"That sounds good. With a cup of tea?"

Ilse left for the station an hour later. She'd realised she couldn't afford to be isolated from the other staff and needed to make peace with her boss, although she wouldn't stop monitoring the Nazi Party's activities. But making peace with Herr Weiss proved to be much harder than she'd predicted.

"We're not running some radical student newspaper here, Fräulein Lipsky! We're a serious broadcaster in an increasingly crowded market, trying to avoid a terminal confrontation with our Board. I abhor the policies of the Nazis, and I accept that for a Jew they represent a particular threat, but they're a recognised political Party that got a million votes in last year's election. Once the Board turned down the case we'd made to them, we had no option but to adjust the way we report on the Nazi Party.

"Your continued challenge to me in this morning's meeting simply prolonged the inevitable and wound up two naïve young colleagues. Some of my senior team want to get rid of you. But... you've done good work since you arrived and I'm prepared to give you another chance, on the condition that there are no more challenges to my authority on policy decisions. Obviously you have the right to express your views on scheduling or production issues."

For a heady moment she imagined taking a principled stand and telling him that she wasn't prepared to compromise over such a blatant attack on journalistic freedom – one that affected her personally. But facing the prospect of losing her job, months out of work, getting into debt, giving up her flat and moving back in with her parents, she said, "I respect you as my boss and don't wish to undermine your authority. Now they've won this concession, it will be interesting to see if the Nazis put pressure on us to make more."

16

SPRING INTO SUMMER, 1926

From the moment she returned to work, Ilse set out to rebuild her relationship with Herr Weiss and restore trust with the other managers, making sure she met her deadlines and was being constructive in meetings. It helped that the new schedules she'd drawn up had led to an increase in the station's audience ratings. Her relationship with John helped her deal with the day-to-day pressures at Funkstade.

But she hadn't forgotten the row with the Board and had begun to monitor the Nazi Party's pamphlets, posters and copies of *Der Stürmer*, a viciously anti-Semitic newspaper that supported the Party. It confirmed her view that their campaign to spread hatred against Jews, liberals and socialists was making an impact on ordinary Germans. John had a shock one Friday afternoon when he let himself in to Ilse's flat before she returned and found her bed covered with Nazi propaganda and two copies of *Der Stürmer*.

"I'm rather surprised by your current reading matter," he teased as she came in soon afterwards.

She laughed.

"I've learnt that the Board have just received another complaint from the Nazi Party about our reporting – as I predicted would happen. I'm going to show Herr Weiss this material and beg him to circulate it to the Board to convince them to reject this new complaint."

"That's a brilliant idea, Ilse. But I don't think you should beg him. Say something like you think 'the Board should be acquainted with all the facts before they make another concession to this Party that's trying to divide us.'"

"That's better, thank you. By the way, I've been wanting to tell you that your spoken German has become far more fluent. And your vocabulary is amazing. I'm proud of you, John."

John slowly realised that attempting to bolster his original research by pursuing the experiments with krypton gas wasn't paying off. After spending two weeks concentrating his efforts on finding a breakthrough – at the expense of everything else – he gave up. He would now focus all of his time on his original hypothesis:

The implications of the Compton effect for collisions between photons and electrons in fixed, bound, orbits.

If he failed to discover any implications he'd write that up as his conclusion, explain the factors behind his findings and propose a new line of research at his review in September. The challenge seemed to renew his enthusiasm for his research.

On the first warm Saturday in May, he suggested to Ilse that they take a picnic to Treptower for the afternoon. He wanted to surprise her.

They found a grassy patch near the lake, took their jackets off and sat on the blanket next to each other. Pouring two glasses of Sekt, John turned to Ilse and said, "How would you fancy a week on the Baltic coast? I've been saving some of my salary every month since October and have enough to rent a small house near the beach in Warnemünde that belongs to the parents of a colleague at work. He's told me we can use it for a small sum. Which just leaves you having to persuade Herr Weiss to give you a week's holiday. What do you think?"

"I think I'm the luckiest girl in Berlin and I will speak to Herr Weiss on Monday!"

John drank the rest of his Sekt and lay back on the grass, hands behind his head, looking up at her in her summer dress. In the sunlight he could make out the fine hairs on her temples and her top lip, the silky hair under her arms and the outline of her breasts under the light cotton material. *I'll hold this image of her in my mind forever.*

A week later, at work, he received a call from Ilse, clearly excited.

"I'm so glad you're there. You know I've been gathering information about the Nazis' activities from their pamphlets and *Der Stürmer*? There's probably going to be a demonstration outside the radio station this evening, protesting about our so-called bias against them. We're all contacting as many friends as possible and asking them to join us for a counter-demonstration. Can you come?"

"Those bastards! Of course I'll be there. What time?"

"It's due to start in two hours."

He packed up his research for the day and ran back to his flat. There were particular items there he needed, ones he'd learnt might prove useful after his last brush with the fascists at Christmas. He tied pieces of cardboard around his shins and put on his hobnailed boots and thick jacket. Overdressed for the weather, but never mind. Finally, he put the knuckle-duster in his pocket, bandages in a small rucksack and set off.

When he arrived at the Funkstade he saw a group of staff and their friends, including Ilse, standing outside the entrance, facing a smaller group of Nazis on the other side of the road. There was no evidence of the police. As more Nazis arrived, their chanting started.

"*Shut down the communist radio station.*"

"*Eradicate journalist scum!*"

"*Jews control the news, they're traitors to Germany.*"

John stood next to Ilse, determined that she would come to no harm. Two policemen had arrived, watching from thirty metres away. Although the group of Nazis now outnumbered the station's supporters, John didn't feel it would get ugly. He began to relax a little, although he could sense Ilse remained tense beside him.

Someone called out, "Look, they're taking our pictures."

Some of the Nazis were taking photos of individual Funkstade staff, one of whom immediately got a camera out and started to do the same, which further enraged the fascists. John recognised the librarian who'd searched him. A few of the Nazis began to advance towards them, shouting, threatening and waving sticks. John reached into his pocket and closed his hand around the knuckle-duster. Ilse and her colleagues shouted back – "*Fascist scum, weirdos, retards!*" – and John tensed, ready to protect her, just as he heard the police whistles. The two original policemen, now joined by six others, were marching down the middle of the road towards the Nazis, truncheons drawn. Most of the Nazis began to walk quickly away, but three who stood their ground and confronted the police in the road were clubbed and arrested.

The sergeant looked at the Funkstade group.

"You lot. Disperse or go back inside."

Ilse and her colleagues looked at each other. There was no enthusiasm for going back to work. Ilse looked at her colleagues and said, "We should stay together in groups until we're well clear of the area. Some of the fascists could hang around the area and attack anyone on their own."

They divided into groups and began to leave, congratulating each other on taking a stand. John and Ilse joined a woman and two men who were catching a tram going in their direction. As they waited at the stop, a group of Nazis walked past, shouting abuse. Ilse's group ignored them, but they turned and began walking towards them. John slid the knuckle-duster through his fingers and said to the others: "If we run and one of us gets caught, they will be merciless. If we stand up to them together, we've got a chance. Just use anything you've got – pens, nails, teeth – against their vulnerable places – eyes, shins, ears, balls. Ilse, please stand behind me."

A stocky man holding a club, around forty years old, was clearly the main threat. If John could put him down, the other three might lose heart. He removed his rucksack, held it in his free hand, fended off the first swing of the club, took half a step back to rebalance and threw a short punch with his full weight behind it to the man's chin. John felt the force of the blow travel down his arm as the knuckle-duster connected with his jaw with a bone-cracking noise. As he staggered back screaming, John connected with a second fierce punch to the man's temple and he went down, unconscious before he hit the ground. Turning, he saw Ilse gouging at the eyes of another Nazi who'd grabbed a clump of her hair. The second woman was kicking his shins, while the two Funkstade men were trading punches with the other two fascists. It was a savage fight – more visceral than his previous encounter with Nazis. These men had to be badly hurt if his group were going to walk away.

John punched Ilse's assailant in the kidneys from behind, then delivered a second blow to his head. As he released Ilse she kicked him hard between his legs and he went down.

Seeing one of the Funkstade men lying on the ground being kicked by the third fascist, John punched down hard on top of the assailant's head, who staggered away, then fell. Three fascists down. When the last fascist saw his comrades lying on the ground unconscious and incapacitated, he broke off and ran.

The five of them looked at each other, incredulous, exultant, bleeding but still standing. John hugged Ilse.

"Are you all right? That bastard has taken a clump of your hair."

"I'll have a headache tomorrow, my nails are a mess but otherwise I'm okay. You were incredible."

She looked around at the other three.

Heinrich had come off worst – he'd been kicked several times when he was lying on the ground. But he could walk, and his two friends, not without cuts and bruises themselves, offered to take him to be checked up at a hospital nearby.

As the sound of police whistles in the distance focussed their attention, the two groups split. John and Ilse started to walk quickly to a nearby taxi rank. Realising he was still wearing the knuckle-duster, he decided to throw it away. If they were stopped by the police before they got to Ilse's flat – they both showed signs of having been in a fight – he would be in serious trouble if it was found on him. It wasn't worth the risk. Before they reached the taxi rank, they straightened each other's clothes and wiped the blood off their faces and hands with the bandages from John's rucksack.

The taxi driver gave no sign that he found their appearance alarming. All the same, they told him to drop them two streets away from the flat so that he couldn't give away Ilse's address. He might be a member of the Party.

Once inside, Ilse went straight to the bathroom and ran a bath. Back in her room, they took their clothes off and carefully examined each other for cuts and bruises. Both of them had sustained more damage than they'd realised, but luckily neither was seriously hurt. In the bath – their first together – they gently washed each other and reflected on a danger faced and overcome.

"You were there for me, John, I won't forget that. Thank you. I'm going to talk to Herr Weiss tomorrow and insist the Board reports this to the police and demands that the station receives police protection. What do you think?"

"They should also explain in person to the staff how they're going to protect you all in the future. You're their employees, being threatened outside your workplace is their responsibility."

That night, John lay awake listening to Ilse's steady breathing, thinking about that day's events. The Nazis were unlikely to forget this. Three of their comrades had been badly hurt; if the librarian recognised him and checked the names of visitors to the library, he could give John's name to the police. He'd go back to his room tomorrow and make sure there was nothing incriminating in case the police came round to question him about the fight. He had to assume they'd taken a picture of him outside the radio station.

So he wasn't surprised by a persistent ringing on the doorbell at eight in the morning a week later, followed by the sound of footsteps climbing the stairs and heavy knocking on his door. He opened it to see two policemen standing there.

"Herr Samson?"

"Yes, officer. Can I help you?"

"We're investigating a fight that took place a week ago near the tram stop on Wilhelmstrasse. Three men were injured, one seriously. Do you know anything about it?"

"I don't. I'm sorry, officer. There are so many street fights in Berlin these days, it can feel like a dangerous place sometimes. I'm a British scientist working at Friedrich Wilhelm University and can't afford to get involved in that sort of thing."

"Where were you around 5pm last Thursday?"

John pretended to think about the question, then said,

"I'd left work at four thirty to meet my girlfriend at Funkstade Berlin. When I got there I saw a group of Nazis were threatening the staff outside, so I joined them to show support. The police came and they fled, but I don't think they should be allowed to threaten innocent people."

The officers looked at each other, disappointed. They'd obviously been given information that he was part of the Funkstade group and were hoping he would make up a story about his whereabouts.

"Can we come in and look around?"

"Of course. I'm afraid it's not very tidy, I've only just got up."

The two police officers spent more than twenty minutes searching his room before grudgingly accepting there was nothing to find.

"That will be all, Herr Samson. I advise you to be careful about getting involved in street protests in future, as you're not a German citizen. Good day."

John relaxed as he heard them descending the stairs. Their warning was clear – clear enough to make him realise that he should exercise more caution in future.

He worked long hours in the laboratory right up to the evening before their holiday. He'd finally persuaded his Head of Department to extend his review deadline by a month so it would now be possible to go away with Ilse and have time to write a thorough report on his year's work. Mark Chastain had accepted that his end-of-year academic review had to be *his* priority.

John gazed out of the soot-darkened window as their train to Warnemünde gathered speed through the northern suburbs of Berlin, shocked by the obvious poverty in the working-class areas of the city he hadn't visited before. Ilse sat opposite, dozing. They'd seen little of each other in the last ten days; Ilse had to prepare detailed instructions for the two colleagues standing in for her and John was focussed on the final chapter of his report. It needed careful crafting to compensate for the inconclusive end to his first year's research.

He'd collected the keys and directions from Warnemünde station to the house from his colleague yesterday.

"The place has been cleaned so please leave it as you find it. I'm glad it's being used. Warnemünde has a fabulous beach, although the sea can still be cool at this time of year. There's a list of instructions about the heating and other things on the kitchen table. I hope you two have a wonderful time."

He looked at John and winked.

"We're both really excited about it, Willy. Thank you, and please thank your parents from both of us."

He'd felt a surge of expectation when he'd seen Ilse standing on the platform that morning. He felt it again now, as he studied her face, eyes closed, lips slightly parted. He checked his jacket pocket for the keys to the cottage for the tenth time that morning.

They'd agreed to buy bread, cheese, sausages and pickled herrings for a picnic, then head straight to the beach after unpacking.

The house was characterful, small but full of artefacts and pictures reflecting a seaside theme. They quickly unpacked, changed into casual, lighter clothing, put towels, swimming costumes, windbreaks and food in beach bags and set off. It was a beautiful early July day, the breeze taking some of the heat out of the overhead sun as they walked towards the beach past a row of pastel-painted immaculate cottages similar to theirs. Ilse was wearing a summer dress that John hadn't seen before; she must have bought it for their holiday. Her legs and arms were bare, her skin glowing in the sunshine. He took her free hand in his, put the bag down and bent his head until his lips met hers.

Their first day in Warnemünde was perfect. They'd hired one of the two-person windbreak basket chairs that stretched out in rows across the sand, then squeezed in to change into their costumes, one after the other. He was taken aback as Ilse emerged from the windbreak in a modern blue woollen bathing costume. Armless and virtually legless, ending a foot above her knees, the material shaped itself to her body. They'd ran into the surf, shocked by the cold water, then splashed each other until Ilse plunged in, shrieking. He had to follow her, of course, and yelled as the water sucked heat from his body. She was a good swimmer, ploughing through the waves, and was soon thirty yards from the shore. He breast-stroked up and down close to the beach for a minute or so then got out, wrapped his towel around him and sat on the sand to wait for her.

He was looking at two children building a sandcastle together when he turned and saw her coming out of the surf. The wet swimming costume now formed a second skin, the fabric highlighting the shape and outline of every curve, bump and cleft. She looked stunning.

They spent each unplanned day as the mood took them, making love, walking, swimming, cooking, laughing and talking about her work and his research, politics, her parents and his family. He knew by the end of the week that he would never feel like this with anyone else, ever, so on their last day he said he wanted to talk about their future together. She'd smiled and said that she wanted that too, but needed time to reflect on her feelings after such a wonderful week.

Back in Berlin, they agreed to spend the next three days apart, acclimatising to normality, and went back to their own flats. Their lives were about to be turned upside down.

17

JULY INTO AUGUST, 1926

He put his suitcase down in the hallway and checked to see if any post had arrived when he'd been in Warnemünde. As he picked up a letter, he was surprised by Frau Hessler opening her door. She respected her tenants' privacy and rarely pounced on him like this.

"Herr Samson, I'm glad I caught you. Two days ago a British gentleman came here asking if I knew where you were. When I told him I thought you'd gone away somewhere, he asked when you'd be back and of course I said I don't know. He seemed very cross about that and asked me if he could leave this note for you."

He looked at the note and recognised Chastain's handwriting.

"Thank you, Frau Hessler. I know the gentleman and I'm sure everything will be okay."

Walking up the stairs to his room, it seemed unlikely that everything was okay – Mark Chastain had never come to see him here before, and was probably annoyed that he'd gone on holiday without informing him. If so, that would be a bloody cheek. *I'm not accountable to them for my every move.*

He slung his suitcase on the bed and opened the note.

Dear John,
I have no idea where you are. There has been a serious incident at
'our house' and we need you to contact us immediately after you
receive this. Don't speak to anyone else about it until we meet.
Regards
MC

The tone dashed any hope he'd harboured that this was maybe just routine. But the train journey back to Berlin had been painfully slow, it was now past six o'clock on Sunday evening, he needed a bath and Mark Chastain could wait until tomorrow.

"Where the bloody hell have you been? We've been trying to get hold of you for three days."

Taken aback by Mark's tone, John looked across at the man beside him, who he assumed to be his boss, if for no other reason than he was wearing a well-tailored suit.

It doesn't take much for the disdain that people like these have for those not of their class to show through, he thought. *Enough is enough, but I'll see what he's got to say before I have it out with him.*

"I went on a week's holiday to the Baltic with a friend. I thought it was time to see what Germany was like outside of Berlin. I told the university I was going, one of my colleagues there knew the address. You hadn't asked me to keep you informed of my movements, and anyway, we agreed that I wasn't going to be carrying out any work for you for the next two months. Do you want to tell me what this is about, Mark?"

Mark glowered at him. He was working himself up, but John sensed there was much more behind this than some trivial cock-up. Chastain was clearly very angry, but with who, and about what, exactly? *Himself, perhaps, and he's deflecting it onto me?*

"We discovered last week that the Embassy has been unknowingly employing an informant. A member of the Nazi

Party, planted by the National Socialists to snoop and feed back whatever information he could. We discovered this on a random check, when a document he had no right to possess was found in his briefcase. That document was the photographic copy of the research paper you made for us five months ago. Our internal investigation has revealed that a junior member of our diplomatic staff, in receipt of that paper for a second opinion, left it exposed on his desk. You are not under suspicion for leaking the document."

Increasingly incredulous, John interrupted.

"Did you say *he 'left it exposed on his desk'*? Forgive me, I know that spying is one of the main activities carried out in this building, but I'd rather thought that meant us spying on them and not the other way round. How can anyone have been that careless?"

The faces of the two men sitting opposite visibly reddened at John's facetious response; the man in the tailored suit sitting next to Mark rounded on him.

"Making a joke about such a serious matter shows what a mistake it was to use an amateur like yourself for work such as this. If you listen instead of interrupting, you will realise that this has serious consequences for you as well."

"That's nonsense. I was asked to track down this kind of research, I handed it over believing the Embassy was a safe place, it appeared to be well received – and you're saying that *I'm* facing serious consequences because one of your employees has been unearthed as a spy and another as incompetent!"

"That's enough, John! If that's all it was, you wouldn't be in trouble. However, it seems that our German spy must have shown the research paper you stole to other members of the Berlin Nazi Party. One of them, a librarian at the Library for Physical Sciences, realised that the document was kept in that library. Unfortunately he also remembered an Englishman who'd visited the library several times, with a camera on one occasion. He got your name from the library's signing in book and took his story to the police.

Luckily, they realised that this was outside of their remit – they couldn't be sure that the document was secret, so possession might not be a crime, and the evidence was circumstantial. So they took it to the German Embassy, who are now demanding to know how this paper came into our possession. You can see the position this puts us in."

As Mark had continued, John's mood switched rapidly from anxiety to calculation to cautious optimism, then back again. The research paper was theoretically in the public domain, so how could possession be a crime? On the other hand, taking it out of the library without permission was against the rules, and it was probably illegal to photograph library documents. The evidence that he'd given the research paper to the Embassy was circumstantial, but a lawyer could build a case that everything pointed to him as the 'thief'. From the tone of his interrogators, he couldn't tell if they were preparing to throw him to the wolves or not. A chill ran through him.

He had a strong card to play, but needed to think clearly before playing it.

"There's no concrete evidence connecting me to the theft, or to the Embassy. Given the area of my research, it would be normal for me to be working in the Library for Physical Sciences, and anyone else using it would have been equally able to photograph the document.

"Can't you throw this back at them? It must be against diplomatic protocols for a political Party to place spies inside a foreign embassy? Surely the Nazis have broken the law. What penalties are they going to suffer?"

At this point the man in the tailored suit introduced himself as Maurice Spencer.

"The Nazis have denied any link to their mole in the Embassy; ridiculous, of course, but that's how they operate. If a truth is inconvenient, they'll just keep denying it and most of their supporters will believe them. The problem we now have – and that includes you, I'm afraid, Mr Samson – is that the legal rights and wrongs take second place to the diplomatic implications. We must ensure there isn't a rift between Britain and the Weimar Government, who fear that the elected Nazi Party members in the Reichstag will demand that someone is punished for this. That someone has to be you, I'm afraid. We need you to go to the police, admit you'd taken the pictures (for your own research) and then brought them to the British Embassy on your own initiative, with no involvement from us.

"I realise this may seem very unjust as you were only doing what we'd asked – and successfully too, I may say. But I guarantee we will extract a promise from the German Embassy that you won't be charged with a crime after you've made this admission."

John had become increasingly furious as Spencer went on; he couldn't believe the injustice of Spencer's proposal, or the arrogant assumption that he'd have to accept it. He took a deep breath and delivered a calculated response that made the two men opposite sit up.

"I'm afraid that's not going to happen. I've got nothing to gain by going to the police and taking the blame for all of this. Whatever promises you get from the German Embassy, everyone knows everyone else in academia. My boss may well want to believe in me, but doubts will have been sown in his mind and he'll regretfully find a reason to fail me at the end of this year. Plus the Nazis could still name me in a story about British spies in the Embassy, to stir up a populist sense of grievance against the Allies. So if I do what you're suggesting, my academic career will be over.

"If you force me to go to the police and take the blame for the Embassy's mistakes – that it was my idea and you had nothing to do with it – there's a very good chance I'll be charged and get a criminal record, on top of ruining my career. My only hope of avoiding a sentence will be to do a deal; tell them what I was doing, why and who I was doing it for, in exchange for clemency. You don't want that, and neither do I. So please stop trying to shift the blame for the Embassy's failure on to me. Start behaving honourably and let's thrash out a better solution."

Spencer looked furious, Chastain surprisingly impressed.

"Do you have any ideas, John?" said Mark.

After two hours, they'd agreed a plan.

John proposed that he'd go to the police with Mark and explain that, yes, he'd visited the library on several occasions as part of his work. He owns a camera and sometimes carries it with him. He'd bought it to take pictures of a group of Nazis who were harassing his girlfriend outside her place of work. He could have these developed and show them. He certainly wouldn't take pictures of another academic's work, that's against his principles.

Mark would tell them that the Embassy had suspected for some time that there was an informant on their staff, so they set a trap. They deliberately left a published document about rocket research in a conspicuous place and waited to see what happened. The informant took the bait and has been dismissed. The document had come into the Embassy's possession through an employee who was interested in rocketry. John had nothing to do with it. As this research paper is in the public domain, the Embassy was sure no laws had been broken.

To John's surprise, both men agreed to his proposal. Mark liaised with his counterpart at the German Embassy, explained how the misunderstanding had come about and informed him that he and the English scientist would visit the police station where the initial report had been made to explain the sequence of events. The German diplomat seemed satisfied with his proposal – less paperwork for him – and said he would let the relevant inspektor know.

Mark and John reported to the police station two days later and had a civilised discussion with two detectives. Apart from some probing about the use of entrapment and the current whereabouts of the informant, the senior detective brought proceedings to a close in under an hour.

"Thank you for coming in, gentlemen. You're free to go, Herr Chastain. If you wouldn't mind waiting, Herr Samson, there are one or two questions I'd like to clear up with you. My colleague will take you to another room and I'll be with you shortly."

They exchanged quizzical glances as Mark left.

John sat at a table facing two empty chairs on the other side, taking in the bare, grubby-looking, cream-coloured walls of the interview room, looking through the door window whenever he heard anyone in the corridor outside. He'd been waiting for over half an hour, increasingly nervous about the questions he might be asked, when the inspektor burst into the room, sat at the other side of the table and opened a file in front of him. He looked straight at John and said, "My name is Inspektor Weisler, Herr Samson. Can you please confirm what position you hold at Friedrich Wilhelm University, and when you started there?"

"I'm a postdoctorate researcher in the physics faculty, currently in my first year of a three-year contract. I started ten months ago in September 1925."

"How is your research going so far?"

"Like most research in the early days, periods of frustration coupled with excitement when you make a breakthrough."

"Are you enjoying Berlin?"

"Very much. It's such a lively and civilised city. I'm used to a large, busy city, being a Londoner."

"So what do you enjoy doing when you're not at your bench researching?"

"Going for walks and the theatre with colleagues, spending time with my girlfriend, going to cabarets. But my research keeps me very busy."

"What about politics? Do you go to any political meetings?"

John paused. *So this is where he's heading. Don't say more than you have to, but don't lie.*

"No, I haven't been to a political meeting since I came to Berlin."

"Would you say that you're someone who takes an interest in politics?"

"Yes, that would be fair. The German system is different to the British, and it's interesting to compare them. The Weimar Republic is only a few years old, whereas Britain has had a parliament for three hundred years."

"Quite so. You British are rightly proud of your democratic tradition. Have you been involved in any political demonstrations or marches?"

"No."

"Are you sure, Herr Samson? Please think carefully before you answer."

John paused again. *He must be thinking about the Nazi protest outside the radio station. I'll mention it before he does.*

"I was present when a number of Nazis were threatening the staff of Funkstade Berlin outside the radio station. My girlfriend works at the station and I joined the staff confronting the fascists to protect her. The police eventually confronted the Nazis and moved them on, but it was a frightening situation."

"What did you do afterwards?"

"My girlfriend and I left the area and walked back to her flat."

The inspektor paused for a moment, flicking through the papers in front of him.

"Did you get into an argument with anybody on the way to her flat?"

"A few of the fascists shouted abuse at us, but we ignored them and carried on."

"Are you certain? Because we've had a report of a serious fight involving a group of people near the radio station soon after the demonstration was broken up."

"I think I would remember such an event, Inspektor. I'm not a fighter by nature, so I was concerned that something like that could occur, given that the police didn't stay with the Nazis as they dispersed."

Inspektor Weisler studied his notes again, appearing – rather unconvincingly – to study each page in detail. Finally he looked up.

"Two men were badly hurt and taken to hospital soon after that protest ended, but they're not co-operating with the police. I think you British have a saying, 'putting two and two together'. When I put two and two together, Herr Samson, I strongly believe that you and others were involved in that fight, but I can't prove it."

John protested his innocence but Weisler curtly told him to save his breath and carried on.

"However, I have made enquiries at your university about their expectations of foreign academics such as yourself, and even if you weren't involved in that fight, the terms of your contract state that joining street demonstrations is not allowed. I understand that your Head of Faculty will be making an appointment to speak to you about the matter, but unless any new evidence comes to light, I won't be getting in touch with you again. However, you should know I've made it clear to Herr Chastain that I don't believe his account of how the document came into the Embassy's possession.

"That is all, Herr Samson. I strongly advise you not to get involved in Berlin street politics in future. It would have negative repercussions for you. Good day."

Mark Chastain had left by the time John's interview finished, which further lowered his mood. He'd hoped – and assumed – that Mark would wait for him to check that everything was okay; but clearly now that the Embassy was off the hook, John's welfare was of little concern anymore. Yet it was his idea that had extricated the Embassy (and himself) from the possibility of further investigation and accusations of spying. To think that he'd harboured hopes that he might get credit for this! He'd been very naïve.

How much damage had the events of the last few days done? He refused to countenance the worst outcome – told to quit the university, leave Germany and lose Ilse. That mustn't happen; his life would unravel. But the police clearly thought that he'd been involved in the fight with the Nazis and had given him an unmistakeable warning that they would be watching him from now on. On top of that, he'd be called before the Head of Faculty to explain his involvement in the confrontation outside the radio station. Combined with the less than impressive end-of-year report that he'd be submitting, he had to face the possibility that his tenure at Friedrich Wilhelm was at risk.

Obviously his role as an amateur spy was over; he was now known to the police and under suspicion from the library. He needed to prepare for being called to a meeting by the Head of Faculty to explain himself; even assuming that meeting went the right way, he still had his annual review with his Head of Department to get through.

His biggest fear was that Ilse would somehow find out that he'd been interviewed by the police. Hopefully she wouldn't hear anything about it, but if she did, he'd convince her that they'd simply been making enquiries about the fight following the Nazi protest, and accepted he'd not been involved.

From the moment John was shown into Mark Chastain's office it was clear there'd be no argument about his decision to quit.

"Good morning, John. I'm sorry I couldn't wait around for you after our conversation with the police yesterday, but I had to get back here pronto to deal with a British citizen who's got himself arrested for assaulting a woman in a nightclub. Normally I don't deal with that kind of low-level stuff, but the chap in question is the son of a British MP, and I happened to be the only one available. Personally, I hope the Germans throw the book at the smug little bastard. I gather that the police haven't charged you, or I would have heard by now. It looks like we've got away with it."

Resisting the urge to reflect out loud what position he'd be in if the incident hadn't been resolved so quickly, he merely said, "If we have, Mark, it's more by luck than calculation. The police interviewed me after you'd left and accused me of taking part in a fight after the Nazi demonstration that left three men badly injured. When that ridiculous idea fell apart – my girlfriend and I had left the area as soon as possible – he said he'd checked with my university and discovered that foreigners like myself working in Berlin universities aren't allowed to take part in street demonstrations. He also told me that he didn't believe our story that it wasn't me that took the pictures and they would be watching me from now on.

"I clearly can't carry on with my work for you if the police are watching me and the university has suspicions I've copied another academic's paper. So I'm afraid our arrangement needs to end."

Mark had been listening intently. After a second's reflection, he said, "I agree with you, and I will do everything I can to make sure that your contract isn't jeopardised. It's the least I can do."

"Thank you, I hoped you'd agree. Of course, I can still alert you if I come across something in the course of my research that may be of interest to you."

Walking from the Embassy to the university later, he felt his spirits starting to lift. Without the need to spend time reading, researching and stealing German research papers, life would be much simpler and less stressful. But his mood slumped again at the thought of the two hurdles he still had to overcome: convincing the Head of Faculty he hadn't broken his contract, and completing his end-of-year research presentation.

He decided not to wait for the Head of Faculty to contact him; as soon as John arrived, he made an appointment to see him at 10am the next day, then went to his laboratory and remained there until 8pm. He hadn't done any work on his presentation since the day before they'd left for Warnemünde, so he spent the day reviewing his work so far, correcting flaws in his data and checking for assumptions he'd made without supporting evidence.

Desperate to speak to Ilse, he rang her just before he left.

"John! I was hoping it was you. I've missed you, even though it's only two days since we parted. I keep thinking about our wonderful holiday, it was blissful, in every way! How are you, what have you been doing?"

Nothing I can tell you about, I'm afraid. I'll never be able to tell you about the events of the last two days, they'd reveal another side of my character that has to stay hidden. Is that so bad? Every couple has secrets from each other, I'll just have to accept it.

They spoke for nearly an hour until he realised he'd hardly eaten anything all day. They agreed to see each other on Friday evening in three days' time. There was a film she wanted to see, *The Clever Fox*.

After a sleepless night, his meeting with the Head of Faculty went more smoothly than he'd feared. Professor Müller made it clear that he was annoyed that the police had thought it appropriate to tell him about John's participation in what seemed to be just a show of solidarity with the staff at the radio station.

"The police detective was surprised when I told him if more ordinary Germans were prepared to stand up against these fascists then our country would be a better place. I applaud you for supporting your girlfriend who works for the station. But please be more careful in future, as your position is obviously less secure than a German citizen's."

By the time John met Ilse in the queue for *The Clever Fox*, he was reasonably confident that his presentation would be good enough to secure his job for a second year; he'd developed further evidence of a connection between two of his experiments and his central hypothesis. Spotting her yellow cloche hat, he walked up behind her and hugged her. Shocked, she yelled and turned to confront her assailant.

"It's you! You gave me such a shock, John. Come here, you idiot."

They hugged and kissed as if they hadn't seen each other for weeks. It was a balmy, warm evening at the end of a hot day, and he delighted in the scent of her clean sweat and perfume. He had a fleeting sense of how fortunate he was, how wonderful his life could still turn out to be. He stood back and looked at her.

Grinning, he said, "Let's skip the film and go back to your place."

"Absolutely not! I've wanted to see this film for ages. You'll have to control yourself. Until then."

That night, they made love for the last time.

John left her flat early the next morning to go back to the laboratory and redraft the conclusion to his presentation. It had to be with the translator in three days.

"Do you have to go in to work so early? I was hoping you could stay longer."

"I promise I'll make it up to you tonight. If I can just finish my conclusion today then I'll be yours for the weekend. And for the future."

"I'll hold you to that, Herr Samson."

18

DOWNFALL

Britischer Spion Gefunden

Ilse usually avoided looking at the front page of '*Der Stürmer*' pasted onto noticeboards all around the city. The mouthpiece of the Nazi Party, it was full of stories inciting hatred against socialists, liberals, artists, Gypsies, homosexuals and Jews. Particularly Jews. She'd never understood what lay behind such unwarranted hatred, which could sometimes make her feel physically sick.

But this week something in the headline *British Spy Found* drew her over to the fly- posted page, in spite of herself. As she read the first sentence under the headline, she almost fainted, just managing to stumble to a bench and sit down. A passer-by came across and handed her a handkerchief.

"Fräulein, what happened? Are you okay?"

"*Danke*. Could you help me up, please?"

The man was in his late twenties, with dark hair and kind eyes. He helped her to her feet and held her as she took a step back to the noticeboard to read the full story.

Patriotic Nazi comrades working at the Physical Sciences library and the British Embassy have uncovered an attempt to steal German research by a British scientist, John Samson. Herr Samson, who is an academic at Friedrich Wilhelm University, was seen entering the library with a camera on several occasions five months ago. When challenged by the librarian, Herr Samson threatened him and refused to open the camera. Subsequently, another member of the Party working in the British Embassy innocently came across a photographed copy of a research paper that was kept in the Physical Sciences library, which had obviously been given to them by Herr Samson. Despite this conclusive evidence, neither the police or university authorities are taking any action against Herr Samson. We demand this British man is interrogated and deported immediately!

She took several deep breaths, thanked the man and reassured him that she'd be all right. *It's obvious,* she thought. *The fascists from the fight after the demonstration decided to take revenge by making up a story that will get him into serious trouble. Remember, Ilse, this is* Der Stürmer. *You can't believe anything they say. But I must let John know about this, he probably won't have seen it yet.*

She walked home as fast as she could and rang John at the laboratory. The colleague who answered hesitated at first, then agreed to get him. When he came to the phone she could tell instantly that he'd seen the poster; he sounded stressed and shaken.

"If you're phoning to tell me about the story in *Der Stürmer,* I've already seen it. The bastards are taking revenge for their beating. It's all lies, apart from the fact that I have used the Physical Sciences library as a normal part of my research. But I'm worried that the physics department here will suspect there's some truth in it, which would be terrible for my reputation, so I'm going to speak to the Head of Department as soon as possible."

"Even if these photographs were found in the British Embassy, why do they think that you're responsible for putting them there? Have you ever been to the Embassy?"

"Not since I first came to Berlin eleven months ago. As I said, the whole thing is made up. I'd better go, Ilse, as I want to make sure I see the Head of Department. Don't worry, I'll sort this out."

"Please let me know what he says, John."

"Of course I will. I love you, Ilse."

The lies had already begun and there would no doubt be more before this was over. He hated deceiving her, but he couldn't risk telling her about his spying.

He'd only been at his bench five minutes when the Head of Department's secretary asked him to attend a meeting at 10am, which was now just twenty minutes away. He'd tried to put off the meeting until he'd spoken to Mark, but he wasn't at his desk. John had difficult choices to make. Should he deny everything except visiting the library, or admit that he'd photographed the document but nothing else, or admit that he'd passed it to the Embassy, potentially revealing his arrangement with the Secret Service?

He answered his own question; until he'd discussed this with Mark, he had to deny everything.

His phone rang; it was Mark.

"I assume you've seen *Der Stürmer*, John?"

"Yes, I've been…"

"The university will want to talk to you as soon as possible. Don't admit to anything at this stage, just stick to the line we used with the police, who've already contacted us. Theoretically, nothing has changed – there's nothing new in the article, evidence is still circumstantial and even the police don't believe most of what appears in *Der Stürmer*. But this has now become a political problem for the government. They'll be under pressure from the press and the Nazi Party to say if this is true, so the politicians will now pressurise the police. We can probably still bluff this out, providing you've told us everything."

Hesitating for a second, John remembered that he'd told Mark he hadn't been involved in a fight with fascists after the demonstration. A lie. But it wasn't relevant to copying German research and giving it to the Embassy, so he said, "Of course, Mark."

Relieved, he confidently assured his Head of Department that the *Der Stürmer* article was a tissue of lies, and prayed the matter would end there. Which it probably would have, were it not for the vigilance of Obermeister Becker, a member of Berlin's police surveillance squad. The British Embassy was on his patch.

The police had been successfully brushing off demands from right-wing politicians and newspapers to reinterview 'Herr Samson, the British spy' on the grounds that there was no firm evidence of a link between Samson and the British Embassy. They could hardly charge him with visiting a library, and their resources were stretched to breaking point by weekly marches and street fights between fascists and communists.

Unfortunately for John, Obermeister Becker, reading about the case in the *Berliner Tageblatt* (he hated the Nazis and never looked at *Der Stürmer*), decided to go back through every picture he'd taken outside the British Embassy over the last five months. If Herr Samson had visited the Embassy around the time the librarian had seen him using the library, this would prove that Samson – and the British Embassy – had lied.

He'd got a picture of Herr Samson from the files – all foreigners employed by the state had to provide the police with a passport photo – then began with his pictures from a month ago and worked backwards. It took him over two hours before he saw the pictures of Samson, both of them close to the time he'd been in the library. In one of the pictures he was holding a small leather case, rather like the one Becker had for his own camera. Obermeister Becker wasn't given to exuberant outbursts, but he'd punched the air with his fist. He'd lost his brother in the war to a British sniper's bullet, so this gave him some satisfaction. He looked up the name of the detective that interviewed Samson, then dialled his station number.

"Inspektor Weisler?"

"Yes."

"This is Obermeister Becker from surveillance section. I have pictures that prove the British scientist Herr Samson visited the British Embassy twice around the time he used the Physical Sciences library. I thought you'd like to know."

Events moved quickly. Weisler was excited; not because he bore the British any particular malice – all nations tried to discover each other's secrets – but because he smelt a rapid and successful conclusion to the case, and he needed that.

His boss agreed that he should bring Herr Chastain and Herr Samson in for questioning immediately.

"Bring them in separately, interview them on their own and see what they say. Do this as discreetly as possible. They won't be surprised to be contacted because of the publicity around the *Der Stürmer* article, and you can imply that it's a routine matter. Don't mention that we've got new information that contradicts their story. Herr Samson can be picked up from his place of work; do that first so that he doesn't have a chance to contact the Embassy. You'll need to be more cautious with Herr Chastain – he has diplomatic protection and you'll have to invite him."

"And if he refuses?"

"I think that's unlikely. He'll want to make sure that we hear the Embassy's version of events first."

Weisler's boss was both right and wrong. Mark Chastain did agree to come to the police station for a follow-up conversation without asking many questions. But he'd guessed before Weisler was into his second sentence that this request was probably about more than the Inspektor was letting on. Assuming that policemen – like diplomats – rarely told the whole truth was ingrained in his very being, so he immediately prepared for a number of eventualities, one of which was that the *Der Stürmer* article had brought new, damning evidence to light. His suspicion was compounded when he'd off-handedly asked if Weisler would also be talking to Herr Samson, and received an affirmative response.

Reassured by his earlier conversation with Mark, John was methodically working through revisions to his conclusion when he was astonished to see the departmental administrator showing two policemen into his laboratory.

"Herr Samson, we would like you accompany us to the police station."

John's heart began to race; he felt light-headed, but tried to sound calm.

"Can you tell me what this is about? Am I being arrested?"

"You're not under arrest, Herr Samson. Inspektor Weisler would simply like to clarify one or two points from your previous conversation."

John realised it would involve more than that, given Weisler had sent two policemen to escort him rather than phoning him. There was no point refusing to come in – it was obvious they'd arrest him if he did.

Controlling his voice, he said, "I'll just put my papers away, if that's okay?"

"Of course, Herr Samson."

"In our previous conversation, Herr Chastain, I believe you and Herr Samson both confirmed that he hadn't ever visited the Embassy, except eleven months ago when he'd just arrived in Berlin?"

As soon as he heard that, Chastain realised the game was up. Weisler had obviously come by new evidence disproving that statement; he wouldn't admit anything until he knew what that was.

"That was our recollection, yes, Inspektor."

Weisler opened a file, took out two photographs and slid them across the desk.

"These photographs were taken one week apart, five months ago, outside of your Embassy. Do you recognise the person entering and leaving the building, Herr Chastain?"

"It looks like Herr Samson. Who took these pictures?"

Weisler sat back. He'd worked out that Chastain was probably not simply a diplomat, but a spy as well. But Weisler had also formed the view that he was someone you could do business with. Deciding to test his hunch, he looked at Chastain.

"Rather than play games, I'm going to be straight with you and hope you'll do the same. These pictures, taken by the Berlin police surveillance unit, are proof that you haven't been telling us the truth. The dates also correspond almost exactly with the dates Herr Samson visited the library. You'll also see that he's carrying a leather camera case in the first picture."

He paused, and Chastain knew he'd seen and heard enough to trust Weisler. He didn't have to tell him at this stage that the dates matched Samson's library visits, nor that he was carrying a camera case. He could have spun that out, trapping Chastain in further lies. Chastain smiled, then said, "It's now my turn to trust you, Inspektor. When you interview John, he may tell you that before he came to Germany he was persuaded by a well-meaning idiot that it was his duty to pass on any promising German research he came across. John took his task seriously and discovered the paper on liquid-fuelled rockets in the library. It's a published paper, not secret and not in itself illegal. But I realise taking photographs of such a document and bringing it to the British Embassy looks bad for relations between our two countries. When this comes out, His Majesty's Government will deny that any such deal was made with John and say that he brought the pictures to us on his own initiative and leave him to his fate. Which makes me very angry.

"I've told you now because I want to prevent him going to

prison, particularly as I doubt he's actually broken any of your laws. Can we work something out that gives you what you want and achieves that?"

Weisler was impressed. He could see the outline of a deal that would give them both what they wanted; a minor punishment for the hapless Samson that avoided charges, while satisfying most Weimar politicians. But he wasn't going to commit to that immediately.

"Thank you for thinking this through, Herr Chastain. You and I have different priorities and paymasters to report to, but I hope we can come to an agreement. I would have to get authorisation from the chief inspektor to go ahead with any such an arrangement. Some of our more rabid politicians might want to make an example of Herr Samson, but they currently have little support outside of the Nazi Party."

"His career as an academic in Germany is obviously at risk, and I understand he's in a serious relationship with a German woman. It's such a mess, the poor fellow doesn't deserve any of this. Are you interviewing him today?"

"Yes, he was brought in from the university this morning and should be waiting in an interview room now."

"Then may I make a suggestion, Inspektor? If he tries to make up a story when you show him the pictures, please save him further humiliation by telling him what I told you several minutes ago, including that the British Government will deny ever asking him to pass on German scientific research. He may not believe you, so tell him he can check it with me. I'll stay in the building."

Weisler thought about it. He'd be cutting corners, but if he could bring this case to a conclusion quickly it would save him so much time.

"If you're prepared to trust me to report your words faithfully, I'll do that. I'm sure he'll want to check it out with you. I'm even feeling sorry for him."

***

"Sorry to bring you here from your workplace, Herr Samson, but I needed to clear something up. Please look at these two photographs that were taken outside the British Embassy five months ago."

Weisler opened the file in front of him and passed the two photographs across the desk to John. He'd been kept waiting in a small, stifling, windowless room at the police station for over an hour, increasingly nervous about why he'd been brought here. *Presumably, the police have new information. But does it concern the removal of the research document, or the fight with the fascists? Or both? If only I'd been able to contact Mark.*

His stomach knotted as he studied the two photographs; they clearly showed him entering the Embassy on different occasions, giving the lie to his previous story that he'd only been to the Embassy once eleven months ago. A horrible, sweaty panic threatened to swallow him up. To give himself time to think, he said, "When were these taken, Inspektor? I may have forgotten that I'd made more than one visit to the Embassy."

"They were taken around five months ago. The dates correspond exactly with those that recorded you entering and leaving the library where the research paper on rocket fuels was kept. You're also holding a leather camera case in the second picture. Can you explain all this, Herr Samson?"

On the point of confessing everything, John suddenly thought of another way to buy some time.

"I don't want to say anything until I've spoken to Herr Chastain, Inspektor."

Weisler looked at him enigmatically. John couldn't tell if he was disappointed, gloating or triumphant.

"That should be possible. Herr Chastain and I spoke at length earlier today. After he'd seen these photographs, he told me how

143

the Embassy had acquired the research paper. We then reached an understanding on this matter and he's given me permission to report the main points to you; would you like to hear what we've agreed? You can speak to him later."

John laughed cynically. *The bastards have done a deal.*

"Please go ahead, Inspektor."

Weisler recounted their conversation faithfully, explaining that Chastain had admitted John had been 'recruited' by a member of the British Secret Service to obtain and pass on examples of interesting German scientific research.

"This you duly did, successfully, but then your document fell into the hands of someone in the Nazi Party working at the Embassy. Herr Chastain also told me unequivocally that the British Government would never admit to their role in this. If you are prepared to say that you acted alone – you could say that you came across this paper by chance, and then decided to hand a copy to the Embassy – I will do everything to ensure you're not prosecuted. I can see from the look on your face that you don't believe me, Herr Samson, so I'll take you to see Herr Chastain now, if you wish."

John felt a rising fury. He believed what Weisler had told him; he seemed to be an honourable man trying to do his job. But his own government were hanging him out to dry – the duplicitous British ruling class. *Well, they've got a fight on their hands.*

"I would like to see Herr Chastain, Inspektor."

He was given coffee then taken to another, more comfortable room, where Chastain was sitting at a desk, writing. He put his pen down and beckoned him to the other chair. The two men studied each other.

"Please sit down, John. I understand that Inspektor Weisler has informed you about our conversation. The problem, as I'm sure you realise, is that the pictures of you entering the Embassy, just after you'd been to the library, have shifted the balance of probability. The police can now make a plausible argument that you brought the photographs of that research to us. It's no longer realistic for our side to continue to claim it's coincidental. Unfortunately for you, the British Government can't be seen to be spying on a friendly country like Weimar Germany. I feel awful about this, but the only way around this problem is for you to say that you came across this research, which was in the public domain, in your normal work as a researcher. You thought it looked interesting, so brought it to our attention.

"If you do that, I have Weisler's assurance that you won't be charged."

John steeled himself to stay calm. Weisler and Chastain clearly feel they'd got everything sewn up. They were going to be surprised – he had no intention of going quietly – but he wasn't about to reveal his hand yet.

"I see. I'm puzzled, Mark. As far as I know, taking a photograph of a research paper that's in the public domain isn't a crime, so there wouldn't be anything to charge me with."

"Apart from a small fine for removing the document from the library without permission, I suspect you're right. However, Inspektor Weisler assures me that passing that document on to the British Embassy without the permission of the original researcher would fall foul of German law. That's where Weisler's discretion comes in."

"But the university is bound to take a harder line with me if they think I initiated this."

"Not necessarily. I agree it doesn't look good either way, but as long as they're pleased with your research so far, they'll try to find a way to keep you."

How can he know that? He's desperate to get me to agree with his plan, so he's almost certainly giving me false hope. Who knows how seriously the university will take this? The British Government wants to hang me out to dry, and they want my agreement on top! Sod them!

Voice trembling, John replied, "My future will depend on how this ends up, and I'd be stupid to take the inspektor's word that he'll be able to clear everything. At least if I tell the university the truth I'll keep my self-respect. I'm being treated disgracefully, Mark, and you know it. I want to go back to my work."

Chastain paused, then said, "Inspektor Weisler will want to hear what you've just told me first hand, John. Please wait here, I'll tell him we're finished for now. I advise you to think very carefully about your decision."

Thirty minutes later, Weisler came in.

"Herr Chastain has told me that you need time to consider whether to publicly support the version of events that he and I have agreed. I can only tell you that making life difficult for your government and mine is only going to make the outcome worse for you. I'm exercising my authority to detain you overnight, Herr Samson, to give you time to reflect on your decision.

"Also, a young woman called Fräulein Lipsky is here and is asking to see you. Do you wish to see her?"

John was astonished to hear Ilse's name suddenly mentioned in this awful place. What was she doing here? His first reaction was to say that he didn't wish her to see him like this. But it would be a relief to see her, to explain his side of the story, to tell her the truth and have no secrets between them at last.

"Please tell Fräulein Lipsky that I would love to see her, Inspektor."

His mood lifted as he waited for her. His relationship with Ilse was more important to him than anything; as long as he could persuade the Head of Faculty to let him continue with his research, they could be together. Nothing else mattered.

She burst into the room, flinging the door open then embracing him.

"Are you all right, John? Why are you in the police station – have you been arrested?"

"Not yet. It's wonderful to see you. Please sit down, I want to explain everything. It's a long story that begins nearly eighteen months ago in England, when I heard I'd been accepted for my postdoctorate at Friedrich Wilhelm University."

"If that's important to you, John, then of course I want to hear it."

Over the next thirty minutes he told Ilse everything, starting with being asked by certain people in London to gather interesting examples of German scientific research and then hand them over to the British Embassy.

"I didn't feel comfortable agreeing to do it, but it was a way that I could help my country."

He was concentrating so hard on getting every detail right, he failed to notice the increasingly fraught expression on Ilse's face. Finally, the dam burst.

"Stop! I have to know if I've understood what you're saying. And be honest with me. Who were the people that approached you eighteen months ago in England?"

Surprised by the hard edge to her voice, he said, "They worked for a government department; the Foreign Office, I assumed."

"Would it be fair to say they were involved in spying on other countries?"

"I didn't realise that at first, but that gradually became clear to me."

"And when exactly did you start looking for examples of German research that you could hand over to the spies in the Embassy?"

Suddenly, John realised how this looked, but he could only push on. She had to know the truth.

"About five months before we met."

"So for the whole time we've been together, intimate with each other, trusting each other completely?"

"Yes, but…"

"Don't you realise what you've done? I trusted you, and you've betrayed me. I'm German, John. My father fought for Germany in the war. I'm proud of the country where I grew up, in spite of the fact that some Germans don't want me here. Which makes what you've done so difficult to accept. I really thought you understood that for a Jew in Germany today, trust means everything. Deceit equals betrayal, and there's no way back from such a betrayal."

"Ilse, please. I've been stupid and made a terrible mistake. I know I should have told you what I'd been doing. I almost did several times. After this blew up, I told the Embassy that was it, I wasn't going to carry on, and they accepted that."

"So if this little spying adventure hadn't been discovered, you would probably still be carrying on. And be honest, John, you wouldn't have told me, would you?"

Ashamed and distraught, he struggled frantically to find the words to salvage the situation. But they wouldn't come.

"Ilse, please. I was only passing on published research. We can't split up over this. There must be a way back – I love you."

They looked at each other. Tears were streaming down Ilse's face, dark lines of eye make-up streaking her cheeks. But he could see she'd made up her mind; there was no way back.

"I love you too, John. I thought we could be for keeps. But I know myself well enough to realise that I will never be able to accept what you've done. Trust is so important for me, there will always be doubt at the back of my mind. No relationship can survive that. I'm so sorry, but I'm also angry because you've been so stupid and ruined the future we might have had together."

Standing up, still crying, she put her hand on his shoulder and kissed his cheek.

"Goodbye, John. I'll put everything you've left in my flat in a bag and leave them with the landlady for you to collect. Can you please do the same?"

His sense of who he was, of time, place and a future, had left him. He heard himself speaking words he wasn't consciously aware of constructing.

"You should know that the deal Inspektor Weisler and Mark Chastain have agreed means that I will almost certainly have to leave Germany, so we're never going to see each other again. I will always remember you, Ilse, I've never felt so alive. Be happy, and…"

At that point he began sobbing so loudly that the policeman outside the door looked in. Ilse kissed John once more and walked out of the room, barely aware of her surroundings as she left the building.

Over the next few years she would become a well-respected Head of Production at Funkstade Berlin. After several boyfriends and a brief affair with her boss, she got engaged to Johan, a successful musician, marrying him in 1932.

19

STAGNATION

Sitting in his sleeper compartment on the express to Paris as it pulled out of Berlin Hauptbahnhof, John tried to make sense of the last six days. A week ago, Inspektor Weisler had told him that he would avoid being officially deported as long as he left Germany by the end of the week.

"I advise you to take up this offer, Herr Samson. Otherwise, if you ever wanted to return to Germany in the future, it would be very difficult. I'm sorry events have turned out this way – you've paid a significant price for the hubris of your British diplomats. If that's what they are."

He'd been kept in a cell at the police station overnight until a decision about his case had been agreed between the British Embassy, the university and German authorities. He'd hardly slept, his mind churning through feelings of despair, anger and self-loathing.

After that, the outcome of his meeting with the Head of Faculty at Friedrich Wilhelm was a forgone conclusion – he had to clear his desk immediately and have no further contact with the university.

In his bed-sitting room the following day, he sat staring at a picture of Ilse on the wall. The events of the last few weeks seemed unconnected from his life, an irrelevant distraction from living. What was the point of his life from now on?

There'd been a note waiting from Mark Chastain on the table in the hall.

Dear John,
I'm very sorry that things have turned out this way. Can you please come to the Embassy tomorrow at midday; I may have some better news for you.
Yours etc
Mark Chastain

He'd nearly thrown the note in the bin, then decided he might as well spend half an hour with Mark. What else had he got to do? Nothing had any point, so he'd just sat listening, disengaged, while Mark explained the marvellous opportunity he'd managed to secure for him.

"I know you're angry with us at the Embassy and it probably won't make you feel any better to know that Major Lawlor, who hatched this idiotic idea, has been disciplined. But I contacted an old university friend of mine in London who heads up the research and development team at Mullard, a London electronics company. They make thermionic valves and his department is currently recruiting people with precisely your qualifications. On my recommendation, he is willing to offer you a job on his team, subject to the usual trial period of three months. You don't have to give me your answer now, but please think about it. His name's Peter Thornbury and he's a good chap. Here's his contact number at Mullard."

It was pure chance that he'd got the compartment to himself; the sleeping-car attendant told him the other fellow hadn't turned up.

Although he doubted that it would make sleep any easier. He'd been unable to sleep for days now, the pointlessness of his life ahead tormenting him. Completing the simple tasks he needed to accomplish before leaving – clearing his bench, returning library books, settling his rent, buying his train and boat tickets – had proved so challenging that he'd almost run out of time. Worst of all was sorting through Ilse's belongings. He'd got very drunk, gone round his room grabbing everything of hers, stuffing them into a laundry bag and leaving it with Frau Hessler. He posted a letter telling Ilse where they were, asking her to give his stuff away to a hostel for war veterans.

He'd withdrawn all the money from his bank account, intending to take his fellow academics out for a goodbye dinner. But word had quickly gone around the physics department about the reason behind his unexpected departure and few of his colleagues wanted to have anything to do with him. Some even regarded his activities as traitorous, while others were worried their careers could be damaged by association. Karl was the only one who'd initially agreed to go out with him, but then backed out at the last moment following pressure from others in the department.

"I'm sorry, John. I hope you understand; they've made it clear that I will be shunned if I go for a drink with you. I like you and hope you manage to rebuild your life back in Britain."

He hadn't given much thought to anything as constructive as rebuilding his life. Quite the opposite; he'd avoided making any plans or decisions. He hadn't tried to contact Peter Thornbury, or told his father and sister that he was coming back. After living as a single man in Berlin for a year, accountable only to his Head of Department, he couldn't face returning to live with them in Kentish Town. There were a few decent guest houses in the streets around Mornington Crescent in Camden; he'd rent a room for a month and then contact Peter Thornbury. Whatever life held for him now, he'd need money. He felt no gratitude to Chastain for setting him up at Mullard; it was the least he could do given the circumstances. Only when he'd sorted out a place to stay and started the new job would he contact his father.

Near Potsdam, he left his train compartment to relieve himself in the lavatory at the end of the carriage and saw a worn-down, middle-aged woman with a teenage girl standing in the adjoining coach. They both looked close to tears. *Almost certainly, my problems are nothing compared to theirs.*

"Excuse me, Fräulein, are you travelling far?"

The woman looked at him suspiciously, then told him that she was travelling to Amsterdam.

"Don't you have seats?"

"Unfortunately not."

"I see. I'm the only one occupying my compartment, and that doesn't seem fair. Would you two like to share? It's a sleeper but I'll leave the top bunk raised so the three of us can sit on the bottom bunk. I'll tell the attendant and we'll leave the blinds open if you're worried."

"Thank you, but we couldn't possibly…"

Her daughter butted in. "Please, Mother, you'll collapse if we stand here any longer. That's very kind of you, sir, if you're sure."

"Good, that's settled. I wouldn't have slept anyway thinking about you two standing out here all night. Please, follow me."

They carried their heavy suitcases along the corridor back to his compartment. At John's suggestion, the daughter took the window seat, her mother in the middle and John sat nearest to the door.

"That way I won't disturb you when I go to the dining car."

They both immediately fell into a deep sleep. As he passed the attendant on the way to the dining car he explained the situation and gave him five marks to leave them alone. The dining car was crowded, there was only one vacant table and the waiter approached him soon after he took his seat and gave him the menu.

"What would sir like to drink?"

"A glass of claret, please."

He scanned the menu, quickly decided on pork schnitzel with bean stew, then looked around the carriage. His fellow diners were solidly middle class, mostly couples but with a smattering of businessmen and Wehrmacht officers. One or two were looking his way; he supposed he did stand out, as he clearly didn't fit any of those groups. After he'd ordered, he lapsed into another of his increasingly frequent abstracted states, staring out of the window as dusk slowly blurred the outlines of the North European Plain.

He suddenly became aware of the waiter's voice, who'd clearly been there for several seconds.

"Your pork schnitzel and bean stew, sir."

As the waiter placed the dish in front of him, John noticed a well-dressed, middle-aged woman standing behind him. The waiter bowed slightly, looked at the woman and said, "Would you mind if this lady joined you, sir? There is only one other place available and that's opposite a gentleman smoking a cigar."

She smiled at John.

"I would be most grateful. I'm allergic to cigar smoke, you see, and my coughing would ruin the meal for both of us if I sat at his table."

John found himself involuntarily returning her smile.

"Please, do join me. I'm not comfortable near cigar smoke myself."

John watched her as she studied the menu and ordered her meal. She was conservatively dressed, by Berlin standards, in an expensive-looking navy-blue silk skirt and matching fitted jacket. He guessed she was around forty years old.

"I'd like a glass of wine, please, waiter. Can I ask what you're drinking?"

"It's claret. I don't know much about wine, but I'm enjoying it."

"A glass of claret then, please, waiter."

John agreed when the waiter asked if he wanted his meal kept hot until the woman's was ready.

"That's kind of you, thank you. I think we should probably introduce ourselves. I'm Margareta."

Far from being irritated, John realised he was pleased to be taken out of his introspection by engaging with this stranger. He noticed that the little make-up she wore emphasised her large, dark-brown eyes.

"I'm pleased to meet you, Margareta. I'm John Samson, from London, England."

"I realised you weren't German from your accent, but I couldn't place it exactly. I'm from Berlin, travelling to Amsterdam to see my sister and her family. What do you do, John? Are you going back to London for good, or just visiting family and friends?"

I'm never going to see her again, so I could tell her the whole story and see how she reacts. But why would she care?

"I'm going home to see my father and sister. I haven't seen them since I came to Friedrich Wilhelm University as a postdoctorate researcher a year ago. It's been an eventful year. How about you, what do you do in Berlin, Margareta?"

Before she answered the waiter returned with their meals and her wine.

"*Prost.*"

They chinked their glasses. Margareta took a sip of her wine and screwed up her face.

"I see you were telling the truth when you said you didn't know much about wine, John."

She looked at him and laughed.

"I'm sorry, that was rude of me. We don't know each other well enough for teasing, but this is awful. Do you mind if I ask the waiter what else they've got?"

"Not at all, please do. This could be the start of my wine education."

She called the waiter over.

"This is dreadful. Please take them away and bring us two glasses of your best red, thank you.

"Now, to answer your question, I manage a nightclub. Don't look surprised; I assume you must have visited a few during the last year?"

"Yes, a few. It was quite a revelation, there's nothing quite like them in London. I remember the first time I went I ended up having my wallet stolen."

"I'm sorry to hear that, but it happens all the time in the clubs. Did you lose a lot of money?"

"Not that much, thankfully. To be fair, it didn't actually happen in the club."

As he remembered the circumstances, John felt his face reddening. Margareta noticed, then smiled at him and said, "Oh, I see. Well, I hope the experience was worth it."

They looked at each other and laughed. The ice had been broken between them, and for the next hour or so they exchanged stories about Berlin's 'liberated women', his research, politics, being attacked by Nazis and the challenge of managing a club as a woman. He was surprised that he only thought about Ilse and his disastrous career briefly. She insisted on paying the bill – "Believe me, John, I earn a lot more than the average scientist" – and thanked him for a lovely evening as they said goodbye outside her compartment.

"You must visit my club when you return to Berlin, John. I promise that you won't be accosted by any young women intent on stealing your wallet," then she kissed him on the cheek.

Walking back to his compartment, he realised their conversation was the first time he'd felt like a normal human being since leaving the police station. Luckily the mother and daughter were still asleep in the same positions in his compartment, leaving him just enough room to squeeze into the remaining space. He took a blanket from the top bunk, pulled it over him and finally sunk into a deep sleep.

He'd missed saying goodbye to Margareta as they'd left the train, distracted by repeated thanks from the mother and daughter. He only just made the connection with his train to Calais and from there on to the ferry.

As he stood watching the White Cliffs of Dover draw closer, almost a year to the day since he'd seen them recede, his sense of despondency completely returned.

20

THE 'PRODIGAL' RETURNS

It took him longer than he'd thought it would to find a room to rent; all of those he'd looked at around Mornington Crescent were either too expensive or too depressing – or both. The landlady in the last room he'd seen advised him to head eastwards to Hackney, where he'd get more for his money. He took her advice and found a self-contained basement flat in a three-storey house overlooking Hackney Downs. The rest of the house was rented to a family of five; a husband, wife, their two children and her mother. He discovered all of that on the day he moved in as the wife, Doreen, had knocked on his door, introduced herself and given him a bottle of milk, a loaf of bread and a large pat of butter.

"That's very kind of you, Doreen, thank you. I'm John Samson, and of course I'll repay you in full."

"Is it just you living here, John?"

"Yes, I'm single and unattached. A scientist, actually, and I've just returned from a year studying in Berlin. I hope to be starting a job at Mullard in Balham next week."

John saw the look of concern on Doreen's face when he mentioned Berlin.

"My husband, Leo, was badly injured in the war. He hates Germans and everything to do with them, so please don't mention that to him, or there'll be a row."

"My brother was killed in that war, Doreen, so I understand. I won't mention it."

The flat was better than he'd expected, although admittedly he'd set his expectations low. The living room and bedroom were both spacious compared to his Berlin flat, there was a gas fire, the small kitchen had a gas stove and a small hot water heater over the sink. Most of the furniture was usable, although shabby and worn. But the flat smelt musty and damp and the mattress was badly stained; he'd have to spend most of his first pay packet on a new one and get cleaning materials for the bathroom, which had a lingering odour of human waste.

Once I've made the flat decent, I'll contact Thornbury and arrange a meeting, assuming that the job wasn't a figment of Chastain's imagination. I'd better find out everything I can about Mullard beforehand, I need to make a good impression. Dad and May will be expecting a visit after the letter I sent them before I left Berlin. That won't be easy, I've hardly written to them over the last six months and I can't lie to them about what happened. Maybe just leave a few details out. Should I write to Ilse? It was a horrible way to end everything, but what would be the point?

He rang the Mullard number from the call box at the end of the street the following morning and asked for Peter Thornbury. He was taken aback when the receptionist said, "Hello, Mister Samson, Mister Thornbury has been expecting your call. I'll see if he's available, please don't hang up."

Expecting my call? That's a surprise. Presumably Mark had contacted Thornbury again and told him I was on my way back to England.

"Hello, is that John Samson?"

Thornbury sounded normal, not at all like the Oxbridge-educated Chastain that he was expecting.

"Yes, it is. It's good to make contact, Mr Thornbury. I'm ringing to arrange a date and time for us to meet. You must be very busy, when would be convenient?"

"It's good to hear from you, John. Straight to the point, I like that. Can you tell me a little about yourself – what you've been doing in Berlin for the last year, what you did before that, how you know Mark Chastain?"

John realised how stupid he'd been. Of course Thornbury would ask him about his time in Berlin, yet he'd never thought to ask Chastain what he'd told Thornbury about their 'arrangement'. He had to assume Chastain wouldn't have raised it, as that wouldn't look good for him.

As he finished telling Peter about his PhD, his year in Berlin, his research at Friedrich Wilhelm and life outside of the university, Thornbury jumped in.

"So why did you leave after one year?"

"It wasn't a snap decision. I'd been growing increasingly disillusioned with theoretical physics research for some time. My boss had asked me to set up a visit to a Berlin radio station for interested members of the physics department, the connection being that we study the behaviour of electrons in vacuum tubes and their equipment applies it. From that moment I was increasingly drawn to working on the practical applications of my research. One year felt the right time to go."

"That's interesting, I'm with you there. Let's fix that meeting, then. How about ten o'clock this Thursday, at our factory in Balham, South London? Just go to the main gate and say you've got an appointment to see me. Stay on the line when we've finished and Dorothy will give you our address."

"Thank you, Peter, I look forward to seeing you then. Should I bring anything with me?"

"There's no need at this stage. Where will you be coming from?"

"I'm currently living in Hackney, while I find my feet in London."

"Keep your wits about you, then, John," he said, laughing.

The conversation with Thornbury raised his spirits. After Dorothy had given him the address, he decided to walk around his new neighbourhood. *I might even go for a pint in The Three Sisters at Hackney Downs.* He started at Hackney Downs station and followed the direction south through London Fields, Bethnal Green and Whitechapel. While he'd heard about these places and knew roughly where they were in relation to his father's house, he'd never been there.

As he left London Fields behind and headed towards Bethnal Green he noticed that many of the larger houses, though similar to those in his street, seemed to be occupied by several families, not just one or two. In many of the streets near Whitechapel, groups of children, some as young as two, were playing games they'd made up themselves on the grimy pavements. He was shocked to see that they were mostly barefoot, filthy and dressed in clothes haphazardly sewn together from various pieces of cloth. The eldest in each group, often no older than ten and usually girls, kept a semblance of order. There were no responsible adults in sight.

In the narrow side streets off Commercial Road that led towards the docks, rows of squalid terraced houses faced each other across dark alleyways no more than ten feet wide, the gutter down the centre clogged with waste of an indeterminate nature. Some of the children shouted at him, begging aggressively and cussing him when he walked on.

He'd seen enough. As he retraced his steps he felt ashamed to see the effect the huge rise in unemployment must have had on these communities – it hadn't crossed his mind before now. *Their lives are so much harder than mine was at their age; we had little money, but compared to them, I always felt cared for and secure.*

He bought cleaning materials in a general store in Shacklewell Lane, then spent most of the evening washing and scrubbing the worst areas of the flat. As he reflected on what he'd seen earlier, he longed to tell Ilse about his impressions and thoughts of the day. He missed her dreadfully.

Standing outside his old home the following evening, he hesitated for a moment. A little earlier, he'd hoped he'd be able to surprise his father having his usual early evening pint in the Admiral, rather than turning up unexpectedly like this at their door. But his father had just left, according to the barman, so here he was.

The noise from the knocker reverberated around the house. The sound of voices was followed by footsteps in the hallway – his sister's he guessed – and suddenly she was standing at the open door, a mixture of joy and disbelief on her face, before launching herself into his arms, shrieking.

"Johnny! Where have you been? Why didn't you write? Dad and I were getting worried about you. I managed to find the address for that Friedrich place in Berlin and wrote to them, but I didn't get a reply. I've missed you, it's wonderful to see you. Come in. Be prepared to get a hard time from Dad. He's furious that you haven't written for so long, but please just let him have his say, he'll calm down and we can have a lovely catch-up. You look different somehow; not surprising – it's a year since we saw you."

And you're very different too, May. No longer the anxious and unconfident little sister I left behind.

"Where the bloody hell have you been? You must have known that May and I would be worried sick. We haven't heard anything since Christmas and had no idea whether you were alive or dead. The son that left here a year ago would never have behaved so thoughtlessly. I'm ashamed of you, John. What have you got to say for yourself?"

John followed his sister's advice. He apologised once, apologised again, and then gave them an edited story of his year in Berlin. How he'd initially been lonely but grew to love the vibrant culture once he'd made friends. How his research had begun well, then started to pose questions he hadn't been able to answer. How he'd met a woman and fallen in love. How there'd been a misunderstanding about his use of another scientist's research. Finally, how all those things seemed to come to a head in the last two months – including breaking up with his girlfriend – and he realised that life as a research physicist wasn't for him.

"I'm really sorry I've caused you both so much worry. I promise that I've written twice since Christmas, the last time just two weeks ago. I've no idea why they haven't arrived."

He glanced at May, who gave him an affirmative wink. She was dying to know more about this woman he'd fallen in love with, but she'd wait until they were alone before asking. Instead, she said, "So what are you going to do now? Have you got a job?"

He felt a sense of relief; he could give them some positive news.

"I was lucky. I managed to line up a job with an electronics company called Mullard before I left Berlin. They make valves for radios and transmitters; I'm seeing one of their senior managers tomorrow to discuss the job in more detail. I'm hoping to start next week."

His father didn't speak for a while. This wasn't necessarily a good sign, but on this occasion he seemed pleasantly surprised.

"I hope you're not feeling too downhearted about leaving the university job or breaking up with your girl. Good on you for bouncing back, John. Have you got somewhere to live yet?"

"I have! I moved into a basement flat in Hackney Downs. It needs a bit of cleaning but otherwise it's fine. Do you two fancy coming to the pub with me? I think I owe you both a drink after what I've put you through. You're allowed to now you've turned eighteen, aren't you, May?"

May beamed at John, but his father looked disapproving.

"Please, Dad. It's a special occasion to celebrate John's return. We could go into the saloon bar at the Admiral."

His father smiled, then said, "There's got to be a first time, I suppose. But nothing strong, mind you. Half a pint of shandy is your lot."

"Aren't you coming with us, Dad?"

"Not this time, May. Go and have a grown-up talk with your long-lost brother, then tell me all his news later on."

The few disapproving glances when they walked into the lounge bar disappeared as soon as the landlord recognised John.

"Well, well, I see the prodigal has returned – and he's brought his sister with him. How are you, John? it's good to see you. And you too, May. Your first time, I hope. Let me get you a pint of London bitter to wash the taste of that German stuff out of your mouth. And what will May be having?"

Before John could answer, May pointedly butted in and said, "I'll have a lemonade, please, George. John's my brother, not my keeper, and this is 1926."

The two men exchanged glances, leaving John uncomfortable, feeling disloyal that he'd connived with George's patronising attitude towards his sister. He could only imagine what Ilse's response would have been if she'd been there – she would have torn into both of them. Thinking about her brought on a surge of sadness for everything he'd lost; not only Ilse, but his academic career, life in Berlin and his standing in the scientific community.

"John, where have you gone? George asked you what beer you wanted?"

He roused himself from his thoughts.

"Sorry, George, I'll have a pint of London Pride, and please have something yourself."

"I see they must have been paying you well over in Hun-land."

It was said with humour, but it was clear that some people still harboured a lingering resentment towards Germany and Germans. He ignored the remark and they took their drinks to a quiet corner of the bar.

May came to the point straight away.

"Well, darling brother, before I tell you about what things have been like for Dad and me over the last year, now we're alone I'd like to know the truth about how you ended up leaving Berlin in such a hurry. And please remember that I'm no longer the wilting violet of a sister you left behind a year ago."

Taken aback by her maturity and new-found confidence, John told her the truth about almost everything that happened to him during his time in Berlin, including the reason he'd left Friedrich Wilhelm, falling in love with Ilse and then breaking up. She listened intently, occasionally letting out a gasp of surprise. As he finished, he said, "I'm not planning on telling anyone else the whole story, May, but I wanted you to know what an idiot I've been. I hope I can trust you."

"Of course you can. I'm sorry your year in Germany turned out so miserably in the end. I can see you're not the same optimistic Johnny that left us. But I must be honest, I'm very pleased to see you back. I understand why you didn't write much, but worrying about whether you were all right, on top of our other troubles, was hard to take, if I'm honest."

Not only have I wasted a year of my life, I've made theirs worse into the bargain.

"I'm so sorry, May. Tell me how it's been for you and Dad, I want to hear everything you've got to say – I deserve that."

"Don't worry, I'm not going to go easy on you. For your sake as much as mine – it's important you know how tough things have been here since the General Strike. I assume you know how that ended, but the mood has been particularly nasty around here because so many men work on the railways. They all came out in support of the miners, and then demanded that workers in other industries join them in solidarity. The trouble was, even though Dad's in a union, his union didn't call out their members and the managers at his works told all of them they'd be sacked if they went on strike. There was a picket of miners and railwaymen outside the factory gates, but he felt he had to cross it, along with almost everyone else.

"It broke him. His old drinking friends in the Admiral won't speak to him anymore. There's a horrible atmosphere when we meet people in the street who came out on strike. Many of them have been sacked, they've no money and their children are starving. They blame the men who went into work – they say that if everyone had gone on strike, the bosses and the government would have caved in. That's why he didn't want to come with us to the pub; he's worried that we'll be labelled as scabs as well."

May went on to describe their precarious financial situation; wages were stagnant, the landlord had put the rent up and it looked like she would have to leave the Camden School for Girls before she completed her typing course. She explained that her father had regretfully told her a week ago that she'd probably have to give it up and take unskilled work in a shop, if she could get one. There were thirty people going for every job at the moment.

The longer she spoke, the angrier he felt, but he knew the real focus of that anger was directed at himself. While he was having a comfortable and fulfilling life in Germany (until the end), his father's and sister's lives were becoming increasingly precarious. He didn't know because he hadn't bothered to write and ask. There was only one thing to say.

"You won't have to leave that course, May, I promise. I start my new job next week. It's a good wage and I'll give you and Dad whatever you need to get your lives back on track. I don't need that much to live on, and we're all family. We've got each other."

May's eyes had become increasingly moist as he spoke; tears were now running down her cheeks. She tried to speak but couldn't get the words out, so just threw her arms around him.

21

AUTUMN 1927

John jolted awake as his bedroom suddenly flooded with light. There was a throbbing pain above his eyes, a sour taste in his mouth and a woman wearing his dressing gown tugging the curtains open.

"Why are you opening the curtains – what time is it?"

"Some of us have got to go to work, lover boy. It's eight thirty and I've got to be back in Soho by ten. Is it okay if I have a quick bath?"

John nodded his assent, trying to remember her name and anything else about last night.

"Of course you can. I'm so sorry, but I've forgotten your name?"

"Oh, the romance! You certainly know how to woo a girl. I'm surprised you can't remember, because you must have repeated 'You're very attractive, Sophie, would you like to come back to my place?' at least five times last night."

"But you are an attractive woman. Very attractive. Did we...?

"Oh yes. More than once, in fact. No fireworks, but I enjoyed it, and you appeared to be having a good time. Is there any soap?"

"There's a new bar in the bathroom cupboard."

She wrapped his dressing gown around her, walked over to the bed and kissed him, putting her hand under the sheet.

"Signs of life already, I'm impressed. But then you can't be more than twenty-eight."

"I'm twenty-seven. How old are you, Sophie?"

She stood up and did a twirl. She had a beautiful body and knew it.

"How old do you think?"

"Well, you've got the body of a twenty-five-year-old."

"And the face of?"

She held one of his nipples between her thumb and forefinger and tweaked it a little.

"Ow!"

"Be very careful with your next answer, John."

"An angel."

She laughed and released his throbbing nipple.

"For your quick thinking, I'll buy you a cocktail if you ever come back to the Golden Slipper."

She sniffed his dressing gown.

"This could do with a wash, by the way."

She picked up a towel and went to run a bath.

Over the last year he'd fallen into the habit of visiting the West End once a week and trying out a different nightclub each time. Occasionally, he might meet a woman and they'd go back to his flat. He enjoyed the uncommitted sex, though not the feeling of post-coital emptiness; he'd never wanted to see any of them again, and the feeling had always seemed mutual.

But his feelings this morning surprised him. Sophie ran the bar at the Golden Slipper in Soho and once her shift ended she'd joined him at his table. She was smart, thoughtful and they'd talked for hours about Berlin, votes for women, her job – *"Not every woman who works in a club is a prostitute, John"* – and his low moods. He'd bought them both a drink every hour in order to keep the table and they were both drunk by the time they left. Her quizzically raised eyebrows and little smile in response to his question – "Would you like to come back to mine for a nightcap?" – left him in no doubt what would happen later.

He wanted to get to know her, to take things further, but was that realistic? She looked a few years older than him, they moved in very different worlds and wanted different things. To be specific, she wanted to manage a nightclub and he still had little idea where his life was going. The self-loathing and sense of pointlessness of a year ago had evolved into an aimless pessimism, tempered by periods of optimism following breakthroughs at work.

The meeting with Peter Thornbury had gone well; at the time, it had helped him through the troughs of his depression. They'd liked each other from the start; Peter didn't want to know the story behind his abrupt departure from Berlin and made it clear that this was his opportunity to make a clean break.

"Mark and I knew each other well at Oxford. Our lives have since gone in very different directions, but we've always trusted each other, so I'm very happy to offer you a post on the basis of his recommendation. Plus, we desperately need more research scientists – the explosion in radio broadcasting has brought the need for smaller, more efficient and cooler-running valves. A challenge, but one that all our competitors are trying to meet. In some ways, you might even find that it's more exciting than pure physics."

John liked his enthusiasm and was grateful for the opportunity, though he doubted that building a better valve would enthuse him quite as much as pure research. But he had to admit that Thornbury's remark had proved more prophetic than he'd thought possible. He worked in an office with three other researchers; two focussed on the practical feasibility of the ideas that John and his colleague researcher came up with. It worked well; so well, that after six months Mullard had developed and patented a redesigned cathode that meant their valves ran cooler and could therefore be made smaller. Thornbury was delighted and had raised the salaries of John and his colleagues. That was one of the things he'd grown to appreciate; there was more collaboration and less competition here, compared to Friedrich Wilhelm.

His reflections were interrupted as Sophie walked back into the room, her skin lobster red from the hot bath, a thoughtful expression on her face.

"Thank you for a lovely evening. You're a nice guy, John; you respect women and that's not easy to find these days."

She paused, deciding what to say next.

"If you ever visit the Golden Slipper again, it would be nice to see you. I feel we've made a connection, so I'll leave you with that thought. If I don't see you again, I wish you good luck and hope you find what you're searching for."

He hesitated, unsure how to respond. *She's clearly saying that she wants more than a one-night stand. But what exactly?*

Scooping up her drawers from the floor and putting them on, Sophie filled the lengthening silence. She looked disappointed.

"I see I've caught you off guard, my mistake. Can we pretend I didn't say that, please? I'll get dressed and see myself out."

Wrested from his indecision, he scrambled to catch up.

"Wait! I would like to see you again. Truly. You did catch me off guard; I haven't had anything more than a one-night stand for over a year. But this has been… different. I feel there could be something between us, too. It's only fair to tell you that my last proper relationship was very intense, it ended horribly and I don't know if I'm ready for anything more serious yet. But if that doesn't put you off, I'd love to take you out to dinner one evening and continue our conversation."

Putting her camisole on, she caught him looking at her breasts under the loose fabric and gave him a wry smile.

"I'd be delighted. My next free evening is in five days' time, if you're free then?"

"I am. Where shall I meet you?"

"Come to my flat at eight o'clock. If you give me a pen and paper, I'll write down my address."

John had the rest of the day off and had arranged to take his sister out for one of their regular lunches together. The family finances were now in reasonable shape thanks to his frequent contributions, May had finished her course and was now a qualified typist earning a reasonable wage. She was worried about their father; he was sixty years old and in increasingly poor health. His lungs had been damaged by prolonged exposure to caustic fumes from the acid bath chemicals used at his factory, and an infected ulcer on his leg was proving stubbornly resistant to treatment.

"He's amazingly uncomplaining, John. I would be going round with a sour look on my face if I had to put up with his woes, but I know he gets low sometimes. I think he'd really welcome the occasional visit from you; you could take him to the pub, he hardly goes anymore since the strike."

"For God's sake, is that nonsense still going on? That's so unfair; I'll go round to see him one evening next week. What time does he usually get home?"

"About six o'clock. I get his supper ready around seven, then most evenings we sit down together and listen to the radio. I haven't thanked you enough for buying it for us. The evenings used to really drag, but now there's something interesting on most nights. It is weird having someone speaking to us in our front room in such a posh voice, though."

As they carried on talking, John was reminded of the extent to which he'd taken the inequality between his sister and himself for granted, as if it was the natural order of things. She was younger than him, yet it was May who was cooking and caring for their father, with no privacy or real independence at home. He had an independent life, his own flat, no responsibility for anyone other than himself, able to invite women back when he wanted. Yet she was grateful to him for the gesture of buying them a radio! *But be honest with yourself– you're not going to start going round to their house several times a week so that May can go out and have fun, are you?*

Turning the corner into Agar Grove, John was surprised by the well-kept street lined with two- and three-storey Victorian terraced houses. As he walked towards Sophie's address, he noticed that while many of the houses had been converted into flats, they were in a good state of repair. Her flat was on the first floor of a larger than average house.

"Hello! Come upstairs while I finish getting ready. Did you find the place all right?"

"I didn't have any trouble. My old house in Gospel Oak isn't far away – two stops further along from Camden Road station."

She had less make-up on than she'd worn in the nightclub and was wearing a sapphire-blue, silk-like dress that really suited her.

Sophie picked up the surprise on his face as he looked around the flat – two bedrooms, a well-lit front room with a floor-to-ceiling sash window, a tiny kitchen and separate bathroom and water closet.

"This is lovely, I'm impressed."

"Just because I work in a nightclub doesn't mean I don't like nice things. I'm also particular about keeping my home clean – my three brothers and I were brought up by our mother on her own, living in two rooms. She was incredible, keeping us warm and fed on the pittance she made from cleaning other people's houses. But cleaning and tidying our rooms came at the bottom of the list, and when I eventually managed to save the rent for this place, I promised myself I'd never live in such squalor again. If you don't mind me saying, I think your flat could do with a spring clean – no offence intended."

"None taken. You'll be pleased to know that my dressing gown has now been washed. You can wear it safely now."

She looked at him, raising an eyebrow. Realising the assumption, he hastily said, "I'm not assuming that you ever will, of course." She laughed, but didn't reply.

"I hope you don't mind me asking, but the rent can't be cheap on a flat like this. How can you afford it?"

"Punters always seem to assume that women who work in nightclubs earn so little that we're available to be bought for sex. Some are, but counting my tips, I bet I earn more than you. You're only the third bloke I've met in the club and then slept with – because I wanted to, not for money. Before you ask, you're the nicest out of the three. Once I'd saved up enough for a deposit, I searched for weeks until I found this place."

John felt himself blushing, as she carried on.

"Have you decided where you're taking me? I'm getting excited."

"I have. We're getting the Tube from Mornington Crescent to Leicester Square. I've had to guess the sort of place you like, so I hope you like it."

"So, tell me more about Ilse. You've obviously got some way to go before she's just a sad but lovely memory. I understand that you're grieving, but you seem angry with yourself, too, when she was the one who ended it."

They were finishing their main course, and conversation between them hadn't stopped since they'd sat down at their table. About twenty minutes ago he'd told her more about his relationship with Ilse in Berlin and she hadn't seemed to pay much attention. Yet she'd obviously picked up his anger and stored it for later. Her perception impressed him.

"I'm not sure I said that I'm feeling angry with myself."

"You didn't have to, it's clear from what you don't say and the way you express your feelings for her. You don't have to talk about it, but I'm a good listener; you have to be in my job."

"It seems you're a very perceptive listener, too."

He paused, sensing this could be a significant moment for their relationship.

"You're right, she finished it with me. But I'd betrayed the trust between us. Trust was very important to her, for good reason."

He carried on, struggling to find the right words as he told her about hiding his undercover spying from Ilse, getting caught, ending up in a police cell and having to tell her what he'd been doing. As his eyes moistened, Sophie reached across the table, covered his hand with hers and left it there.

"So why did that matter so much to her?"

"She's Jewish, and the way things are going in Germany right now, knowing you can trust your lover means everything. You see, Sophie…"

She'd gripped his hand.

"I understand. My father's Jewish. He came to Britain in 1886 as a young man, fleeing the pogroms in Russia along with thousands of other Jews. He met my mother two years later, it was love at first sight and they married eight weeks after that. I was born in 1896. Several members of his family who stayed behind were killed or driven out of their village; I've read about the situation in Germany, it sounds horribly familiar."

"Have you or your father ever experienced prejudice in this country?"

"My father did when he first arrived. But he moved into an area in the East End where there are other Jewish families, so there was solidarity. He's not particularly religious, we didn't observe many Jewish rituals or customs when I was growing up and so didn't stand out. It's not something I mention to people until I've got to know them – there's definitely anti-Jewish feeling in this country, too, unfortunately.

"Why did you agree to do that – to spy on other scientists? I hardly know you, but it seems out of character."

"I was naïve and arrogant. When I got to Berlin I discovered it had been the idea of one mad individual in London; staff at the British Embassy thought it was ridiculous – I could have backed out. But part of me had got carried away with the excitement. Me, a spy! What an idiot. I thought I was a better person than that and I've been disappointed in myself ever since. I've now told you more than anybody; I wouldn't blame you if you walked away."

Sophie finally took her hand away from his, and said, "I'm going to the toilet. Why don't you pay the bill and hail a taxi back to my flat. We can carry on talking there, or alternatively we can go to bed, make love and fall asleep in each other's arms. In the morning, I'll tell you the things about me that I'm not very proud of; if you haven't walked out by the end, I'll make us a lovely breakfast. After that, who knows? How does that sound?"

A wide grin had stretched across his face. He hadn't felt so uncomplicatedly happy since his stupid escapade in Berlin was discovered. Maybe even earlier.

"That's the best proposal I've had for a long time. I'll collect our coats and meet you at the exit. Don't be too long."

He woke slowly to the morning light filtering past the bedroom curtains. Her head was lying on his shoulder, strands of hair falling across her face, one of his thighs snuggled between her legs. The smell of their sweat was a heady reminder of their boisterous, abandoned fucking a few hours ago. Afterwards, she'd insisted on telling him the list of things she was ashamed of; drug taking, sleeping with the wrong men, two abortions. He'd only once been shocked, when she'd told him that a group of women in the club – her included – had paid a bouncer to beat up a punter who'd raped one of them. He'd reassured her it didn't change his feelings just before they'd fallen asleep.

He watched as her eyes flickered open, gradually focussing on his.

She smiled, then put her hand up to the side of his face.

"Good morning, John. Are you feeling hungry?"

Shifting his shoulder under her head, her breast falling softly into his hand, he kissed her and said, "What's on the menu?"

"Scrambled eggs, bacon and mushrooms, on toast."

"That sounds wonderful."

After eating breakfast around the tiny kitchen table, they'd taken a bath, sponging each other with her lavender soap, then walked to Parliament Hill Fields with the autumn sun on their faces, her arm in his. At the top of the hill, looking out over London, he took her hand in his, held his breath and said, "It feels just right being with you, Sophie. I know we've only been out together twice, but I'd like to see you more in the future. Regularly. If you would like that too, of course."

She looked at him, her expression unreadable, except for the faintest lowering of her eyebrows.

As the silence between them lengthened, his stomach gave a horrible lurch. He had to say something.

"You think it's too soon then? I know we've only spent a few hours together."

"It's not long, but we could always take things slowly at the start, so that's not why I'm hesitating. I think most people know after they've spent several hours with someone if it could lead somewhere romantically or not. But I want to be clear about what you're proposing. Are you asking me to become your companion and lover, and be open about that?"

She stopped and looked at him, a questioning look on her face.

"Yes, Sophie, I suppose that's exactly what I'm proposing."

"You're a lovely, attractive man and I'm flattered – very flattered – to be asked. But you're being naïve about relationships between unmarried men and women. Perhaps Berlin has misled you. You need to understand the damage such a relationship with me could do to your reputation. I work in a nightclub, and for most middle-class people that's no different to being a prostitute. Working-class people, too. Many of your friends could disapprove. More importantly, what will your family think? Their son and brother going out with an older woman who works in a nightclub, in a sexual relationship? It's the double standard – men are expected to have sex before they marry, but keep quiet about who with."

"But what about your reputation, Sophie?"

"I don't have one to lose. My parents were horrified when I told them where I would be working, but we were desperately poor before the war, I used my good looks to get the job, brought in money and they accepted it. I put up with the nasty comments directed towards me as part of the job."

"I won't care what my family says, and I've only made a few friends in the last year. I don't think they'll give a damn."

"Friends maybe. But I'm not going to be responsible for causing a split between you and your father and sister. I'm also thinking of myself. I've been let down in the past by a man promising lifelong commitment, only to run a mile when mummy and daddy threatened to disinherit him."

"Well, that won't be an issue for me – there's nothing for me to inherit."

"These are my conditions. Take me with you the next time you visit your father and sister. I'll be open about my job, we'll make it clear we're in a relationship and then let's see what happens."

22

THREE YEARS LATER, 1930
HIGHGATE CEMETERY

Holding Sophie's hand in the front pew of the chapel, May crying softly beside him, John sat reflecting on the last three years. His father's lung condition had deteriorated rapidly over the last four months, and his death a week ago had brought a blessed relief from the constant pain. Peter Thornbury had told him to take all the leave he needed to care for his father as it became clear there was nothing the doctors could do to slow the cancer's growth, so he'd spent most days at his father's house with May and the district nurse. His sister had been amazing, taking the lead organising their father's care. A few days before the end, John, May and Sophie worked their way through everything that had to be done – informing his father's siblings and drinking buddies, booking the wake and liaising with the church and undertakers.

John had worked hard to build a closer, more honest relationship with his father over the last three years, bringing him peace of mind. That had begun the day he'd taken Sophie to see his dad, just two weeks after she'd insisted they had to tell his father about their relationship before she'd agree to be his 'companion'. He'd arranged for May to meet Sophie first so that she knew the nature of their relationship beforehand, as he needed his sister to be on his side from the start.

He hadn't planned for what to do if their meeting didn't go well. They were very different – in age, experience and temperament. But he needn't have worried; the two women had gone to a tea shop in Camden Town and left as friends. Sophie worked hard to make sure that her maturity and experience didn't unconsciously overwhelm the younger woman.

His father had clearly been taken aback when he'd opened the door to see this older, glamorous woman standing next to his son in the doorway, but Sophie charmed him from the start. Holding out her hand, she'd said, "Hello, Mr Samson, I'm Sophie and I'm very pleased to meet you. Thank you for seeing us this afternoon, I hope we haven't interrupted any of your plans?"

His father had given a friendly laugh, shaken her hand and said, humorously, "I don't make many plans these days, Sophie. It's lovely to meet you – and to see my son, of course. I don't see him that often. Please come in, and do call me Harold."

As May got their tea together, John opened the conversation.

"Dad, Sophie and I are here to tell you that we've decided we want to be together as companions, and wanted to get your approval before anybody else knows. We've already told May and she's happy for us."

"You don't need my approval to start courting, John, you know that. You must be nearly thirty by now?"

As John hesitated, Sophie had politely taken over. She'd made a quick judgement about Harold and decided he would respect frank speaking.

"We know we don't need your approval, Harold, but given the decision John and I have come to, it would mean a lot for us to have it. You see, I've been engaged before and my fiancé went off with another woman. John fell in love with a woman in Germany over a year ago, and he was heartbroken when she ended the relationship. Because of those experiences, we're both cautious about making a lifelong commitment at this time. But we make each other happy, we're attracted to one another and want to be together – like a husband and wife. But discreetly, of course."

She'd stopped there, suddenly aware of the blood pumping in her chest, and waited.

Harold looked at them both, then turned to May.

"I assume you know about this, May? What do you think?"

"I want my brother to be happy, Dad. Sophie makes him happy and I like her, so I'm pleased for both of them."

Harold didn't say anything for a while, just sat looking out of the window.

"Thank you both for coming here and asking me. I can't say I'm overjoyed, but as long as you're discreet then you have my approval. I'm pleased that you've found each other."

He'd made a point of seeing his dad at least once a fortnight since then, and Harold hadn't ever mentioned the issue again, aside from asking after Sophie's health and happiness.

During the first few months of their relationship, they would stay at her more spacious flat whenever they wanted to sleep together. Which was more often than not. The limitations of this arrangement – lack of personal space, use of the bathroom in the morning, never having enough of his clothes at Sophie's place – began to chafe on both of them.

"John, have you seen my special soap? You'd better not have used it as shaving cream again."

"You remember we agreed that you wouldn't shave your armpits in the bath, Sophie?"

"When was the last time you washed the clothes you keep here? They're starting to make my clothes smell."

"If you don't want me staying in your flat so often, just tell me."

After another similar exchange turned into a furious row, John had stormed out and didn't contact Sophie again for three days. But for most of that time he was working out how much it would cost to buy a bigger flat with a mortgage. Since he'd started working at Mullard he'd been promoted twice and his salary had almost doubled. With the help of the company's finance manager, he'd worked out that he could afford a two-bedroom flat in De Beauvoir, Hackney, paying only a few pounds a month more than the rent he was currently paying. When he'd finally gone round to Sophie's flat with a large bunch of flowers, she'd thrown her arms around him and said, "I hate it when we row, John. I'm sorry. It's always about stupid things, too. It's just that this flat's too small for two of us and yours is even smaller. I don't know how to solve it."

"I agree. So I'm taking out a mortgage on a two-bedroom flat in Hackney. I'd like you to help me choose one. What do you think?"

"I think you're a very decisive man who's full of surprises."

There were lots of flats for sale due to the Depression and banks calling in their loans. As soon as he found somewhere with a garden that he could afford, he made the owner a good offer which was immediately accepted. Sophie was adamant about keeping her own flat, even though sharing John's flat would have saved her money, which would have been useful. Although she'd been promoted as the manager of the Golden Slipper, takings were down because of the Depression so she earned no more than two years ago.

Sitting in his garden with Sophie and a group of their mutual friends on the day after he'd moved, he watched her talking animatedly to two of his work colleagues and their wives. *Look at her, she's amazing. I'm so lucky to have found this woman to share my life with. We're happy, we love each other, still have a passionate relationship and always manage to sort out our differences amicably. But the children question came up again last week, when I'd thoughtlessly said that bringing a child into this increasingly uncertain world was a massive responsibility. But how can I ever be sure that I'd be a good father? Taking on that commitment scares me.*

I can't forget her response.

"That's all very well for you, John, but I'm almost thirty-four and don't want to end up an old maid. Some of my friends think you're being selfish."

Since then he'd made himself think long and hard about his justification for not wanting to be a father. He remembered that he and Ilse had begun to talk seriously about having children just before the truth about his spying had come out. *If I'd felt that then, what's changed? Do I still have unresolved feelings for Ilse? Having lost the opportunity of having children with her, do I somehow feel – unconsciously, maybe – that I'm being unfaithful to Ilse if I have a child with Sophie? Or is it simply that thirty-year-old John has different hopes and dreams to the one who was madly in love with Ilse?*

It was clear that Sophie's desire to become a mother had grown stronger. If that continued and his feelings remained the same, there was only going to be one outcome.

23

1934-1936

April 1934

"Thanks for agreeing to meet, John. I've got some big news and I wanted you to hear it from me first. Tom and I are trying for a baby, so we're getting married this July, and I'd like to invite you to the wedding. It's not going to be big, just immediate family and a few friends. I really hope you can come. Can you pass the invitation to May as well, please? I would say bring a 'friend', but Tom and I want to keep things small, and I'm not too sure who you're with at the moment...?"

John smiled at her last remark, a gentle tease about his most recent affair. He'd suspected it could be something like this the moment she'd called on his shared phone line asking to meet in Victoria Park. She looked as strikingly attractive as ever and he remembered how he'd felt the first time he'd seen her at the Golden Slipper.

"Congratulations, Sophie, that's wonderful news. I'm so pleased for you both. I know it's a cliché, but I'm going to say it anyway – Tom Johnson's a very lucky man. May I kiss the bride-to-be?"

"You may."

Their kiss involved firmer mouth-to-mouth contact than would be usual in the circumstances, given he was kissing another man's wife-to-be.

Around two years ago, Sophie had finally accepted that her patient attempts to understand John's reluctance to start a family and change his mind weren't ever going to bear fruit. Thirty-six years old, her desire to become a mother had grown to such an extent that the choice between staying with John or marrying a man who wanted to be a father overwhelmed her thoughts.

Inevitably their relationship had begun to suffer and on a surprisingly sunny April afternoon on Parliament Hill Fields she forced John to face the consequences honestly, admit that his doubts about having children weren't ever going to change and accept that they couldn't remain lovers – it would be too complicated and too painful.

He was distraught, but not shocked, having realised for some months that this day was bound to come and feeling increasingly guilty about the role his indecision was playing in Sophie's unhappiness.

Struggling to find the words, he'd said, "I'm so sorry, Sophie. I suppose I knew it would come to this one day and I'm sure you'll find a good man who'll give you the children you long for. I love you and please remember that I'll always be here for you, if ever you need me."

"I know you will, John. I think the saddest part about splitting up is that I know you'd make a wonderful father, if only you could conquer your doubts, wherever they come from. No one knows until they take the leap. The irony of it all is that our wonderful relationship convinced me that I could, with the right husband, provide a child with a loving, happy home."

She'd paused, composing herself.

"I'll ask Bill at the Golden Slipper to help me move my stuff back to my flat when you're out at work, then I'll put your keys back through the letterbox."

"There's no need to do that. Keep the keys for now, you never know what's coming down the track, Sophie.

As his composure finally cracked, they'd tearfully hugged each other goodbye.

Now here they were in Victoria Park, still good friends eighteen months later. His relationship with Sophie had changed his life. The pre-Sophie John – the aimless pessimist, whose only satisfaction in life had come through his work – had become an optimist. Their life together had been based on mutual respect, laughter, enduring sexual attraction and love for each other.

He was still only thirty-four, earning a good salary and living in a comfortable North London flat. He and Sophie had got to know a number of married couples when they were together and he'd managed to stay friendly with some of them after their break-up. In fact, he found himself in regular demand at dinner parties as the single man the hostess needed to set up with one of her unmarried female friends. He accepted the cattle market implications with good grace – his attendance had led to two of his recent affairs.

As he walked back to his flat along the Regent's Canal that afternoon, he reflected on why her invitation had made him so happy. Of course, it was normal to feel good at being invited, but Sophie was his ex, he wasn't in a relationship and apart from Sophie's parents he would be on his own among a crowd of couples and relatives he'd never met before.

Four months later, watching Tom and Sophie dancing together at their reception, the answer was obvious. He was still in love with her, and the fact that she'd invited him – against Tom's wishes, apparently – said much about the feelings she still had for him. Several times during that warm July day he'd looked at her, only to catch her looking at him. He'd raised his glass, smiled and mouthed, "*Be happy, Soph*" across the room. He left the reception when the party was in full swing, went back to his flat and cried into a large glass of whisky.

December 1934

When Mullard was taken over by Philips Electronics in October 1934, many colleagues had lost their jobs. But as the Deputy Head of Research, working under the direction of the Air Ministry on the development of a system to detect incoming enemy aircraft, his team's jobs were protected. It was demanding, fulfilling work, particularly given the potential threat posed by the rapid rearmament in Germany.

He'd been following news from Germany since Hitler had been elected Chancellor over a year ago and worried what life must be like for Ilse and her family. *It's unbelievable – the thugs that had beaten me up and attacked Ilse eight years ago were now running the country.* Boycotts of Jewish shops, doctors and lawyers had begun almost immediately after Hitler had come to power and Jews were being targeted in the street, although British newspapers hardly mentioned this. The exception was the *Daily Worker*, the Communist Party's paper, which he ordered every week from his local newsagent as it carried stories about Nazi Germany. He was expecting to be met with a refusal from the newsagent, only to discover that he was a Party member.

His concern had grown after listening to a speech by Winston Churchill on the BBC, warning that Britain needed to be better prepared to defend itself from a growing German threat. Churchill seemed to be a voice in the wilderness, ignored by Parliament and several of John's friends, who thought Churchill was a warmonger; they were desperate for peace at all costs. Arguments in the pub with his colleagues could get heated, but he refused to be silenced.

"I was beaten up by Nazi supporters in Berlin; Hitler is a fanatic, utterly ruthless, who came to power by whipping up hatred against anyone who was different or opposed him – Jews, socialists, journalists and trade unionists. If he builds a big enough army, God knows what he'll do to countries that stand in his way."

Sophie phoned him every Sunday from a public phone box at the same time each week. They were determined to keep in touch, in spite of Tom's disapproval.

"I so look forward to our phone calls, John. Tom and I don't really have conversations where we talk about our feelings and the state of the world. He lacks your self-assurance and compensates by trying to control me. Unsuccessfully, I should add. He even followed me to the phone box last week and demanded to know who I was speaking to; I told him it was none of his business. Now he's saying I should give up my job at the Golden Slipper while we're trying for a baby. No news on that score yet, I'm afraid."

September 1935

> *Germany introduces harsh new laws against Jews*
> *New laws remove right to citizenship, work and marriage to non-Jews*

John stood outside the newsagents, staring at the *Daily Worker* headline. Hitler was moving faster to isolate and stigmatise Jews in Germany than anyone had thought possible. Desperate to know more, he bought copies of *The Times* and *The Manchester Guardian*, but was astonished to see that their coverage downplayed the viciousness of the laws and even blamed the Jews for bringing this on themselves. He resolved to find out more about the reality of anti-Semitism in Britain. Where to begin? With Sophie, of course.

"Does your dad ever talk to you about what's happening to Jews in Germany at the moment?"

"Often. But he talks even more about this British MP Oswald Mosley who's set up a British Fascist movement. I couldn't believe it until I read more about them – they're even worse than he said. Why do you ask, are you worried about Ilse?"

"I am. I'm going to write to her at her parents' address in Germany and ask if there's anything I can do. I just hope they pass it on. I think the family should get out of the country as soon as possible."

"Please let me know how she is if you hear."

Sophie's question about Ilse's situation had made John feel guilty. Yes, he'd often thought about her and their passionate, intense time together in Berlin nine years ago. It had changed him forever, he realised that now, and he'd never forget her. But that's not the same thing as taking the trouble to find out what's happening to her and her family in Nazi Germany.

Dear John,

It was wonderful to receive your letter and hear your news. I'm not living with my parents now but they passed your letter on to me. I often think about you and what your life is like in England. Life for Jews in Germany has become intolerable since 1933, which I see you know about from your letter. I have been trying desperately to convince my mother, father and sister to leave Germany for more than a year and I'm glad to say that the new race laws have finally woken them up. We're emigrating to Holland in a month when we've finally got all our papers together. It's a nightmare – you would think the Nazis would make it easy as they want to get rid of us. We're going to stay with my uncle, my father's brother, in Amsterdam. It will be a squeeze, and we'll lose almost everything, but anything is better than staying here.

I got married to a lovely man called Johan three years ago. He's not Jewish but the race laws would make it impossible for us to stay here anyway. Thank goodness there's no sign that Holland is going to persecute Jews. I was forced to leave my job at the station last year – I'd been promoted to Editor-in-Chief – because several of my ex-colleagues refused to work with a Jew. Can you imagine that, John? I'd worked with these people for ten years, I thought some of them were my friends! It was a horrible experience and I was depressed for a long time, but Johan helped me to get over it. That's the worst thing about the current situation; friends and acquaintances who you've known for years are ostracising you, or even denouncing you to the police for a fabricated petty crime. Once that happens, you can lose your home and then they just take it. There's no protection under the law for Jews anymore, so you can see why we must leave.

I would love to hear more about your life since you left Germany. I hope you don't think too badly of me for the way I behaved at the end. I was very upset and shocked when I heard about your spying and couldn't imagine ever feeling the same about us again. Perhaps if you hadn't had to leave Germany I might have changed my mind over time? But I don't believe there's any point regretting the past – we have to be strong and face whatever the future brings at uncertain times like this.

My parents have asked that you don't write to their address again, as we don't know if mail to Jews is being opened. I'll write to you at this address when we get to Holland, and then you can tell me more about your life. I hope you're well and happy.

Best Regards,

Ilse

Ilse's letter arrived four weeks after he'd written to her. He hadn't expected her parents to pass his letter on – they must have been furious with him for what he did – so he was surprised and delighted when she'd replied. But his joy changed to anger as he'd read on, imagining what life for Ilse, her husband, her sister and her aging parents must be like. What kind of regime does those things to its citizens?

Yet he felt no yearning to return to that time, or jealousy that she was now married to another man. Time, it seems, really can be a healer.

But if we don't stop these British fascists we'll end up like Germany.

April 1936

May had suggested they meet for afternoon tea at Brasserie Zédel, Piccadilly. He knew that she'd been seeing Eric for over a year so he wasn't surprised when she announced that they were getting married in four weeks' time.

"Will you walk me down the aisle, please, John? I'm not asking you to 'give me away', though – it's so degrading."

"I'd be honoured, May. Congratulations to both of you. What's the date – I hope I can make it, it's rather short notice?"

She smiled a little coyly.

"I know. I'm two months' pregnant. You're going to be an uncle, Johnny."

"That's brilliant, May. So much to take in; me, an uncle! Where will you and Eric live?"

"We've worked out that we can afford to rent a small house in Kentish Town. I think you know that Eric's a solicitors' clerk? He's been studying to pass his accountancy exams and once he's qualified the money should be enough to keep the three of us. I'm making sure he keeps up with his revision!"

As he walked her down the aisle a month later, slightly nervous about his speech, he suddenly felt furious with himself for not fighting harder to keep him and Sophie together. *Too late now, John. That boat has well and truly sailed.*

Like many brothers, he didn't think that Eric was worthy of his sister. Rather dull with a chip on his shoulder, John had never seen him show any overt affection for May during the three occasions they'd met since her announcement. He'd even refused John's offer to organise a stag night.

Ceremony over, sitting on his own at the reception sipping his third pint, a woman pulled up a chair and sat next to him.

"Hello, I'm Daphne, Eric's aunt on his mother's side. That was a good speech, well done you. Your sister seems a lovely person, John, I think Eric's very lucky. You and May are clearly close; I imagine it can be difficult for a brother to relinquish responsibility for his only sister to another man."

He'd noticed her a couple of times during and after the ceremony, assumed she was family on Eric's side but couldn't decide which generation. She looked too young to be an aunt but too old to be a cousin. May's new mother-in-law's sister, then. Attractive, his type, and clearly not dull like her nephew. Quite the opposite. *Be careful.*

"Thank you for those kind words. It seemed to go down okay. I'm not sure how my sister would respond to the notion of responsibility for her passing from one man to another, though. I was told quite clearly not to use the phrase 'given away.'"

"Ah, a modern woman. Oh dear, I'm afraid that I'm even more pessimistic about this marriage than I was five minutes ago. Sorry, that was rather flippant. I just mean that Eric…"

"That's really okay, Daphne. I know exactly what you mean and I've had similar doubts myself."

"Is your wife here this afternoon?"

"I'm not married. Never have been, although there have been a couple of missed opportunities. And you?"

"I was married. Believe it or not, I'm now divorced. One of the few hundred women in the country that have successfully petitioned their husband for one. With his permission, of course, and 'fabricated evidence' of his adultery. Our marriage was a sham from the start, although I didn't realise that until the wedding night. I wasn't a virgin, so I knew something wasn't right. He preferred men. Nothing wrong with that, I just wish he'd told me beforehand.

That was seven years ago and caused a huge schism in our family; this wedding is only the third time I've seen my sister and Eric since then. I was amazed to be invited."

"That's quite a story. It must have been traumatic, going through the divorce and then being cut off from your family. Here's to you, cheers!"

She was silent for a moment, then said, "Do you mind if I ask you a personal question?"

"Oh dear, I've always regretted saying no to this question, but go ahead anyway."

"Are you queer?"

John burst out laughing, so loudly that some of the wedding guests on tables close by turned and looked.

"My God, Daphne. Is that your usual pick-up line? Does it ever work?"

"Well, are you?"

Lying next to him later that evening, she lit a cigarette, turned to him and said, "I think that's a 'no', then. You really enjoy women's company, don't you? In and out of bed."

They carried on seeing each other irregularly for sex on a casual basis for the next two years. There was never any pretence on either side that their relationship would ever be more complicated; they just had fun and cheered each other up. Daphne was killed in one of the first German bomber raids on London in September 1940. By then, John was working full time for the Air Ministry, with a notional rank of Group Captain, leading a team of scientists and engineers responsible for Britain's radar defences.

September 1936

Relaxing in his flat on Sunday afternoon with the *Manchester Guardian*, listening to classical music on the radio and self-satisfyingly enjoying the freedom of bachelor life, he groaned as the phone rang. He got less time to himself these days, his work on radar systems now a priority since the Nazis invaded the Rhineland four months ago. Irritated, he put the paper down and picked up the phone.

"Hello, John, it's your long-lost friend. I'm sorry I've not been in touch for a while, but Tom and I have been going through a difficult time and I haven't been feeling very sociable."

"It's lovely to hear your voice, Sophie. I was thinking about you the other day, wondering how you were. What do you mean, 'going through a difficult time'?"

"Well, it's sort of personal, but I think we know each other well enough by now. Tom and I have been trying for a baby, as you know. After eighteen months of frustration I finally found out I was pregnant, only to lose the baby after ten weeks. We were both heartbroken, but since then Tom has been blaming me for miscarrying, not thinking how I must be feeling; which is devastated, of course. What I need from him is love and affection, but he can't seem to connect on that level."

"I'm so sorry, Sophie, that sounds really hard. I know he's your husband and I should probably keep my opinions to myself, but I think he's being very selfish. He should be supporting you, putting your feelings first and not looking to find blame. Maybe he just needs time to adjust to the disappointment."

"I know, that's what I tell myself, but it's been going on for several weeks now and I'm getting worn down by the arguments. Anyway, I haven't rung to bother you with my problems. Did you know that Mosley is planning to march through the Jewish area of the East End with a large crowd from the British Union of Fascists?"

"I'd heard that, yes."

"There's an organised campaign of Jewish groups, socialists, trade unionists, Irish dockers and Labour Party members to confront the march and prevent them passing through. My dad's on the organising committee – of course – and I know that he's planning to be at the front of the barricades. I'm worried about him. It's not only his age, his heart's not brilliant, as you know. I know this is a big favour, John, but would you be prepared to join him on the barricade and make sure he doesn't get hurt?"

Any hesitation was swept away by the accounts of Nazi atrocities in Ilse's last letter. Mosley's fascists must be stopped.

"If he's all right with that, of course I will. How can we set this up?"

"I've got an idea about how to put this to Dad in a way that he'll accept. I'll say that you've contacted me about joining the campaign to prevent the fascists marching through, but would feel more confident if you were with someone with knowledge of the area. What do you think about that?"

"I'm okay with it, though your father might think I'm being rather pathetic."

She started to say something, then laughed and said, "You're right, he may think that. But he likes you, so I think he'll let you tag along. You're a big lad and you've gone up against Brownshirts before, so I'll convince him you'll be useful. I'm seeing him tonight anyway, and I'll let you know what he says by tomorrow evening."

"Do you know exactly when this march is taking place? I think I should see your dad before then. I'm really busy at work these days, so it would have to be late evening or on a Sunday."

"It's on Sunday, 4th October, in the afternoon, so that fits. I'm sorry, John, I just realised that I haven't asked you anything about your life. How are you?"

"I'm doing okay, Sophie. I've got a fulfilling job, some special friends like you and a roof over my head. It would be lovely to meet soon and catch up."

"Is there a woman in your life at the moment? Silly question, really."

"I think we should finish this conversation before it goes any further. I'll wait for you to phone me tomorrow; better leave it until after eight o'clock."

"Spoilsport. I love you, John."

"I love you, Sophie."

What did we just say to each other?

Sunday, 4th October 1936, Sophie's parents' house.

John looked around at the nine men squeezed into the small parlour. Some were younger than him, some a lot older. All working-class Jews, as far as he could tell. They'd just nodded when Sophie's dad had introduced him – "A good friend of Sophie who's already seen action fighting fascists in Berlin." The leader of the group – a trade union organiser in the Communist Party – had just finished briefing everyone in detail about what to expect. The headlines weren't reassuring:

"We're expecting that between three and five thousand fascists will try and march through our area. Comrades have already barricaded most of the main streets through the East End, but we know that large numbers of police are going to try and smash a path through for the fascists to march behind. It's going to be brutal."

He felt the weight of the knuckle-duster in his coat pocket, the cricket box around his genitals and the shin pads wrapped around his legs. *The last time was ten years ago, and that nearly ended badly for me and Ilse. Here I am again, this time trying to protect Sophie's father instead of my girlfriend; my life seems to be going in circles.*

"We've been assigned to the east end of Cable Street. It's one of their planned routes, so we've built a substantial barricade, and assembled a huge stockpile of bricks, staves and iron bars behind it. Female comrades in houses lining the street have been storing up their chamber pots for days and will be making a present of the contents to the police from upstairs windows. All that should be enough to stop the police; if individuals get over, hurt them but be careful not to kill them. If they break through completely, run like hell – you don't want to get arrested."

John turned to Sidney.

"Make sure we stick together, Sidney. I don't want to end up on my own around here, I'd be lost in seconds."

He looked at John archly. "Who do you think you're fooling, John? Sophie asked you to come so that I don't get hurt, not the other way round. Don't think I'm not grateful, I am. We'll stick together, and we'll be okay. I've been meaning to say, I was sorry when you two split up. Tom's all right, but you two had something special together."

Later that day

Slumped in his armchair, bruised, exhausted but with no broken bones, he nursed a scalding cup of tea. He'd got home nearly an hour ago, having avoided any gangs of Blackshirts furious at being denied their right to march through the East End.

The determination of the police to force a way through the Cable Street blockade to allow the fascists through had led to a much higher level of violence than he'd anticipated. He and Sidney were pressed together in the crowd about ten feet behind the barricades. As the police tried to dismantle the assortment of wooden sleepers, lorry tyres and iron bedsteads they came under attack from rocks thrown over John's head. The mounted police tried to move their horses around the barricades, lashing down on any heads in range with frightening blows. The crowd jostled and shoved at random, making it difficult to keep upright. Sidney was gripping his arm tightly, shouting every profanity John knew, and then some. A woman emptied two chamber pots onto the group of policemen standing under her window, provoking them into a frenzy. They immediately started to pick up anything they could find and hurl it back at the crowd. Two rocks flew perilously close to John's head, his apprehension now turning to fear; the next he knew Sidney yelled out and collapsed against him, hit by a cobblestone on his left shoulder.

He hauled Sidney upright by his right arm and started to push slowly to the back of the crowd, Sidney screaming in pain every time someone bumped into him. Eventually they came out into a clear space and sat down on some crates.

"How far is your house from here, Sidney?"

"About half a mile, I think."

"Do you think we can make it?"

"Bloody right we can. Thanks, John."

The half mile felt more like two with Sidney's weight to bear as well, but they made it back to the house without further trouble. Sophie answered John's knock.

"Oh God, come in. What happened? Is Dad all right?"

"I'm fully conscious and can answer for myself, Sophie. I'm okay, I just need someone to look at my shoulder, see what the damage is. Your John's been brilliant, half carried me back here."

John and Sophie looked at each other and smiled; neither corrected Sidney's reference to 'your John'. As soon as Doctor Simon had checked Sidney out and proclaimed him to be "badly bruised and cut, but no worse as far as I can tell," John said his goodbyes.

"If I'm no longer needed I'll go back home now and lie down. I've got to get up early tomorrow and go to Oxford."

"Be careful on your way home, John. There'll be lots of angry fascists and policemen roaming the streets."

"Thanks, Sidney, I will. I hope your shoulder's okay."

"I'll show you out, John."

Sophie walked with him to the door and took out a handkerchief.

"Let me clean up your face, you look like you've been in a brawl."

She spat copiously on the handkerchief and started to wipe the smudges from his face.

"Saliva can spread germs, you know."

She looked at him, smiling.

"I think we've left it a bit late to worry about sharing our germs, don't you? Please listen to what Dad said. Mosley's thugs will be out for revenge. Apparently they had to abandon every march."

"That's great to hear, it makes a few cuts and bruises worthwhile."

She gave his face a final wipe, brushed dirt off his jacket and kissed him on the cheek.

He woke to the persistent ringing of his doorbell.

Fearing it could be the police, he cautiously left his flat and peered through the glass in the front door. There was only the outline of one person.

"I've still got my key, but I thought it would be presumptuous to let myself in. I wanted to check that you got home okay, but I can see that I've woken you up, I'm sorry."

They stood on the doorstep, neither taking their eyes off the other, until he held out his hand. She held it and followed him into his flat, closing the door behind her. Kissing him softly, she undressed then got into his still-warm bed.

"Come here, lie with me."

He trembled as he held her, running his fingertips down her arm, kissing her chastely. *"What on earth are we doing?"* he whispered.

By way of an answer, she pulled down his pyjamas and lifted herself on top of him.

After she'd washed, dressed and tidied her make-up, she sat on the bed and said, "That brought back some lovely memories. There will only ever be you, John. Just my luck to fall for the one man that didn't want a family. I was a fool to marry Tom but I can't undo that now. We mustn't ever do this again, or I think I'll lose my mind – but please stay in touch. I'd better go home now, my darling."

She kissed him deeply, then let herself out.

24

MARCH 1937-NOVEMBER 1938

"Can we meet somewhere in the next few days? It is important or I wouldn't be asking."

"It's lovely to hear from you – is everything all right? I'm free this Saturday, just tell me where and when."

He felt his heart speeding up.

"Victoria Park, by the bandstand, three o'clock. I'll see you there. Try not to be late, please."

She rang off, leaving him puzzled; it wasn't like her to be so abrupt. Maybe she wasn't alone in the house – but why not ring him from the nightclub?

"So who's Sophie?"

Daphne took a long drag on her cigarette and looked at him in faux accusation. She was about to leave for the South of France for the summer with a friend and wanted to see John before she left.

"Sophie's an old friend, and a good one. It's not like that between us; it was odd, she sounded tense about something and asked to meet."

"Lucky girl. Now, where were we?"

He'd been waiting less than five minutes when he saw Sophie about two hundred yards away, walking straight towards him. She was wearing a loose-fitting print dress and cardigan. It struck him as a little odd, rather conservative for her. But there was something else unfamiliar that he couldn't put his finger on. Until he could.

She was pregnant.

His surprise was replaced by a feeling of unfiltered, unselfish joy. She'd wanted this so much, and now it was happening. She was having a baby.

He began to walk towards her with a huge grin on his face. She was about thirty yards away when he realised how stressed she appeared; it wasn't the look of someone about to share good news with a close friend. In fact, he thought she'd been crying. As they came closer she managed to force a smile.

"Sophie, if this is about what I think it is, I'm really happy for you. But is something wrong?"

"Let's just walk together." With a bitter laugh, she said, "Oh God, John, why aren't things ever simple between you and me? Yes, I'm pregnant and of course it's wonderful. I just don't know who the father is."

There are moments in everyone's life when they receive news they know means life from that point won't ever be the same. How they react at these moments says much about them. Perhaps everything you need to know about them.

In less than a second, John had done the maths, remembered them making love nearly six months ago and realised what she meant and why they were meeting. He decided that whatever her decision, he would support it.

He gave a sympathetic laugh, reached out and clasped her hand.

"I see what you mean about nothing ever being simple. I'm assuming that the father's either me or Tom?"

She nodded.

"Then please listen. I promise I will support you, whatever you want from me."

"How can you say that when you don't know what I'm about to ask?"

"Sophie, I mean it. Just tell me so that I can stop trying to guess."

"It's completely selfish and unreasonable. I want you to give up your right to contact the child directly until they're twenty-one. After that, assuming you're still speaking to me, I would like us to work something out. I also want you to give me your word that you won't ever mention this to anyone, even your wife, if you ever marry. Tom must never doubt that the baby is his. It would probably destroy him and our marriage if he found out."

He recovered quickly from the pain her words caused him, and said, "Of course I agree, Sophie. I would enjoy having the occasional glimpse if we could arrange moments when we just happen to be in the park at the same time. That's my only wish."

Her whole body relaxed and her face softened into a smile.

"I would love to arrange moments like that, for both of you. Thank you, John. You're a wonderful man. It's ironic, you could never commit to starting a family with me, and yet here I am carrying your…"

He smiled, and she stopped, realising what she'd given away.

"So, you think it's probably ours?"

After a long pause, she said, "That last time we made love was the perfect time in the month. I just know it's yours. Ours."

On 16th July 1937, Sophie gave birth to Alice Johnson in the Mothers' Hospital, Hackney. Three weeks later, pushing her daughter around Hackney Downs in a pram that an anonymous well-wisher had provided, the two of them ran into John Samson who happened to be walking in the park at the same time.

"Alice, this is your Uncle John. He's someone who's very special to Mummy and I hope will be to you, one day."

"She's beautiful, Sophie. You're looking very well for someone who gave birth a few weeks ago. How was it?"

"Horrendous, but no different from what every women goes through – horrible cramping pain for hours, feeling you're going to be split apart, flesh tearing as the baby comes out, stitches where you don't want to think about, not to mention the blood and shit. Then it's all worth it in the end."

She picked Alice out of the pram.

"Would you like to hold her?"

"Can I? I'd love to."

He carefully took his daughter and held her against him, cradling her head in his hand, absorbing the meaning of this moment.

"She's perfect."

He left the park later with a big smile on his face and tears in his eyes.

November 1937

Freezing in the east wind under huge blue skies, John looked out over the flat Suffolk farmland stretching towards the English Channel. He'd been waiting on Westerfield station platform outside Ipswich for the Felixstowe train for over half an hour. Once there, he was due to be met by an Air Ministry car, have his papers checked and then be driven via the ferry to Bawdsey Manor. A year ago, all research and development teams working on Britain's radar system had been brought together at a manor house on the Suffolk coast and now it was his team's turn to join them. He wasn't looking forward to it. He enjoyed his life in London; seeing Sophie and Alice, spending the occasional night with Daphne, beers in the evening with friends and colleagues from work. Moving to this godforsaken corner of East Anglia didn't appeal. But there was no choice; his team was making significant progress developing an interface for the men and women who'd be operating the land-based radar detectors. Their work had to progress in sync with everything else.

Time was crucial. Hitler had been making increasingly bellicose speeches about the rights of 'German-speaking people' in Austria and Czechoslovakia and was continuing to rearm the army, air force and navy at an unbelievable rate. Every politician and commentator whose opinions he respected believed that war with Germany was now inevitable. The only two questions that mattered were when, and would Britain be ready in time.

His visit today was a reconnaissance; to check the working environment, the accommodation and sleeping quarters – and the journey. The plan was to have two teams, each working ten days on and ten off. But as the Head of Research, he knew that he could be called back at a moment's notice in emergencies, so the journey time mattered. Over three hours wasn't good.

At last, he heard the piercing whistle of the approaching train.

12th March 1938

Walking drowsily to the communal washrooms for his morning shave, John was brought abruptly awake by shouting erupting from the dining room.

"Christ almighty, Hitler's just invaded Austria."

"What, all on his own?" Laughter.

He abandoned his shave and ran to the dining room, catching the end of the BBC newsreader's report.

"*German troops began marching into Austria early this morning. We understand that they aren't encountering any opposition and no fighting has been reported. The BBC will bring news of further developments as they occur.*"

Most of his colleagues remained quiet, letting the implications for themselves, their friends and families sink in. All of them understood this meant that the odds on war with Germany in the future had just got much shorter; they were infinitely better informed about the growing strength of the German armed forces than the rest of the population.

Every time that John heard news about Hitler crossing another line, he thought about Ilse and her family. But this was different; the Nazis had marched into another European country, annexed the territory and installed the Austrian Nazi Party in power. If this could happen in Austria, why not Czechoslovakia, or even Holland? He hadn't her from her since her family had moved to Holland, and that was over two years ago. But what could he do?

Because his team was now under the overall control of the Air Ministry, he felt a responsibility as their team leader to say something. Looking around the room, he cleared his throat and started to speak.

"I hope I'm not overplaying this, but surely no one can now doubt the expansionist intentions behind Hitler's huge arms build-up. Austria today – who tomorrow? I suspect we're going to be under increasing pressure – and scrutiny – to deliver workable solutions within a year. I'm confident this team can do it."

As he walked back to the washroom, self-doubt crept in. He'd never wanted to hold a rank, let alone one that was significantly superior to the team of men he was working with and was uncomfortable in the role of 'motivating the troops'. *God, I hope I didn't sound like one of those overbearing, pompous public-school officers I meet on a daily basis.*

He cringed at the thought as he looked at his reflection in the shaving mirror.

A week later, he met May and his nephew for lunch at a café on Parliament Hill Fields, a short train journey across London from his flat in Hackney. After recent events in Austria, he wanted to persuade May and her family to move out of Kentish Town, which was criss-crossed by vital railway lines and an obvious target for German bombers. But he didn't want to alarm her.

"What's it like commuting between Suffolk and London every two weeks? I think I'd hate it, John. Of course, I couldn't leave Philip with Eric for that long anyway."

"I thought I would, too, but I've adjusted to it. There are advantages – the countryside air is refreshing after London, we're by the sea and there are no distractions, which is good for making progress with our work. I make sure I use my time in London to keep in touch with friends and the people that matter to me – like you and Philip."

"I know you have to be secretive about your work, but you must hear things. Should we be worried about this man Hitler? I couldn't believe the German Army just marched into Austria and took over the country!"

This was his opportunity to impress the gravity of the situation on May.

"We were all shocked, May. You're right, I can't say too much – and this is only my opinion, anyway – but a lot of well-informed people I meet through my work believe that Hitler isn't going to stop with Austria. He wants to create a 'Greater Germany' and has built a huge army. The question is, why would he do that? If, God forbid, he tries to take territory from France or Belgium, then Britain will be drawn in. Hopefully he won't be that stupid, but as you've asked me, if Hitler marches into another European country, it would make sense for you three to move to outer London."

May looked thoughtful, not shocked, which surprised him. *Underestimating her again.*

"Gosh, that's given me something to think about. It would be an upheaval, but Eric's qualified now, as you know, so he could probably get another job easily. I'll talk to him about moving if the situation in Europe continues to get worse. I remember now it was German bombers that killed those poor people in that Spanish village. What was it called? Guernica, I think."

"I think that makes sense. How are you and Eric?"

"We're managing okay, probably better off than most working-class families. We don't lead an exciting life like you, but Eric's earning decent money now and I'm going to start taking in typing work at home. He loves Philip to bits and looks after me, though I find him a bit smothering at times. We're all in good health, luckily. As you know, the Co-op insurance paid out for Dad's funeral, so Eric and I took out health insurance with them afterwards, just in case."

They left the café, pushed Philip to the top of Parliament Hill in his pram and went over to the duck pond. He'd begun to talk a month ago and took great pride in pointing to things and calling out their names. John was fascinated by his nephew and his daughter, watching signs of their future characters beginning to show – less than a year in Alice's case. He saw more of Philip, as there was no need for any subterfuge.

Sophie had become more cautious about their meetings, particularly with Alice. Tom's controlling attitude towards his wife had become apparent soon after their marriage. She'd pushed back against his constant questions and suspicions about her movements, but that led to bickering and a joyless daily life together. They argued frequently; no issue seemed too trivial to start a row, though Sophie often backed down in the end to avoid exposing Alice to her parents' arguments. She'd thought about divorce, more so after the last year's Matrimonial Causes Act of 1937 had introduced insanity, cruelty and desertion as grounds to end a marriage. But none applied in her case – Tom had never been violent towards her – and it was very expensive. Her biggest reason, though, was fear of the effect a split might have on Alice. Tom would fight her request for a divorce every step of the way, and it could backfire. She'd recently read about a divorce case where the man had insisted on having a paternity test to check their child was his. The blood test had showed there was a significant chance the child wasn't, so he'd divorced his wife on the grounds of her cruelty and she lost custody of the baby. That mustn't happen to her.

As long as Alice couldn't speak more than a few simple words John would arrange to bump into them in either Victoria or Finsbury Park. But the day that Alice innocently said, "Alice see man today" – almost giving her mother a heart attack – was the point when the park meetings had to end. From then on they could only use public phone boxes to keep in touch. Except for one time.

To make his journey from London to Bawdsey and back easier, John had bought a second-hand Morris Eight. He would drive to Ipswich station, leave the car and catch the London train, then reverse that to get back to Bawdsey. Not only did this cut out the increasingly unreliable train service from Bawdsey to Ipswich, but it allowed him to occasionally drive colleagues to the Shepherd and Dog for a pint in the evenings. So when Sophie casually mentioned that Tom was taking Alice to see his parents this coming Sunday in Slough "and what bad luck you're in Suffolk," his reply was immediate.

"If you get the nine-thirty train from Liverpool Street station to Ipswich, I'll meet you on the platform, then we'll drive to a nice country pub for lunch, go to the beach near Orford Ness, have a swim and make passionate love in the sand-dunes. What do you think?"

The man waiting outside the phone box was startled by the shriek of laughter from the woman inside.

"I think it's a wonderful idea. I'm afraid the last part might be off the menu, but if the rest of the offer stands, I'll see you on the platform this Sunday."

They changed into their costumes behind a dune, oddly coy about the sight of each other's bodies. They whooped and screamed at the shock of the North Sea in April, hugging each other for warmth. Gasping for breath, John got out after less than two minutes and wrapped a towel around him. As Sophie walked out of the surf a minute later, nipples protruding like cherries under her costume, he was fleetingly taken back twelve years to Warnemünde. He only had good memories from that period of his life now; the sorrow and hollowness he'd felt after he and Ilse had split had been eased away by his relationship with Sophie, the fact of Alice and his fulfilling job.

They towelled themselves dry and dressed; there was no question of sex. Besides, he'd never fancied the idea of making love on a sand-dune.

They caught up with the events in each other's lives as they feasted on thick bread, cheese, pickle and pie in the Old Coach House in Aldeburgh. After persistent prodding – "Come on, John, you must be able to give me some idea what you're working on – there's only one ex-spy at this table and it's not me" – he told her more than he should have, forgetting how perceptive she was. She was fascinated, and jealous, when he mentioned his infrequent liaisons with Daphne.

"You've got no right to be jealous, you've got Tom."

"Bedding Daphne when the mood takes her isn't the same as me sleeping with Tom and you know it – I'm married to him and I'm obliged to."

"That a ringing endorsement of married life, I must say."

His sarcastic remark hurt. She was about to give him an angry reply, then paused.

"I'm nearly forty-one, Tom's forty-three. We've been together for over five years, sleeping in the same bed for four, the last eighteen months with a baby to care for. So no, Tom and I don't have a passionate relationship; we rarely have sex, if ever. I can live with that – I suspect most married women of my age do – but it's the lack of affection that upsets me most. I don't even know what he feels about me any longer. We no longer really talk to each other or share thoughts – if I try, he closes down. Are we happy? Not really. But that's married life. Have I thought about divorce? Yes, but the consequences would be horrible for everyone, particularly me and Alice!

"Be honest with yourself, John. If I'd waited to have a child with you, I'd still be childless. When I ask myself whether I'd rather be living with Tom and have Alice, or be with you without her, my answer every time is to be a mother to Alice. I'm sorry if hearing that hurts you. It hurts me to say it."

In the silence that followed, he reached over, held her hand, then finally said, "I'm so sorry, Sophie. That was a stupid, insensitive remark from a John I thought I'd grown out of. Unfortunately, bits of him still pop out from time to time. I've had such a fortunate life, maybe too fortunate. When really good things have been put in front of me – research in Berlin, Ilse, you – I mess them up. I'm thirty-eight but going on twenty-one sometimes, and I know it's time I finally grew up. I'll always be here for you and Alice when you need me."

Tears welling, she said, "You're a wonderful man, John Samson. You haven't messed up with me and I treasure our friendship. Just promise me you won't get too serious and lose your sense of fun. Now, what's for pudding?"

9th–10th November 1938

> *Violent Pogroms against Jews across Germany*
> *Thousands of Jewish Homes, Businesses and Synagogues Attacked*
> *Over 90 Killed, Thousands Injured in 'Kristallnacht'*

There was only one story running on the front pages of every newspaper when he collected *The Times*, so he bought the *Manchester Guardian* as well and read their coverage quickly before returning to Daphne, who'd stayed the night after an evening at the theatre.

"Where've you been, darling? Apparently you were too tired last night, so I've been patiently waiting here hoping that you'd replenished your energy."

"There've been horrendous attacks on Jews right across Germany, so widespread they must have been organised by the Nazi Party. It's unbelievable, Daphne – nearly a hundred murdered, people attacked in their homes, Jewish shops looted and synagogues burnt down. They're calling it *Kristallnacht* because of the amount of broken glass on the streets. This is all happening in a supposedly civilised European country."

"It sounds horrible for those poor people who've been attacked in their homes. But I'm afraid that I think the Jews have only got themselves to blame for a lot of this. They don't make much attempt to integrate, yet do very well in business and the professions. I can understand why German people get resentful."

Why am I involved with this vacuous, prejudiced woman?

Barely controlling himself, he said, "You really do talk rubbish sometimes, Daphne. Most of the time, in fact. Firstly, these people are Germans! Most of them third or fourth generation, some far more. I spent a year in Germany and met a number of Jews. Fell in love with one, even. They're like everyone else – good, bad and in between. Hitler cleverly exploited Christian anti-Semitism to pin the blame for Germany's defeat in 1918 on the Jews, even though many served in the army. Friends and colleagues from my time in Germany could have been murdered, and you lie there and tell me that they've got themselves to blame."

Daphne had already got out of the bed before he'd stopped speaking.

"You know, you really are a bore these days, John. You always had a serious side, but when we first met you were fun as well. Over the last two years you've become more engrossed with politics and threats of war, and frankly, it's tiresome. If you wouldn't mind letting me get dressed in private, I'll go now."

"Goodbye, Daphne. I'm sure there'll be plenty of Nazi sympathisers around to keep you amused."

He never saw her again. She died in September 1940 in her bed, stubbornly ignoring the air-raid siren during one of the first German bomber raids.

After she'd left, he made a coffee and read the papers from cover to cover, sending him into a deep depression. *Hitler has obviously calculated that he can inflict limitless suffering and degradation on German Jews without triggering protest from other European states. It's horrific, but true; I bet there won't be any significant protest.*

His belief that Hitler was determined to expand Germany's borders in Europe 'by any means necessary' hadn't been changed by the signing of the Munich Agreement between France, Britain and Germany two months earlier in September. That agreement 'gave' Germany the German-speaking part of Czechoslovakia, in exchange for Hitler agreeing not to annex the rest of the country. Unlike many of his countrymen and women – desperate to clutch at any chance for peace, whatever the evidence from Hitler's previous promises – he knew that Hitler had played France and Britain for fools and sold out Czechoslovakia.

25

MARCH-AUGUST 1939

Vindicated six months later on 15th March 1939 when Hitler invaded the rest of Czechoslovakia, John had no time for basking in self-righteousness. Hitler had reneged on a deal with the two major European powers, changing the calculations about the likelihood of war in every European country. On 20th March, John was summoned to a meeting at the Air Ministry near Aldwych in London to brief the top brass on progress. There were about a dozen serving officers in the room, their uniforms adorned with copious gold braid and strips of medals. He guessed that between them the group represented every Command responsible for the defence of the country against air attacks. The man sitting at the head of the table introduced himself and began to speak.

"Good morning, gentlemen. The government is now assuming that there is a grave risk that this country could soon be at war with Germany. Given the huge expansion in Luftwaffe fighter and bomber numbers, the purpose of our meeting today is twofold: to establish the state of readiness of our defences against attacks from the air and from there to identify our weakest links. I'm going to ask Air Chief Marshall Dowding, head of Fighter Command, to begin."

John felt the temperature in the room fall several degrees. Dowding was a national figure, the top man. He'd had no idea that the meeting would include such a figure, though he should have guessed. He was way out of his league; an imposter who was sure to be found wanting. Dowding began.

"The good news is that we're in a far better position now than a year ago. The Hurricane fighters have been in production for over a year and fifteen squadrons are now fully equipped. Spitfire production is ramping up and we will begin equipping squadrons in September."

John tried to listen as Dowding continued, painting a reassuring picture of fighter strength in the coming months. But he couldn't concentrate; he was rehearsing the key points he needed to make about radar defences when it was his turn.

Repeated tests in the Channel show the radar system is working effectively; there are now a chain of towers in place from Ventnor to Hull; there's a potential risk of overloading pilots with too much information from operators at different radar stations.

He became aware that the Chair was speaking again.

"I specifically asked that a scientist with knowledge of progress on our radar defences be present today. John Samson from the Bawdsey Research and Development facility has agreed to attend at short notice. Over to you, John."

During the following twenty minutes John outlined a positive, realistic and – he hoped – accessible picture of the Chain Radar Microwave system. He had a good story to tell and the senior officers assembled around the table listened attentively. The questions at the end focussed on his point about solving the problem of fighter pilots becoming confused by too much contradictory information.

"How serious is this, Samson?"

"I believe there is a fix, sir, although it's likely to be costly in human resources. If every report from each radar station in each sector can be fed through to one place, then analysed, filtered to a few key points about each attacking formation and only then sent to the airfields, we can focus our resources efficiently."

Once he'd outlined how he thought this could be practically achieved, he was thanked and dismissed. Stepping out of Adastral House as dusk was falling, he realised where he was. Ten minutes later he was standing outside the Golden Slipper. *This is a bloody stupid idea – any of the others at the meeting might see me. But then they'd have to explain what they were doing, too.*

He pulled his greatcoat around him and descended the stairs. Nothing had changed. It was still early; there were few girls and even fewer customers, all of them drinkers. He went to the bar, ordered a gin and tonic and asked the young woman behind the bar to have one herself.

"Quiet tonight, I see."

She looked at him, figuring out if he was just a friendly bloke in for a drink on his way home to his wife and children, or a punter looking for a girl. Or both.

"This is usual for a Tuesday. I haven't seen you in here before, have I?"

"Probably not. I was last in this place twelve years ago. Though I was a regular back then."

The club was quiet and she fancied a chat. Good-looking guy, well spoken. She was intrigued. And fancied pushing her luck.

"Regular with who? One girl all the time or lots of girls one at a time?"

He was amused by her chutzpah, and smiled. *Cheek with charm.*

"That's very forward, we hardly know each other. But as we're getting along so well, it was the former. She did your job back then."

He could see that she was intrigued, but not sure how to take the next step.

"Twelve years ago, you say. Worked behind the bar. Give me a clue."

"She was funny, gorgeous, smart, cheeky – like you – and is now happily married, but not to me, sadly."

He could see he'd given too much away. She was searching her memory for all the possible girls she'd heard about.

"Sophie! Was it Sophie?"

His smile told her everything.

"She was great. Everyone loved her, apparently. And you two went out together? All I can say then, sir, is that you were a bloody idiot to lose her."

"And on that we can agree, Miss…?

"I'm Clare. Pleased to meet you."

She shook his extended hand, saw a woman coming down the stairs and called out, "Hey, Frances, come over here. This gentleman says he was Sophie's boyfriend years ago. You worked here with her, didn't you?"

As Frances approached, trying to place him, John saw the moment recognition flickered across her face.

"You're John, ain't you? Blimey, looks like you've done all right for yourself, posh coat, fancy briefcase. Sophie told me you two had split up years ago over having kids. She was so upset at the time, she really loved you. Still does, I reckon. I bumped into her by chance a while back after she'd stopped working here and we went for a drink. She said that she and her husband – I got the impression it was a loveless marriage – had been trying unsuccessfully to have a baby for two years and time was running out – she was almost forty. Then she'd had the idea of getting pregnant by sleeping with you again. I'm not sure how that worked out, but you might be a dad by now."

Frances realised from the look on John's face that her mouth had run away with her – again! Clare had quickly turned away and was making a show of rearranging glasses behind the bar. In a hard, callous tone, John said, "Well, Frances, I can update you. She had a little girl two years ago," then he turned to leave.

As he climbed the stairs he heard Clare saying, "You stupid cow, why did you tell him that!"

He walked all the way back to his flat, consumed by so many emotions that every time he tried to focus on one – anger, betrayal, disgust, humiliation, loss – another pushed in.

He thought he really knew this woman, believed her when she'd said she still loved him, trusted her when she'd said that she'd just come round after Cable Street to check he was all right, completely taken in by her act in the park when she'd told him she was pregnant. *How could she deliberately deceive me all this time? There'd been so many occasions over the last eighteen months when she could have told me the truth about Alice's conception, but she let me go on thinking that Alice was just a joyful, accidental outcome between us – and she couldn't even be totally sure she was mine. Whatever she feels for me, it isn't love.*

Of course, there was Alice. He had no regrets about Alice – how could he, she was totally innocent. But his feelings for her mother could never be the same. Sophie's professed love for him had helped convince him that he was a decent person deep down, in spite of his betrayal of Ilse. But if her avowals of love were based on deceit, how could he believe in her love for him anymore?

Was her deceit any worse than his with Ilse? Irrelevant, so no point going down that rabbit hole.

He didn't sleep that night, trying to get everything in perspective. They'd become lovers nearly twelve years ago on the night they'd met, stayed together as a couple for six years, then loved each other as friends ever since. The thought of not having Sophie in his life was unbearable, but if he wanted their friendship to carry on, he had to confront her and have it out. Saying nothing didn't seem possible; he couldn't keep up the façade of normality.

But confronting her carried the risk that she'd deny everything, or fracture their friendship beyond repair.

But there was really only one option.

"So, when exactly did you have this conversation with Frances?"

They were walking side by side through Victoria Park. Tom had taken Alice to see his mother for the day and they'd arranged to meet at two o'clock. It was a midweek afternoon, the trees were just beginning to come into leaf and thoughts of war were far away for the couples and families enjoying the first mild day of the year.

"It was eight days ago. I'd been called into the Air Ministry in Aldwych to brief some high-ups about progress. It had gone well, I was feeling good and when I realised how close I was to the Golden Slipper I decided to drop in for old times' sake. I was having a drink with Clare, the girl behind the bar – who remembered you – when a woman called Frances came in, who also did. She mentioned she'd seen you by chance over two years ago and you'd told her that you'd decided to 'have a fling' with me to try and get pregnant."

"And you believed her?"

"Because of the way it came up naturally in the conversation, I did, yes."

Sophie said nothing and the silence lengthened between them. Eventually, John said, "Well, did you tell her something like that, or was she lying?"

Her fine, soft features had become hard and scornful. He couldn't recall her ever looking at him like this, and at that moment it occurred to him there might be no going back between them.

"First, you need to know that there was no love lost between me and Frances. But she wasn't lying. I was desperate to get pregnant again, but nothing was happening and I was nearly forty. I kept thinking how if we'd stayed together I'd probably have a child already, how selfish you'd been and how if I slept with you it might happen if I timed it right in my cycle. And I did think you owed it to me, for fuck's sake, and of course I'm glad I did it. Look at the outcome – Alice wouldn't be here otherwise."

"But you kept the deceit going, telling me what a wonderful piece of luck it was. I could forgive you if it was on the spur of the moment, but there have been so many times in the last two years when you could have told me the truth, starting with your Academy Award performance in the park. So I now have to live with the knowledge that our loving friendship has been based on a lie for the last two years."

She erupted.

"You could forgive me!! That's so magnanimous of you, so gracious, kind sir. Be honest, John, what would you have said if I'd come to you after my miscarriage and suggested having your child? And how would you have reacted if I'd told you when I became pregnant, or even after Alice was born? And now she's here, do you regret that? Your distress in finding out our friendship over the last two years was based on a deceit doesn't compare to the misery of spending the rest of my life childless with a boring, possessive man. Okay, that was my choice, but you should have told me you'd never want children sooner than you did."

"I swear that if you'd told me the truth about that night at any time since you got pregnant, I might have been angry, but I would have understood, and respected you for telling me."

"I don't believe you, John. But this row isn't getting us anywhere, is it? I've given you an honest response, so what do you want to do?"

"I wish I knew."

August 1939

John was now spending more of his time attending briefings at Adastral House as increasing intelligence from MI6 came in, much of it pointing to the certainty of Germany invading Poland. When he'd suggested seeing May after one such meeting, she'd invited him round for supper. He'd walked to Leicester Square then taken the Tube to Kentish Town. It was almost six o'clock and the Tube carriage was hot, noisy and full of cigarette smoke, but he couldn't help hearing some of the conversations around him.

"All this talk of war is nonsense. Hitler's not barmy, he knows our navy will obliterate his."

"He's not going to declare war on us anyway, he sees British people as kinsfolk."

"It's that bloody warmonger, Churchill, that keeps stirring things up, he should keep his sodding trap shut."

As he walked from the Tube station to her house, he decided he had to tell May and Eric about the situation as he saw it. If they were talking to idiots like his fellow Tube passengers, they wouldn't have a clue what was going to happen.

"So you're saying you think that Churchill is right. Hitler is preparing for a war in Europe?"

Eric had listened attentively as John went through the evidence he'd heard an hour ago at Adastral House, being careful not to reveal anything classified.

"I do, Eric. You said a few months ago that you and May were thinking of moving out to the suburbs? If I'm right, I hope you do, for Philip's sake in particular. Hitler may start a bombing campaign against England – London particularly. Kentish Town will be a target – it's criss-crossed by railway lines running north, east and west."

When he returned to his flat that evening he saw an envelope addressed to him on the mat with Sophie's handwriting. She'd sent him another photo of Alice, as she'd said she would.

After their row in the park they'd agreed that it would probably be better if they contacted each other less for a while. As he was leaving, he'd asked her to send him pictures of Alice from time to time.

"Of course I will."

She'd kept her word, sending him regular photos, each with a few lines from her on the back. He opened the envelope and read:

Dear John,

I had the photographs of Alice's second birthday party developed and managed to put one aside for you. She's growing up fast, starting to run about in the park, putting words together and asking for things. Tom thinks she's a genius – but how would he know? Ho! Ho!

You were right, as usual, it looks like war. I'm so scared that we could lose Alice, and I miss talking to you. Tom's going to see his parents next Wednesday, so you could phone me then if you can do that from work.

All my Love, Sophie.

John fully intended to call Sophie from work that day, 23rd August 1939, but his plans, like those of many others, were overturned by the news that the Soviet Union and Nazi Germany had signed a non-aggression pact. The implications were clear; Hitler was making sure that Russia wouldn't intervene if Germany invaded Poland. Everyone in John's team stopped work to listen to the radio throughout the day, dreading news that German troops were massing on the border with Poland.

Nine days later on 1st September 1939, Germany invaded Poland; two days after that, Britain and France declared war on Germany.

John finally spoke to Sophie two weeks later and told her that she, Tom and Alice could always use his flat in emergencies. He didn't need to spell out what he meant.

26

WORLD WAR

By 6th October, just five weeks after Germany invaded Poland, the Polish Army was defeated. *Blitzkrieg* was now part of the vocabulary of the average British man and woman. The British Army hadn't been able to provide the Poles with any significant support and was now stuck in France. It was clear that France would be next, and he felt the need to do something – irrational or not. He arranged to meet Peter Thornbury to ask for his support.

"Don't be fucking stupid, John, the idea is out of the question. You'd make a lousy field officer, anyway, and your knowledge and expertise are needed here at home."

"Be fair, Peter, since I was transferred to Bawdsey Manor my position in the scheme of things has never been clear, to say the least. Philips still pay my wages, you're still my boss – notionally – but I report to the Air Ministry. There was talk some time ago of giving me a notional rank but that went nowhere. Be honest, apart from our monthly meetings we hardly see each other. The radar chain is up and running, the snags are almost ironed out, my role is less vital so I thought I should join up."

"For an intelligent scientist you do reach some ridiculous conclusions. Of course, I see what's driving this, but at thirty-nine you're almost over the hill for active service anyway. In my opinion, after seeing the German Army sweep through Poland in thirty-five days, I think the odds that the French and British Armies will stop the Germans taking France are no more than fifty-fifty. That's not just my view, by the way. If they do reach the Channel, then our air defences are going to be crucial to preventing an invasion. So no, I won't support your application, which means there's no point in you making one. I will suggest to the Air Ministry that they give you a notional rank, though. 'Group Captain Samson' sounds rather good, I think."

John knew Thornbury was right. It was obvious to both of them that he would be far more useful to the war effort helping to develop Britain's coastal radar defences than he would anywhere else. His team were doing vital work, and doing it effectively, and he was proud of that. The chance to play an important role in the coming conflagration should be giving his life meaning. So why the recent sense of purposelessness, faint echoes of those that had plagued him years ago?

It was Sophie, of course; or rather the lack of Sophie since their big row. She'd helped to give him a grounded sense of himself, an equanimity, in a world that now seemed to be heading for catastrophe and chaos.

His spirits had lifted ahead of their phone call two weeks ago, but not for long.

They'd talked about the war, what Hitler would do next, will the Germans invade Britain and keeping Alice safe – but not about their feelings around the issue that had come between them. They both knew that it was too early, that it could risk reopening their quarrel. To keep the conversation going he'd asked her about Tom; John actually knew little about him.

"What does Tom think about the war – do you talk about it much?"

The silence seemed to go on and on; eventually Sophie said, "I hope you're not being provocative, John. Tom's a builder – well, a sort of handyman – not a thinker. So he approaches the question of whether the war may come to Britain in terms of what opportunities it might open up for him. Our last conversation, when the Germans were bombing Warsaw to smithereens, involved him pointing out how the Germans would need lots of local Polish builders to repair vital structures they'd damaged. 'So if they bomb London, Sophie, I'll be rich'."

"Christ! What did you say?"

"Something like 'If they bomb London, Tom, we might all die. Including Alice. Has that occurred to you?' Can we not talk about my marriage, please, John? I think you know it upsets me, so let's leave it."

"I'm sorry. I shouldn't have asked. But please just tell me this; he doesn't mistreat you, does he?"

"What fucking business is that of yours? Maybe I haven't made this clear. You and I had our chance of happiness, John, but it meant you making a compromise that you weren't prepared to make. You didn't want children; that was your right and it broke my heart. But I did – desperately – and so I married the first acceptable-looking bloke that asked me to marry him. That's pretty much the only choice left for a working-class woman going on forty in that situation.

"Please let's never speak about my marriage again. Is that understood?"

"I'm sorry, Sophie. I was a selfish, blinkered man and that's the biggest regret of my life, too."

"But we have Alice and I promise I'll make sure she knows how important you are to her."

Remembering that conversation three months later, John realised that in a perverse way it had been responsible for helping him to recover from his low mood. She was dealing with her cheerless, dispiriting marriage with resilience, seeing the glass half full, and he'd felt ashamed at how easily he'd succumbed to depression. He had a rewarding job, his own flat he loved going back to and financial security. The future was uncertain, but that was the same for almost everyone in the country. He'd noticed how the possibility of an existential threat to the country had begun to bring communities in London together.

There was one thing missing in his life. It was eighteen months since he'd seen Daphne and he missed the combination of repose and excitement of sharing physical and emotional intimacy with another human being. Living a peripatetic life in two places with meetings at odd hours of the day and night limited his opportunities. Of course, he could have gone to the Golden Slipper and paid for a one-night stand, but he was no longer interested in that kind of connection.

Three days before Christmas he managed to steal some time away from Bawdsey to spend an afternoon present-shopping in London; a necklace for May, a posh fountain pen for Eric and a push-along wooden toy for Philip. Everyone in his team got a bottle of whisky. He knew what to get Sophie and Alice, but how could he give them their presents?

He hadn't seen May in weeks and was looking forward to spending Christmas Day with his sister and her family. He hoped they could avoid dwelling on the war for just one day. He'd given May five pounds so that they could all have a Christmas dinner to remember "and put what's left towards clothes for you and Philip." She'd looked embarrassed, but he'd noticed the look of relief on her face.

"That was delicious, May. I haven't eaten that well in months. Where did you get the turkey?"

"Don't ask and you'll hear no lies. I hope you're not implying it might be the black market."

She gave him a wink.

"Would I suggest that my sister would do such a thing? I'll clear the plates."

They'd managed to maintain an unforced, upbeat spirit throughout the meal, helped by sufficient quantities of beer and sherry. This eventually ended when Eric said, "I reckon Chamberlain and those other politicians have been exaggerating the threat that Hitler's posing for their own ends. Everyone at work is saying that this so-called war seems phoney, and I agree. I've not seen any German bombers over London or German battleships sailing up the Thames. May agrees, don't you, May?"

Eric looked at her for affirmation, but she stayed silent.

"I can understand why people might think that, Eric," John began diplomatically, "but I don't think your workmates are seeing the whole picture. Not by any means, I'm afraid. I don't want to come across as a doom merchant, but here's what I know. Two of our warships have been badly damaged by German mines in the Thames Estuary; Hitler's moving enormous armoured columns towards the Belgian and French borders; Nazi battleships are sinking thousands of tons of British merchant ships in the Atlantic as I speak; from intelligence that I receive as part of my work, the Germans are preparing to invade Norway and we've sent forces to help the Norwegians defend their country. I'm afraid there's nothing phoney about what the Nazis are doing at the moment."

He looked at May and Eric. Their expressions told him that he'd just dampened their Christmas, but he couldn't let Eric's comment go unanswered.

The awkward silence was broken by a knock on the door, resulting in May jumping up to answer it with a look of expectation and relief. John looked up as she came back, followed by Sophie with Alice in a pushchair.

"I thought it would be nice to invite some old friends round. Unfortunately Tom can't be here, but you're very welcome, Sophie. And little Alice, too, of course."

"Thank you so much for inviting us, May. Happy Christmas everybody!"

Beaming, she looked at John and said, "Hello, stranger, how are you?"

He felt so happy to see them he was lost for words, feeling ridiculously nervous and trying not to show it. Looking from Sophie to Alice and back again, he eventually said, "Completely amazed and delighted to see you both. Gosh, how much you've grown, Alice. You're looking well, Sophie."

She laughed. "Thank you. It must be down to the fact I'm getting some sleep again these days, thanks to this one going through the night. And maybe the extra attention I paid to my make-up for Christmas Day."

She winked at John.

"How long is it since you've seen Alice, John? It must be at least a year. Alice, this is Mummy's friend, John. Do you remember him?"

Alice's face screwed up in a look of concentration, then she shook her head.

"She's beautiful, Sophie. You and Tom have got an absolute cracker there."

There was an indefinable shift in the atmosphere in the room, and he moved the conversation on.

"I wasn't expecting you two to be here, so I haven't wrapped your presents yet. If you've got any spare paper and string, May, I could wrap them now."

"Follow me, John, there's some in the kitchen."

"That's lovely of you, but it's not fair. I haven't got you anything."

"Seeing you two is present enough. Who knows where we'll all be by next Christmas."

The rest of the afternoon slid by. As if by unspoken agreement, the war wasn't mentioned again. Presents were exchanged, toasts drunk and toddlers passed around. Eventually, seeing Eric and

May starting to look at the clock and Sophie preparing to take Alice back, he decided that now was the time to tell them.

"There's something I'd like to tell you before I leave. The Air Ministry has decided that Bawdsey Manor, where I'm based, is too vulnerable to attack from German commando raids. Given the nature of our work, they're moving us. It was originally going to be Dundee, and some staff and equipment have already been moved there. But apparently that isn't suitable either – thank goodness – and they've found another place for us near Swanage, in Dorset. I'll be moving down there in the spring. It's over four hours away by car or train, so you'll be seeing even less of me. I know you'll all be heartbroken," he said with a laugh.

His announcement meant that this evening would be the last one they'd all spend together for a long time. Sophie felt bereft, although perhaps it was for the best; seeing John only shone a light on the limitations of her relationship with her husband and stirred up emotions and feelings that were probably better left buried.

For John, Eric's delusional thoughts on the war's progress had only confirmed his view that there was still a dangerous mood of complacency in the minds of many of his countrymen and women, encouraged by opportunist politicians who wanted Britain to negotiate a peace with Hitler. He had a small role to play doing what he could to ensure that the country was as prepared as it could be should the German Army conquer France, facing Britain across the Channel.

End of the Phoney War

Before his team completed their move to Swanage, the German Army had invaded France, Belgium and Holland on 10th May, then fought their way across France in thirteen days to encircle the British and French forces at Dunkirk. Neville Chamberlain was forced to resign as Prime Minister and Parliament voted for a coalition government led by Winston Churchill.

300,000 British troops were trapped on the beach.

He felt like sending Eric a letter: *Not much phoney about the war anymore, is there?* but thought better of it.

Suddenly the war against the Nazis was personal. Robert Mayhew, a softly-spoken Cambridge graduate in his team, had joined up in time to be sent to France with the British Expeditionary Force. John had heard from Robert's parents that he was one of those stuck on the beach, at the mercy of German dive-bombers. He desperately hoped that the lottery of war would fall in Robert's favour, but he was killed when his destroyer was bombed as it left the beachhead.

At the end of May his team finally joined other scientists at their new base in the village of Worth Matravers, four miles from Swanage in Dorset. The number working on radar research had grown as new applications were discovered; John's team were now specialising on systems to jam enemy radar. Additional accommodation of questionable quality had been hastily built to house the increased numbers, but luckily John had his own room in one of the older buildings. Sadly, he'd been overly optimistic about the length of the journey back to London; it was at least five hours by car – longer at night in the blackout – and passenger trains were frequently held in sidings to allow goods trains to go through. The first time he'd gone back, the train had taken seven hours, and he realised he wouldn't be making the journey very often. The only pub in the village – the Square and Compass – did good business from the scientists stuck on the base.

One evening in early July, nursing the last of his pint in the Square and Compass, alone after two colleagues had left early for their night shift, he was approached by a casually dressed woman in her thirties.

"May I join you? I don't want to interrupt your thoughts."

"Please do. My thoughts would benefit with an interruption; I was thinking about a young man I used to work with who died at Dunkirk."

"I hate those bastards. I'm so sorry for your friend. I'm Sophie, pleased to meet you."

He was startled to hear that name in such unfamiliar surroundings, and it was a moment before he replied.

"A pleasure to meet you, Sophie. I'm John. Do you come from around here, or do you work on the base?"

His casual, friendly manner belied that his guard was up. Every man working at Worth Matravers had been warned to be suspicious of unsolicited approaches from strangers.

"I live in Swanage and work in an antiques shop. I love walking the coastal path to the pub on the light evenings. I think it's a wonderful part of the country. What do you do?"

"I've been attached to the army base for three months, helping to organise the construction of extra accommodation. Nothing very exciting."

Sophie probed him a little more about his work; not too obviously, but rather more than small talk between a man and a woman meeting for the first time would justify. He filed the thought away and they carried on talking about Dunkirk and the likelihood of invasion, until she left to walk back before dusk. Later that evening in his room, he worked out what had left him feeling uneasy about their conversation. Most people wouldn't have picked it up, but he'd remained fluent in German. Her pronunciation of her name sounded the way a native German speaker, fluent in English, might pronounce it. The 's' had a slight 'z' sound and the 'ph' a slight 'v'.

Half the country is seeing German spies around every corner, for fuck's sake. Just leave it.

But when the same thing happened the next time they'd met by chance in the Square and Compass, he found he couldn't forget about it. *So what if your last espionage escapade turned out so badly. What's the right thing to do in this case?*

He decided to speak to the senior officer in charge of security on the base, even if it probably meant being patronised and told that half the country is seeing spies around every corner.

Group Captain Nicholls listened carefully, sat back in his chair, took several deep puffs on his pipe and said, "Have you arranged to see this woman again?"

"No."

"Then I want you to arrange to meet her somewhere in Swanage. Tell me where and when and I'll get MI5 to follow her back home. Once we know where she lives, we can search the place. We'll probably find nothing, but it's worth making sure. Thanks for this, John, you did the right thing."

Nearly a week went by until he saw her again. There was some flirtation between them over drinks, so he wasn't surprised when she agreed to meet him for a meal out at a pub in Swanage. He passed the time and place on to Nicholls and left the rest to him.

During their passable but flavourless meal, John had struggled to appear relaxed. Watching Sophie as they exchanged undemanding conversation, he couldn't squash the thought that he was playing a game with this woman that could end up with her being exposed as a spy. Then he shocked himself as he began to realise that he felt the same sense of excitement he'd last experienced when smuggling pictures of German rocket research out of a Berlin library. They left the pub and agreed to "do this again" before going their separate ways. A week later, he got a message to see Nicholls immediately.

"Come in, Samson. I wanted to update you about your young lady, who we now know to be Fräulein Sophie Brandt. When the police searched her flat they eventually found a well-concealed radio transmitter. She was immediately arrested, and under interrogation eventually admitted to being a German agent. Not only that, she took a pistol off one of her guards when he was distracted and shot him before being disempowered. He'll live, but her trial will be expedited and she'll be executed before the end of the month."

John's stomach heaved; he just managed to control the urge to vomit.

"I understand it's upsetting but that woman could have caused the deaths of thousands of our countrymen. You did the right thing and you should be proud of yourself. There's something else."

He let his queasiness settle, then said, "What's that, sir?"

"She asked to see you. You don't have to oblige, but she may reveal something of use to us. You will be closely guarded, of course."

He needed time to collect himself again, then answered calmly, "I will see her, yes, sir."

"I rather thought you would. It's not often we get the chance to grant someone's last wish before they die. Just be prepared for her to say anything."

As he entered the cell, Sophie was sitting manacled to the arm of a chair that was bolted to the floor. She looked directly at him, a half smile on her lips. The corporal beside her indicated he should sit in the chair positioned six feet away from her. He couldn't see any signs of a beating on her face or arms, but he knew that didn't prove anything.

"Hello, Sophie. You asked to see me."

"I have one question. What gave me away?"

Ever since he'd agreed to it, he'd been wondering why she wanted to see him. She'd just answered his question. She had to know, even in her final weeks on Earth, whether she'd slipped up in some way. Whether she'd betrayed her beloved Führer.

I'll never fully understand human behaviour, he thought.

"You weren't to know that I'd lived in Berlin during the 1920s. Not only did I become a fluent German speaker, but I had to become a forensic listener. Unfortunately for you, once I returned to England I had a long-term girlfriend called Sophie. I realised early on that your pronunciation of your name had a German, not English, accentuation to it."

Her eyes narrowed, her face now a mask of hatred.

"So you told them of your suspicions. Well, you English fool, enjoy the next few weeks of freedom. Your pathetic little country will soon be invaded and your army, having scurried off the beach at Dunkirk, will collapse in a few weeks, just as they did in France."

John smiled back.

"Spoken with the arrogance of a fanatic and true believer. But I suspect that invading Britain across the Channel will prove to be a challenge too far, even for the master race. Unfortunately, you won't be around to find out if I'm right.

Goodbye, Sophie."

As he got up to leave, her eyes gave away her fear for the first time. She'd managed to hide that up to now and he couldn't help feeling a moment of compassion.

"English cunt."

He was moved by her bravado in spite of himself. A month later, on the day she was hung, he marked the end of her life and his undercover role in bringing that about by dwelling for some time on the unexpected exhilaration he'd felt carrying out his subterfuge and what that suggested about the boundary between decency and treachery.

The mood on the base grew increasingly sombre during August and September as the Luftwaffe's massive daily bomber raids over southern England began to impact on the ability of the RAF to get enough fighter planes into the air. For a few weeks it looked as if the German bombers might succeed in crippling the airfields of Kent and East Anglia; John had the sickening thought that Sophie's wish might be granted. The radar site near Worth Matravers was a frequent target and he often had to drop his research instantly and join the repair team. He was amazed at how little serious damage most of the bombing caused, and the mast was usually working again the following day. *I just hope they can repair the runways as quickly.*

27

KEEPING IN TOUCH WITH THE ONES YOU LOVE

In the middle of September the Luftwaffe's focus suddenly switched; the bombers started to target London and other main cities instead of the airfields. The aim was to destroy Londoners' morale and provoke a mass evacuation to the countryside – but it proved a huge miscalculation. While the docks were badly damaged, whole streets flattened and thousands killed and badly injured, production in most of London's factories quickly recovered. He hadn't been back for weeks and pestered his boss to be given leave "to check that my flat and my friends are okay." Three days' leave was finally granted after news of a particularly heavy bomber raid on the East End around Dalston and Kentish Town; exactly where Sophie, Tom, Alice, May, Eric and Philip lived. He let May know he was coming and arranged to meet her; checking that Sophie and Alice were okay wouldn't be so easy.

Sophie and Tom had intended to move to a bigger place after they married, but with Tom's inconsistent earnings as a jobbing builder and her wages from the Golden Slipper, they only managed to save a few pounds each month. Once Alice came along and Sophie stopped working, they hardly broke even; moving to a bigger place was out of the question. As Alice got older, Sophie's small flat became increasingly claustrophobic and they argued constantly. Calling round on the off-chance she might be alone was out of the question, as Tom had made it clear that he wasn't welcome. Sophie had given up their phone line to save money, so all he could do was make sure their flat was undamaged.

Driving up to London on the A3 trunk road proved faster than he'd thought it would; several sections had been made into dual carriageways which gave him enough time to coax the Morris up to fifty-five mph and edge past the frequent military convoys. But everything changed when he got lost driving through Kingston. He cursed the removal of road signs and drove around several roundabouts three times before finally guessing the right exit. He'd hardly ever been south of the Thames in London before and was hugely relieved when he saw the Houses of Parliament across the river. Keeping the river on his left until Waterloo Bridge, he crossed over to North London and immediately felt more relaxed. He was a North Londoner, after all.

From Waterloo Bridge onwards he started to notice scores of homeless men and women sleeping rough in the doorways of bombed and undamaged buildings. At first, the bomb damage didn't look too bad, but as he got near the Euston Road the landscape became a horrendous conglomeration of decapitated, windowless buildings and huge piles of brick, stone, steel and rubble. *I've seen the reports, but this is worse than anything I'd imagined.*

Shocked, he began driving at a snail's pace towards Hackney along the Balls Pond Road, barely able to pick out the kerb side in the growing dusk with the feeble beams of light from the car's hooded headlights. The tension in his body wound tighter as he got closer to his street. What would he find?

It was dark by the time he pulled up outside his flat, which to his great relief appeared undamaged. As he walked up the steps to his front door, the piercing sound of a siren broke the silence; the thought that there could be an air raid hadn't crossed his mind during his drive across the capital. *How stupid can I be?*

He had no idea what to do and stood planted to the spot until the door to the neighbouring house opened. A family of four rushed out, looking at him quizzically. The father said, "You live next door, don't you? You'd better join us in our shelter, mate. This sounds like a big one."

He steadied himself and followed them into their back garden. The air-raid shelter was half buried in the ground; there were three curved sheets of corrugated iron for the roof and brick walls at the front and back, one with a small metal entrance door. He squeezed in next to the father who switched on his torch then bolted the door. The two children, who looked about seven and nine, stared at him.

"Thank you so much. I've come back to London to check on my flat and have no idea where the nearest community shelter is."

"We've hardly seen you since Christmas. That's an RAF uniform you're wearing – where are you based? Or can't you say?"

"I'm afraid I can't, sorry. It's about a hundred and sixty miles away, so I can't get up to London very often. I hear the bombing has been terrible here over the last few weeks."

"Bloody Nazis. They don't care how many women and children they kill. It's totally indiscriminate – we're nowhere near the docks here."

"What do you do, mister?"

John looked at their daughter. Many children her age had been sent to the countryside and he wondered why she hadn't. What a frightening experience it must be for her and her brother, bombs falling from the sky night after night. He thought about Alice and Philip. They were too young to make any sense of it, but old enough to be scared out of their wits every night. The constant worry for their parents must be unbearable; compared with them, he had a relatively easy life.

About to give her an edited reply, he suddenly heard the terrifying whistling of bombs falling above the drone of aeroplane engines and thump of anti-aircraft guns. Everyone tensed as the explosions came closer in rapid succession; he realised it must be bombs from one aircraft as they hit the ground one after the other, each explosion shaking the ground more than the previous one as the bombs got closer. He tried to remember the bombload of a German bomber; eight, ten, twelve? He'd heard at least six and the last one shook the ground beneath his feet. Number seven was deafening and caused debris to crash on top of the shelter, but it held. Both children were crying now, terrified. As was he. But there were no more, for now at least. An odd number of bombs? He'd either miscounted or one was a UXB – an unexploded bomb.

He knew the drill; wait for the all-clear. When it came, they slowly emerged from the shelter and took in the damage. His side of the street was largely intact, with just a few broken windows, but thirty yards down the road on the opposite side, three houses had taken a direct hit. As one, John and the father set off towards the devastation and began to search the rubble. When flames from a fractured gas pipe shot out from beneath a pile of bricks, the father shouted, "We need to go, now. This could explode and bring what's left down on our heads."

They heard the bell of the fire engine as they ran back to safety.

"Bastards. That was close. I'm going in to check the house over and I suggest you do the same. My name's Henry."

"Pleased to meet you, Henry. Thanks for the shelter. A lifesaver, literally. I'm John Samson. If I give you my work number, would you mind calling me if anything happens to my flat?"

"Of course I will. Although the phone lines are often down."

Everything inside his flat seemed intact. The electricity and gas supplies still worked, there were no leaks and nothing had fallen down. When he switched the bedroom light on he noticed everything was covered in a layer of dust. Of course – the air in London was now full of fine particles from the explosions and damaged buildings.

Suddenly feeling hungry, he made himself baked beans and scrambled powdered eggs then checked every room thoroughly. First thing in the morning, he'd go round and check on his sister, as he hadn't been able to get through on the phone. He climbed into his damp bed and fell asleep immediately.

"John! What are you doing here? Why didn't you let me know you're in London, I'd have got some lunch together – or at least the best I could manage with my ration coupons."

"I heard about the raids in this area and wanted to check you were all okay. I tried to call but the line is dead."

"I know, bomb damage apparently. Come in, it's so good to see you. It's been weeks."

Over cups of tea and two rock-hard scones with homemade blackberry jam – "there are wild blackberries all over London" – May updated him on the joys of living in the Blitz.

"The worst part is the effect it's having on everyone's nerves. It's awful – nobody knows if tonight's going to be their last. Just thinking about anything happening to Philip reduces me to jelly. It's much worse if you're a parent, although I think a lot of young people are having a whale of a time. They think they're immortal and anything goes: *'If today's our last, then let's make the most of it and go all the way'*."

John raised his eyebrows and smiled.

"I didn't know you were so easily shocked by young people having sex."

"Don't tease me, I'm not. But there's going to be a lot of babies born in the next few years who don't look much like their supposed fathers. Changing the subject, have you seen Sophie and Alice yet?"

Smiling at her possible quip about Alice's paternity, he said, "No, and I'd like your advice. I know Tom hates my guts, so I can't just turn up like I did this morning. But I'd love to see them both. Do you know if there's somewhere she regularly takes Alice?"

May looked concerned.

"I saw her with Alice two weeks ago in the park. She looked very tired, drawn and unhappy. When I asked her if everything was okay, she said that Tom and she were having money troubles and problems in their marriage, but she clammed up when I pushed further. She's always taken pride in her appearance, but I noticed that her hair looked greasy and her clothes were dirty. She also had a bruise on her arm. Alice seemed to be happy and healthy, though; Sophie's obviously giving most of her rations to Alice."

"Would you mind if I walked with you and Philip if you go to that park tomorrow? That's my best chance of meeting her without causing any trouble."

She thought for a moment, then said, "Okay, come around here tomorrow about eleven. You can push Philip on the swings, he'll love that."

John saw the startled look on Sophie's face the moment she recognised the three of them in the park. She hesitated, then carried on towards them. There was no sign of Tom.

May hadn't been exaggerating; if anything, Sophie looked more haggard than she'd prepared him for. Dark bags under her eyes, clear skin now turned grey, hair lank and dirty. He was shocked; it was obvious that she'd stopped caring for herself and he realised that his reaction must also be obvious.

May looked at her son and said, "Why don't Mummy and Philip go to the swings, then Uncle John and Sophie can have a chat, and catch us up."

She strode off with Philip in the pushchair before they had a chance to object. Alice carried on playing with her doll.

"I wish you hadn't done this, John. I know you want to see Alice, but I'm embarrassed for you to see me looking like this."

She paused, thinking about whether to carry on, then spoke in a rush.

"Tom knows Alice isn't his daughter. He gave blood recently – a surprisingly unselfish thing for him to do – and the nurse told him his blood type. He checked on Alice's health records and discovered that someone with his type was very unlikely to be her father. When he confronted me I admitted it; even though I won't tell him who the father is, he assumes it's you. He's not giving me any money for Alice – '*I'm not paying to raise that bastard's kid*' – all I get is a pitiful welfare handout for her. My parents give me what they can. I've even thought about prostituting myself, but I can't do it. Who'd pay money to have sex with me looking like this, anyway? Tom's moved out to live with his mother, but says he won't divorce me because I'll be free to marry someone else. So I'm trapped."

John could only stand there, seething with anger and shame. *I've been so selfish, so unthinking. These two mean everything to me and I've let them down once again – I should have been giving Sophie money for Alice's care all this time. Do something, now, and don't make this about you.*

"I'm so sorry, Tom's being a complete bastard. Please listen to me, Sophie. Alice is my responsibility, you're exhausted and I want to help you both. I can send you money every month. It's not a gift, it's what I should be doing – she's my daughter and I can afford to do this."

"I will accept your help, John, on the understanding it's for Alice and not me. Thank you. But you can't send cash to my flat. Tom has a key and sometimes walks in unannounced. He even tried to exert his 'marital rights' once, and only backed off when I threatened him with a kitchen knife. How can we make this work?"

"I'm only doing this if you agree to spend money on yourself as well. If I send money to May by registered letter on the same date once a month, you can collect it from her. I still expect to come to London sometimes, and when I do I'll arrange to meet you and give you a larger amount. I'll withdraw twenty one-pound notes and coins from my bank this afternoon and meet you here tomorrow. If that gets low before the month is out, phone me from a call box and I'll send another ten pounds."

"Don't be ridiculous, John, that's a huge amount. I have to be careful – people will talk if I suddenly start spending money I didn't have before."

"So be careful. I know you can – you looked after the books at the nightclub for months. How about I give you back your key to my flat and you could keep the money somewhere safe there, if you're worried about Tom finding it."

Sophie looked at him, smiling. She already looked less haggard and overwhelmed.

"I feel like a weight's been lifted from my shoulders. Thank you from the bottom of my heart. I can buy decent food for us both, use as much hot water as we need, heat the flat, replace some of the rags I've been wearing and get Alice a couple of nice outfits. But I'll be careful, don't worry. I would love to give you a hug but you never know who's watching in this park. And I don't think I smell very fragrant – but that's going to change tonight!"

"Please take care of yourself. I wish I was living in London and able to support you more. How does Alice cope with the explosions? Is there an air-raid shelter near your flat?"

"She gets scared, of course, but luckily our streets haven't been hit yet and she hasn't seen anything horrific. We always go to the shelter as soon as the siren sounds. I can see May and Philip coming back, so I'll say goodbye now. Take care of yourself, John, and thank you again."

She surreptitiously brushed her fingers against his as she walked off.

There were fewer and fewer opportunities for John to get to London over the next eighteen months; the pressure to improve Britain's radar systems was unrelenting and London was still subjected to sporadic bombardment. Most Britons lived from day to day, desperately hoping for signs that Hitler might eventually be defeated. He treasured the letters he received from his sister and Sophie, and replied whenever he could. His replies to Sophie were sent via his London address, where she collected them.

Breaking the pact that he'd made with Stalin two years earlier, Hitler ordered the invasion of the Soviet Union in June 1941 and began a lightning advance towards Moscow, leading many to feel even more pessimistic about Britain's chances. John didn't share this view; he'd started to devour books about military strategy and had a hunch that Hitler had finally overreached. As the German Army's progress slowed with the onset of the Russian winter and news came of Japan's attack on Pearl Harbour – leading Hitler to declare war on the USA – John allowed himself to hope that Germany would eventually lose the war.

Shortly after Pearl Harbour, at the beginning of 1942, rumours started to circulate around the base about an imminent move to another location. The Dorset coast, like Bawdsey, was now considered too vulnerable to a raid from the sea. A week later the Officer Commanding, Radar Research, confirmed they would be moving to Malvern College, a boys' private school near Worcester, an even longer journey to London. He couldn't give Sophie or May details of his new location, of course, save to tell them he'd be in London even less from now on. Transferring all of the equipment and preparing Malvern College for its new role took over two months and wasn't finally completed until July.

He had to admit there were advantages. He was billeted in a grand room in the senior master's wing; built in the 1860s, it had a huge, comfortable bed, a washbasin and views over the Malvern Hills. The demands on his team were relentless; they were now developing improvements that would give a clearer image of planes flying through poor weather. It was proving tricky, but they were all driven by the knowledge that their work saved countless lives.

His team had remained almost unchanged since they'd moved to Bawdsey; only two had left, out of the original fifteen men and four women. To his knowledge, there'd been no intimate liaisons between any of them – and he was pretty sure he'd know if there had. He bought everyone a drink in the masters' bar every Friday evening unless there was an emergency. While he tried not to get close to anyone in particular, he often ended up talking with Ruth and Wilfred, the two other senior scientists, after the rest had gone into town. Both were single and completely dedicated to their work; Wilfred was painfully shy and he suspected Ruth didn't fancy men. The three of them often went to bed slightly drunk, having pored over the latest war news from the Home Front, the Mediterranean, Russia and the Pacific.

John regularly tried to get news about the fate of Jews in Holland. Three months ago in May 1942 the Germans had instructed all Dutch Jews to wear a 'yellow star'; many had gone into hiding as a result. He prayed that Ilse and her family were among them.

As Christmas 1942 drew near he was hoping he'd be able to get back to London for a few days and see May, Philip, Sophie and Alice again. But it wasn't to be. He was ordered to oversee the transport and loading of delicate radar equipment onto a ship in Portsmouth. The ship was bound for Malta, under constant air attack from Italian and German bombers and in danger of being overrun. When he protested that overseeing the loading of equipment wasn't the best use of his time, he was given short shrift by his boss.

"I don't want any old corporal to be responsible for seeing that this gets handled safely and loaded onto the ship. At least I can make sure that we send someone with knowledge and clout. I'm sorry if this has upset your plans for Christmas, John."

He spent Christmas Day in Portsmouth freezing on the dockside, driving the dockers mad as he told them how to do their jobs – at least that's how they saw it. One even threatened to lay him out, until he beckoned the head loader to the boot of his car and showed him the six bottles of Scotch that he'd managed to liberate from the bar at Malvern College.

"It's all yours if you take over and personally oversee this lot safely battened down in the hold."

He couldn't face driving back to Malvern through the night with blacked-out headlights, so checked into a room above a pub and left Portsmouth on Boxing Day at dawn, feeling flat and thinking about those he loved in Britain and Holland.

After persistent lobbying from John and others, the Officer Commanding at Malvern had eventually agreed to hold a New Year's Eve party for everyone at the base plus a selection of the 'right people' from the town. In spite of his continuing low mood, he was determined to get into the spirit and put on his best shirt and jacket. At midnight he found himself linking arms with a glamorous but boring young woman on one side and a sad forty-something woman on the other. As the circle broke apart, the older woman turned to him and said, "Thank God that's over" and started to walk away.

Empathising with her melancholia, he walked after her.

"Enforced jollity can be hell if you're not in the mood, can't it? Can I buy you a drink? There are some quiet tables over there."

She swung round to face him.

"I agree, but not as bad as being propositioned by a stranger when one is desperate to escape. Happy New Year."

Chastened, he went back to his room to nurse his hurt feelings.

At that moment, the woman who'd just rebuffed him – who'd recently heard that her husband's ship had been torpedoed in the Mediterranean – returned to the party to apologise to the man to whom she'd been unforgivably rude. Failing to find him, she went to the bar, gave the barman his description plus two shillings and was told his name and the location of his room.

Cursing the knock at his door – it could only mean there was some emergency that required his attention – he levered himself off the bed, pulled his door open and found himself lost for words.

"Mr Samson, I hope I haven't woken you up."

He shook her outstretched hand.

"Sylvia Thompson; we met earlier and I've come to apologise for my rudeness, which I assure you is out of character, although that's no excuse and I'm truly sorry. I would like to take you up on your offer, if it's still there, but I will insist on paying. What do you say?"

After a moment's hesitation, he said, "I'd like that, thank you, Sylvia. How did you know where to find me?"

"I gave the barman a tip and your description."

He gasped. Wartime had led to some relaxation of pre-war norms of behaviour between the sexes, but a well-dressed middle-class woman asking for a man's name and room at the bar would have previously been a huge risk to her good name. The party was still going with a good crowd when they walked in; John caught the barman's raised eyebrows as he saw them enter. They found a reasonably quiet table, ordered their drinks and toasted the New Year.

"I'm impressed, but weren't you taking a risk?"

"A risk? How so? I tend to sum people up pretty quickly and you seemed a decent man."

"I meant a risk to your reputation."

She looked around the room and noted, unsurprised, that a number of Malvern residents were looking disapprovingly in their direction.

"I moved to Malvern with my husband twelve years ago. It's a small-minded place, and we were an unconventional couple in some ways. I don't really have a reputation to lose, plus I don't give a shit. What do you do here at Malvern College, John? Or is it too hush-hush to divulge?"

He was warming to Sylvia Thompson. He'd always enjoyed the company of unconventional women; with her unfashionably long hair, trousers and little make-up except for a swipe of lipstick, Sylvia fitted that description. She reminded him a little of Katharine Hepburn. He gave her a brief summary of his work, careful not to say anything except what he knew to be common knowledge. She listened attentively, asking questions.

"What about you and your husband, Sylvia?"

"I'm loosely involved in the Women's Voluntary Service. There's a split at the moment between those of us that support the war and those that adopt a pacifist stance. I respect their position but disagree with it strongly. Fascism has to be fought for many reasons – not least because the only roles fascists allow for women are producing babies, homemaking and letting the men make all the decisions."

She paused, clearly deciding whether to carry on.

"My husband was the captain on HMS *Cairo*, a cruiser that was sunk off Tunisia four months ago. I've recently heard from the Admiralty that his name wasn't on the list of survivors and he's now assumed to be dead. I miss Charles terribly, and I'm only just holding on. We'd been together since we met fifteen years ago and realised immediately that we were both square pegs in round holes and had found our soulmates. Singing 'Auld Lang Syne' brought back the memory of singing it with him last year and realising I'd never do anything like that with him again."

"I'm so sorry you've lost him, Sylvia. Do you have children?"

"We both decided we didn't want children, but I don't believe that makes his death any less tragic, do you?"

"No, I don't, that was clumsy of me, I'm sorry. What did you mean by square pegs in round holes?"

"We had an intimate relationship, but also an understanding that we could see other people discreetly. That never affected our love for each other; at heart I'm a lesbian and he's bisexual. Does that shock you?"

"A lot less than you might think. I spent a year in Berlin in 1925 and came across many kinds of relationships there. Later, in my thirties, I fell in love with a woman who ran a nightclub in Soho and had my eyes opened even further. If people are happy and it's not harming anyone else, who am I to judge them, or their life?"

"That makes you unusual. And interesting. I assume you're not still with your nightclub lady? Do you have children?"

"We have a daughter, Alice, but we're not together anymore. I still see them whenever I can, but as they live in London, not enough."

They carried on talking for over an hour, reflecting on how the war was changing so many lives in such fundamental, permanent ways. When Sylvia said that she was tired and wanted to go home, John asked if she wanted him to walk with her and was surprised when she said yes.

As they left the party, she asked how he thought the war was going.

"I assume you get more reliable information and less propaganda than the rest of us."

"For the first time since September 1939, I can see signs that the Allies might eventually win this war, but it all depends on the outcome on two fronts. We're pushing the Afrika Korps back to Tunisia and have relieved the siege of Malta. That will give us greater control over the Mediterranean. More significantly, the Soviets have counter-attacked at Stalingrad and are hoping to surround the German Army there.

"So in a few months, the Germans could be retreating from the

Red Army and the Allies could be about to invade Italy from the sea. If that happens, the only questions will be how long it takes to defeat Germany and how many people living today will be alive to see it."

John and Sylvia kept in touch throughout the rest of the war, becoming close friends. Sometimes, after an evening together in the pub, she would invite him back and they'd carry on talking over a whisky until she went to her bedroom and he to the spare room.

They could talk to each other about anything; one night, after he'd told her of his shame for betraying Ilse's trust, he'd gone on to admit that he was sometimes haunted by a sense that he'd been an imposter all his adult life, believing himself to be a good person while really he was terribly flawed.

"Ah, Freud. The battle between the ego and the superego. Interesting stuff, but I can't stand his archaic views on women's emancipation. And as for penis envy – a ridiculous theory. You're a lovely, decent man, John. A real *mensch*. I should know, I married one of the best. And now he's gone."

When the Allies successfully stormed ashore in Sicily in July 1943, she met him in the bar over a glass of champagne and toasted "to the end of the war, whenever it comes," much to the bemusement of those who overheard.

He'd arranged to have his mail sent to the Malvern post office and collect it three times a week – there were only ever letters from May and Sophie. Shortly after the Sicily landings May told him that a house two doors from them had been blown up. Although their house was virtually undamaged, they'd been told to move out while nearby houses were strengthened. "Could we use your flat while the repairs are carried out, please, John?"

He was given special leave to drive to London and help them move in – he'd been wanting to check on his flat for some time. This was his first time in the capital for several months and it was clear that the rate of bomb damage had slowed, but not stopped. His street in Dalston was still unscathed, and he was relieved to see that his flat hadn't been squatted in by one of the many families who'd been made homeless by the bombing. It would be a relief to have May, Eric and Philip living there. Like most Londoners, they were stoical but worn down, looking unhealthy from a basic diet.

He'd risked sending Sophie a letter proposing a time and place to meet, feeling nervous as he waited in his car at the end of her road at 6pm, as he'd suggested. For all he knew, Tom had come back and seen his letter. She wrote to him regularly, telling him about their daughter, how well she was doing and thanking him for the difference his money made to their lives. He'd seen pictures of Alice, but he hadn't seen her in the flesh for at least eight months. Would she recognise him?

By 6.10pm, just as he was beginning to assume that she either hadn't got his letter or couldn't leave the flat for some reason, he saw them walking quickly down the road. As she came close to the car she gestured with the palm of her hand and walked on past. He watched in the rear-view mirror as they turned left and walked out of sight. Obviously she was worried about being watched; he drove off, turned right and then right again, and there they were, waiting by the side of the road. As soon as they'd jumped into the back of the Morris she began to give him directions and didn't stop until he'd driven for at least ten minutes. He turned around to look at them.

"That was very cloak and dagger! It's so wonderful to see you two, you're both looking so well. Have you been looking after your mum, Alice?"

He looked at Sophie, who was looking much healthier than when he'd last seen her. When he smiled and mouthed, "You okay?" she smiled back and nodded, but he had to restrain himself from leaning across and hugging her. Alice was aged six and she would quickly pick up any indication that Sophie and her Uncle John were being over-friendly.

"We thought it was better to meet Uncle John away from nosey old Mrs Dawson, didn't we, Alice? She sits at her front window all day long, watching everyone. It's creepy, like she's spying on us."

She gave John a long stare to emphasise the meaning of her words; Mrs Dawson was keeping an eye on Sophie for Tom. John remembered Sophie had once told him that Tom was pals with a neighbour across the street. As they sat in his car making small talk, John wondered if it would be better not to see Sophie rather than meet in this clandestine way. Alice hardly said a word to him, obviously confused why her mum had brought her out just to sit in the back of Uncle John's car; she liked him, but rarely saw him these days.

Two days later, back in Malvern College after helping to move May and Eric into his flat, he steeled himself to write to Sophie.

Dear Sophie,

It was lovely to see you and Alice two days ago. She's growing up fast and is so lucky to have you as her mum. But I felt how tense you were and saw that Alice seemed unsure of why we'd met in my car. I hate to say this, but it's obvious that life would be less stressful for you two if we didn't meet again in London until the situation with Tom is resolved. This won't change my contributions to Alice's care and well-being. I love you both very much and hope with all my heart that we can be together again one day.
Stay safe my darling,
John xx

Dear John,

Thank you for your letter. I felt so upset after reading it that Alice kept asking me what was wrong. Now I've had time to think more clearly, I can see, very sadly, that what you're saying makes sense. I will of course continue to write regularly with news about Alice. She's got a place in primary school from this September so I'm going to look for part-time work after she settles into school.

I asked Tom for a divorce again two days ago, trying to persuade him that he won't be able to marry anyone else until he divorces me. He flew into a rage, saying that being married to me has put him off women for life! I know that's a lie, as he sometimes sleeps with a married woman he met in the pub. Her husband is away fighting in the desert and Tom needs to watch himself. God only knows what medical condition he's faked to avoid being called up. I pray that once this war is over we can be happy together again. My feelings for you haven't changed one bit – I've missed you since you went back to Malvern.

All my love,

Sophie xx

During the middle of August John began to pick up news of a huge tank battle between the advancing Red Army and the Germans at Kursk, in Russia. After heavy losses on both sides, the Soviet Army eventually routed the Germans and began advancing again. Soon afterwards, on 3rd September 1943, the British Eighth Army landed in mainland Italy. He was now certain that the Allies were going to win, eventually.

28

VE DAY, 8TH MAY 1945

He'd arranged to meet Sophie outside the entrance to Lillywhites sports store in Piccadilly Circus. John guessed there'd be a large crowd but wasn't expecting anything this size – his bus was stuck half a mile away in Regent Street – so he walked the rest of the way. They hadn't seen each other for over a month and he was longing to celebrate today's news together.

In August 1944, increasingly frustrated and angry with her husband-in-name-only, Sophie had given Tom an ultimatum. He was now living openly with another woman and his visits to see Alice were so infrequent she no longer wished to see him.

"Seeing as it's common knowledge in the East End that you're now permanently sharing a bed with another man's wife, I'm letting you know that when John moves back to London in the next few weeks we will be seeing each other as often as we feel like. Alice will be seeing much more of him too and can make up her own mind what she wants to call him. I advise you not to cause any trouble about this. I've gone to some lengths to find out the name, regiment and posting of your mistress's husband and will make sure he finds out about his wife's affair if you do. I hope we understand each other."

Tom swore and raged at her but she knew it was all a bluff. There'd been no scenes or confrontations with Tom when John began to visit Sophie and sometimes stay the night. It had been seven years since they'd last made love – the night Alice had been conceived – and they joked with each other as they pointed out the changes time had brought to their bodies.

Once the Allies had successfully established a strong beachhead in Northern France after the D-Day landings, John was instructed to relocate from Malvern to London to oversee the adaptions needed to the Chain Radar system in Kent to support the offensive in France. It was wonderful news, as he could live in London, see Sophie, Alice and May and take a train to Dover when needed. He'd paid attention when Sophie had gently warned him not to push things too fast with his daughter, who was now seven years old; he experienced their developing relationship with a sense of joy and wonder.

Finally emerging into the crush of celebrating humanity at Piccadilly Circus, he realised that finding Sophie wasn't going to be as easy as he'd imagined. He needn't have worried – she was holding a sign over the heads of the crowd outside Lillywhites with *Sophie's here* written in large black letters.

As he worked his way through the crowd towards the sign, he'd occasionally catch a glimpse of her head and shoulders in a gap in the crowd, looking excited and anxious. She remained a beautiful woman, but her face now showed, not just the passing years, but signs of how tough life had been for her since Alice was born. They'd met seventeen years ago, been lovers for six and then an elemental part of each other's lives for the last twelve. Against the odds, they'd had a daughter. He'd never loved or admired another human being like this and he told himself every day not to blow their chance of happiness ever again.

Finally together, he kissed her then lifted her in the air, the crowd cheering around them.

After soaking up the atmosphere for a couple of hours, they walked the four miles back to John's flat, enjoying the variations in mood as they went from street to street. Getting out the bottle of champagne he'd put in the fridge specially, they drank to the end of the war in Europe and their future life together. Hearing the family next door laughing in their back garden, they took the bottle outside and shared it with the parents, finally collapsing exhausted into bed at midnight to the sounds of a street party.

"Have you given any more thought to bringing things to a head with Tom?"

John and Sophie were sitting around his breakfast table a month later, having a leisurely powdered scrambled eggs on toast. He'd raised the question they'd been asking each other over the last nine months; when was the right time for Sophie to start divorce proceedings? The marriage had effectively ended years ago, but Tom had always refused to divorce her out of spite. Alice never expressed a wish to see him anymore, although she still called him Daddy sometimes.

"No, I'm afraid not. I just can't face it at the moment, John."

"I understand. But there is something else I wanted to ask you."

He paused, then went on.

"Do you remember I told you that I combined my work as a scientist in Berlin with a sideline spying on German scientists?"

"Yes, John, I believe that you mentioned it once or twice. I also remember that you nearly ended up in a German gaol and lost Ilse," she replied sardonically.

Pausing again at the memory of his final goodbye with Ilse, he carried on.

"Well, there's a strong rumour going around that Army Intelligence is recruiting British scientists to join a team that's being put together to go to Berlin for a couple of months and interrogate German scientists who want to defect to us. Obviously MI6 officers will try to sift out those with dubious motives, but they've realised they'll also need people like me who can interview them and verify their scientific bona fides. If it's true, I was thinking of applying, especially as I speak reasonable German, but I wanted to ask you what you think first, as it means I'll be away for three months."

He could tell from the slight frown on her face that this wasn't the most welcome news, but she quickly recovered.

"I'm a little surprised as you'd said that your work developing radar for civilian airports is really taking off – sorry about the unintended pun. But three months isn't that long, so of course you should apply, if it interests you."

"It really does. If I'm honest, I admit that part of the attraction is the thought of being involved in something that's intelligence-related again. Obviously we'll keep up a front of gaining their trust, while trying to catch them out and reveal something that will give them away. I can't deny it, the deception aspect intrigues me, just as it did when I was involved in unmasking that German spy in Swanage five years ago.

"Which is odd, because I believe I'm a pretty honest person, basically. What do you think?"

Sophie studied him with a teasingly enigmatic look on her face, taking her time.

"I think you are, John, or our relationship wouldn't have survived. But ever since you told me what happened in Berlin and Swanage, I've found it puzzling. It's always seemed out of character."

29

SEPTEMBER 1945, BRITISH SECTOR, BERLIN

"Fancy a pint in the bar at seven, John?"

He turned to his colleague.

"I could definitely use one after that landing, Harry. I'll see you down there after I've checked into my room."

John looked at his watch: 6.15. His flight from Croydon had landed an hour ago and the selected group of scientists had spent most of their time since then being thrown around in the back of an army truck, before finally arriving at their hotel in the British sector. He was still struggling to stop the remaining contents of his stomach from making a return journey. Just as he'd begun to recover from the turbulence over the Channel and adjust to the deafening noise inside the Dakota, the pilot had announced their descent into Berlin's Tempelhof Airport.

"Twenty minutes to landing, gentlemen. I'm afraid it's going to be rather bumpy on the way in, as long as some trigger-happy Russian doesn't get us first."

The thought of a heavy drinking session that evening made him feel queasy again, but he'd sensed a wariness towards him from some of the group and didn't want to seem standoffish. They were all scientists, recruited by Army Intelligence for a three-month assignment in Berlin, charged with interrogating German scientists who were desperate to come to Britain.

Sinking into a chair in reception while he waited for his room to be ready, he reflected on the scenes he'd witnessed on his journey through the city.

The colossal scale of the physical damage hadn't surprised him, as they'd had a briefing on the extent of the devastation caused by Allied bombing and Russian artillery from a junior diplomat at the Foreign Office before leaving.

But the pasty-faced Oxbridge graduate with Brylcreemed hair had been unforthcoming about the human collateral damage, so he'd been shocked by the squalor he'd witnessed amongst people on the streets as their truck made its way slowly from Tempelhof to their hotel along roads piled high with rubble. Almost all looked malnourished, dirty and conveyed a sense of utter hopelessness. Gangs of women clearing rubble by hand, seemingly making little impact on their enormous task, stared blankly at John with expressionless eyes sunk into pale, gaunt faces, lank hair tied back with scarves and rags. Many looked far too old for such hard physical labour. When he'd commented on the women's condition to the army captain escorting his group, he'd replied, "These people have experienced unimaginable trauma during the last six months in the battle for Berlin. Many will have lost either family, friends and home – or all three. Now, they're citizens of a defeated nation that the rest of the world despises. Given that, I would imagine you either fall into a fatal despair, or do whatever it takes to survive each day – no matter how old you are."

They'd finally turned into a large square, dominated by the

bullet-scarred façade of their hotel on the opposite side. He'd thought he recognised it from his time in the city before the war, but couldn't be sure. Many of the surrounding buildings had their front walls blown out, opening the rooms and their contents to public view, like gigantic dolls' houses. Another group of women were clearing rubble in the centre of the square; their collective labour seemed to be forging a sense of defiant resilience as they'd stared straight at the occupants of the army truck.

His thoughts were interrupted by the receptionist calling his name.

"Herr Samson, please collect your key, your room is now ready."

Picking up his battered leather suitcase, he walked up the grand, peeling, central staircase to the first floor. They'd been advised not to take the lift, which – unsurprisingly – still needed new parts five months after the war had ended. The hotel had apparently remained open throughout the war, surviving the Allied bombing almost intact; unlike the majority of buildings in the part of Berlin they'd just driven through, which had been reduced to rubble.

Imagining the worst, he unlocked the door to his room and pushed it open, but was pleasantly surprised to find it clean and tidy, with fresh linen. He filled the sink in the corner by the window with warm water, washed his hands and face and lay on the bed. *Was this a mistake, stuck in Berlin with a bunch of boring scientists for three months, cut off from Sophie and Alice?*

But he knew he was indulging in dishonest speculation. The cloak and dagger aspect of the role continued to excite him. Being in Berlin at this time would somehow tie together the last twenty-year chapter of his life.

Looking up at the fan turning lethargically above him, he forced himself to get off the bed, straightened his tie, locked his room and descended the stairs to join the others.

"At last! There you are, John. Come and join us, what can I get you?"

He walked over to their table and looked around the crowded lounge full of British officers and their female companions. The background noise of clipped middle-class English accents was only interrupted by the drinks orders shouted by German waiters and waitresses to the bar staff.

"Sorry, Mike, I made the mistake of lying down for a second and must have dozed off. I'll have *ein grosse bier, danke schon.*"

"Okay, clever dick, I heard you spoke German. I'm assuming that's a large beer. *Fräulein, ein grosse bier, bitte.*"

The others manoeuvred their chairs to make space for him around the table they'd grabbed earlier. He smiled at them and raised his glass.

"Cheers. Here's to a successful and safe time in Berlin, for all of us."

"Cheers!"

As mugs were banged together across the table, Harry looked at him and said, "Here's to us. But it's an odd toast, isn't it? I mean, the whole area is run by the British Army, it should be safe. No German would risk attacking us."

The others were now all looking at him, questioningly. *If I'm going to disabuse them, now's the time.*

"Before I came here, I tracked down a friend of mine in the police force who'd just returned from Berlin. He didn't mince his words. There are hundreds of thousands of homeless, starving people in the city, many flooding in from the Russian sector or the countryside. Food is scarce, few people have jobs and in that situation they'll do what they have to in order to survive. The black market is thriving, you can buy anything or anyone for a few packets of cigarettes; robberies, murder, rape and prostitution are soaring."

He glanced at the women hanging off the arms of two officers on the next table and carried on.

"There's no police force yet. The soldiers stationed here aren't policemen; they'll try and ensure there's an impression of order on the surface, but that doesn't reflect the reality. Like I said, stay safe."

They were all due to report to Colonel Smart's office at British Army HQ, Berlin, at 08:00 hours tomorrow morning. John had another half litre and then called it a night. His frank remarks had clearly put some noses out of joint; he'd make a fresh start in the morning.

Three weeks later

Their mission was going well; he'd interviewed, interrogated and assessed almost thirty potential German 'defectors' in the last three weeks and approved half of them for transfer to Britain. For many, the US was their preferred option, but even Britain was better than staying put and hugely preferred to the Soviet Union.

He was finding what was left of Berlin more interesting than he'd thought he would, if 'interesting' was the right word given the scale of the destruction, filth, violence and crime. In his time off, he explored the city within the British and American sectors, searching out the streets and areas he hoped to recognise from nineteen years ago. But he was acutely aware this wasn't a safe city; as he'd reminded his colleagues in the bar on their first night in the hotel; British and American soldiers weren't policemen and the officer's uniform he wore offered little protection.

The destruction and desolation were far worse than anything he'd seen in London and made it difficult for him to relate his memory of Berlin in 1926 to the landscape he was exploring now. Unfortunately, his old university and the infamous library were in the Soviet sector. He needed special papers to go there, but Kreuzberg and Tiergarten were open to him. Wandering around an almost undamaged street in Kreuzberg on a surprisingly warm Sunday afternoon, taking in the relatively unscathed homes, he realised he was in the street where Ilse's flat used to be. Walking slowly along the row of tall, imposing houses, he stopped. There it was; the same door, the same casement window to her bed-sitting room on the second floor. It was as if the bombing and shelling had passed this street by.

As he stood lost in thoughts of Ilse living there twenty years ago and the awful uncertainty around her survival, a middle-aged woman appeared at the front door. Seeing a British officer closely examining the building, she unleashed a barrage of obscenities, her features distorted with anger. She finished with "If you're thinking of requisitioning this building you can fuck off."

His response in German surprised her – she'd clearly thought he wouldn't understand.

"I don't want your building, Frau. My girlfriend lived here twenty years ago and I have happy memories of this place."

"Well, she's not here anymore, so you can bugger off now."

Angrily, he shot back, "Of course she isn't. She's almost certainly dead, killed by the Nazis for the crime of being Jewish."

"Jewish! They're responsible for bringing this misery on the Reich. They forced America to enter the war – we would never have been defeated otherwise. We won't ever accept them back in Germany, so she shouldn't think about returning."

He forced himself to stay calm. One or two other doors had opened, neighbours listening with interest.

"I see you're an unrepentant Nazi. Forget what I said about not requisitioning the building; I will put this house on the list as soon as I get back to my barracks. *Guten Tag.*"

He walked away as she carried on shouting, shaken by the strength of her hate.

Furious with himself for rising to her taunts, he was still feeling unsettled when he returned to his hotel. He went to the bar, saw there was no one else around and bought a beer. He needed time to think, alone.

However vile her outburst had been, he shouldn't let the views of one bitter Berliner distort his perspective, even though she might be saying what a significant number of Germans think, but weren't prepared to say out loud. Her words kept nagging at him, though. For several years he'd been assuming that Ilse, her husband and her parents must have perished in one of the Nazi death camps. He knew that most of the Jews in Holland had been discovered or betrayed and transported to death camps. Only a few thousand had survived out of several hundred thousand.

Why hadn't he tried to find out if she was alive? If she – or some of her family – had survived, they would most likely be in one of Europe's displacement camps. There were hundreds of such camps and over five million displaced people. Where could he begin? There was someone who might be able to help, if John could persuade him.

"You must understand, John, that Her Majesty's Government didn't send you over to Germany to start searching displacement camps for a long-lost girlfriend."

"She's not long-lost, for God's sake, Colonel. She's almost certainly been exterminated in a death camp."

"Of course, sorry, awful choice of words. A terrible business. I know that almost all the Jews in Holland were first sent to the Westerbork transit camp, which was liberated by the Canadians in April. I'm prepared to give you an afternoon off to make enquiries with the Red Cross, who I believe are compiling the names of all those found alive in the liberated camps. But that's as much time as I can spare you for."

He spent the next two afternoons at the Red Cross centre in Berlin with a helpful and fastidious Swiss gentleman, going through the records of all inmates present when the Westerbork camp was liberated. When that produced no one by the name of Ilse Lipsky, Ilse Donetz or just Lipsky, the Swiss gentleman then rang the Red

Cross central register for those liberated from the death camps to which the Westerbork inmates had been sent. Again, there was no record of anyone with those names. Finally, he contacted the United Nations Rehabilitation Administration's Central Tracking Bureau. Again, nothing.

"I'm sorry, Herr Samson, but you mustn't give up hope. Thousands will have slipped through the net, so this doesn't mean that Fräulein Lipsky hasn't survived. I will leave this as a live enquiry on our records, so if you leave a contact address the Red Cross will get in touch with you if we hear anything."

He owed Sophie a letter and took an unexpected gap in his schedule caused by a mix-up between the British and French sectors to write to her. They'd agreed that he still needed to express himself carefully; Tom wasn't above returning to her house unexpectedly and going through her mail. He'd just finished when Corporal Best knocked on his door.

"Colonel Smart wants to see you in his office now, sir. I think he's got something up his sleeve for you."

30

THE HAND OF FRIENDSHIP

"Sorry, sir, I don't understand. You want me to go to the Russian sector! Why would they risk giving the British the opportunity of persuading 'their' German scientists to come over to us?"

For the second time, John found himself in Colonel Smart's office on the receiving end of decisions made by the higher echelons of the British Army. Although a trip to the Soviet sector could be interesting.

"Calm down, Samson. We're trying to establish an effective joint administration with the Russians in Berlin, and it's important we build trust. They're obviously doing the same as we are – recruiting German scientists and engineers – but are short of fluent German speakers with a scientific background. They've come to us for help and we're extending the hand of friendship. Your hand, to be precise."

The colonel smiled at his own little joke.

"I'd like you to be ready to go at short notice once your papers are cleared. I've agreed with my Russian opposite number that we can spare you for up to five days; report to Colonel Volkov when you arrive and he will brief you. I understand he speaks some English."

"Do I have a choice, Colonel?"

"Well, you and your colleagues have effectively been put under my command while you're working in Berlin, so no, you don't, I'm afraid."

"Understood. In that case, I'll await my papers and try to learn a few useful phrases in Russian."

John headed straight for the officers' mess, hoping that none of the usual boors were there at three in the afternoon.

"A pint and a whisky chaser, please, Freddy, and have one yourself."

"Thank you, sir. You look as if you've just found sixpence and lost half a crown."

"Is it obvious? I've just been informed by the colonel that I'm being sent to the Soviet sector for five days as part of operation 'extend the hand of friendship'. I hope they don't bite it off."

"Make sure you bring back some Russian vodka, sir. I'll give you a good price for it."

"I didn't hear that, Freddy. Just the one case?"

They both laughed.

Two days later, papers in his kitbag and mentally prepared for the unexpected, he was driven the short journey to the checkpoint into the Soviet sector. He'd guessed that the devastation to buildings and infrastructure in the east would be even worse than the west, caused by Russian tanks and artillery as the Red Army fought its way street by street into the heart of Berlin. He'd also heard that the population would look even more malnourished and desperate, and that there would be very few men under the age of forty as the Russians were allegedly transporting them east to slave labour camps.

But he hadn't been expecting this.

"Welcome to the Soviet sector, Major Samson. The USSR truly thanks you for your support." Colonel Volkov embraced him in a firm hug, kissing him on both cheeks.

"You look surprised, Major. Don't you have women officers in the British Army? I'm Colonel Natasha Volkov, in charge of the programme for the re-education of German scientists. Come with me, please, let's drink to the success of our enterprise."

She was about five foot four, looked barely thirty years old and smelled of lavender soap. Her angelic, slightly Asiatic features made a strange contrast with the austere Red Army uniform. John hurried after her as she turned on her heels and set off towards a bullet-scarred, two-storey brick building, the Red Flag hanging over the entrance. *Keep an open mind, John. The next few days could be interesting.*

"Forgive me, Colonel. My commanding officer told me you were a man. There are women in the British Army, but they don't serve in front-line positions. He also said that you speak some English, but that was an understatement, your English is good. I'm very pleased to meet you, and would be glad to join you in a toast. Although I don't usually drink vodka at this time of the day."

Colonel Volkov looked at him quizzically, then smiled.

"After a week here, I think you will."

As he finally caught up with her, John grasped the opportunity to maintain their conversation.

"Are you named after Natasha Rostova, one of the great characters in Russian literature?"

Colonel Volkov stopped in the doorway. She studied him for a moment, came to a decision and chuckled.

"You're referring to *War and Peace*, of course. I doubt that my parents had that character in mind when they decided on my name – it's a story about cruel, privileged aristocrats and bourgeois individualists."

John groaned inwardly as she paused. Had he misjudged Colonel Volkov?

"However, just between us, I've read it three times."

Relieved, he followed her past the two bored sentries, then up the stairs to the first floor. Her office consisted of a battered wooden desk, two chairs, several filing cabinets and a wine rack holding several bottles of vodka. Stalin stared out from the wall behind her desk, and three unframed photographs stood on the shelf above the fireplace; an old couple in farming clothes, Natasha holding a dog on a lead, and a good-looking man in uniform.

"May I?" he said, indicating the photos and looking at Natasha.

"Of course. The picture on the right is of my parents, taken on their small farm before the war. They were murdered by the Nazis in the first wave of the invasion. That's me with my dog, Olga, on the left, and the third is my fiancé, Vladislav. He was a tank commander, assumed killed in the battle of Kursk two years ago – although his body was never found."

"I'm sorry."

"Millions of my countrymen and women have been killed in the war, Major. Before that, millions died of starvation during the famine of 1930–33. Russian people have a fatalistic acceptance of death. We were planning to have five children and grow old together, but the Nazis wiped out our dreams. I hope I meet someone else one day, but if I don't, life will carry on. Enough of this talk, Major, *Na Zdorovie!*"

John took the small glass of vodka she'd handed him and downed it, knowing there would be several to follow. Three shots later, he waved the fourth one away.

"I think we should discuss my role now, Colonel, while I'm still sober."

Natasha made it clear that he would be accompanied in every interview by a German-speaking Russian officer who would make a verbatim record of all the questions and answers, "Just so you sneaky British don't try and take some of them for yourself."

While there was little chance of that happening, as soon as the interviews began, it was clear to John that the men he was interviewing weren't exactly desperate to emigrate to the Soviet Union. Without being explicit, all of them indicated that they had no desire to be transported to some far-flung scientific outpost in Siberia. He realised that his involvement in these interviews made him partly complicit in their fate; but he still carried on.

Suddenly, the deception inherent in the interviews made him feel shallow and ashamed.

Depressed by the role he'd been playing, he still thought it wise to accept Natasha's invitation to join her and her junior officers in their dining room for the evening meal. The food was surprisingly tasty and well cooked – borscht, beef stroganoff dumplings and pancakes. God knows where they were getting the ingredients; of course, the officers must have channels to the black market and made sure they looked after themselves.

He'd heard stories about the volume of vodka that Russian soldiers consumed and was determined not to be cajoled into keeping up with them. But in spite of joining in with only one in every three rounds, he staggered to bed on that first night, leaving before anyone else, to shouts of derision. On the second evening, he noticed that Natasha had changed into a smarter uniform, a Russian version of a British officer's mess dress. None of the others had bothered and were constantly looking between him and Natasha and joking with each other. He understood little Russian, but he assumed they were teasing her for trying to impress him.

Suddenly, Natasha pushed her chair back, stood up and berated them for several minutes. Whatever she said, there was no more teasing after that.

As they left after the meal, he asked her what she'd said to them. She looked at him with a straight face and said, "I told them that if I wanted to sleep with the British officer that was my business, not theirs, and anyone who disagrees can be transferred to Siberia at any time if they prefer the climate there."

He looked at her and burst out laughing.

"Your directness is much appreciated, Colonel. Thank you for another delicious meal. I wish you goodnight."

There was no sign of Colonel Volkov when he went into breakfast the next morning, but just as he was finishing his fried eggs and pancakes she walked in, came straight over to him and announced that he wouldn't be needed until the afternoon.

"You are free to leave the compound, but make sure you have your papers with you, Major. I don't want you getting shot, it will look very bad for me."

Studying her expression for signs of irony, he had a thought.

"Are we far from Treptower Park?"

Colonel Volkov looked at him questioningly.

"About a kilometre, but why are you interested in going there?"

"I used to go there sometimes when I lived in Berlin twenty years ago. It would be interesting to see what's left of it now."

"What were you doing in Berlin at that time?"

I was spying on German scientists. "I was doing research in atomic physics at Friedrich Wilhelm University, although unfortunately I had to leave before it was completed. Can I go?"

"Unfortunately that area is out of bounds to foreigners, Major."

He felt surprisingly deflated, then had an idea and decided to ask her before she had time to think of the reason to say no.

"Could you spare one of your officers to escort me? I would only need an hour or so."

He could see the word 'Niet' forming on her lips, but she swallowed it and said, "I could escort you. If you want to go, get your papers and meet me here in five minutes."

Twenty minutes later, they were entering the park. He didn't think he'd recognise any of the features; Berlin had suffered constant air raids and bombing for over three years. The park was in a terrible state, huge trees split into massive splinters by the rain of high explosives and a large mound of earth in the centre that was possibly the site of a mass grave. But the lake was there, drained of water by the residents of Berlin as supplies were cut off, its banks still clear enough.

The Colonel looked at him, puzzled.

"Why did you want to see this mess, Major, it's more like a rubbish tip than a park. There must be a thousand more interesting things to see."

He paused. How much should he tell this unreadable Russian officer? Given her role here, she was probably attached to Army Intelligence. He realised that if she'd been a man, there was no chance he'd share personal information. On the other hand, building a less frosty connection might be to his advantage, if she reciprocated. She might let something slip that could be of use to British Intelligence.

"Twenty years ago, I used to meet the woman I was hoping to marry here. We'd walk along the banks of the Spree, then have a picnic by the lake and take out a rowing boat."

Colonel Volkov looked genuinely intrigued.

"So what happened?"

"Adolf Hitler, a World War and the methodical extermination of millions of Jews."

She said nothing for several minutes as they walked on, following what remained of the path that led to the lake. The sickly sweet smell of decomposing human remains became stronger as they approached the mound of earth.

Finally, she broke the silence.

"Vladislav had a Jewish grandparent. He remembered visiting their house as a child with his parents, and they would sometimes all sit down for the Seder meal together. He was very proud that the Bolsheviks outlawed anti-Semitism, which was encouraged under the Tsarist regime. Did you know that, under the Tsar, Jewish families had to hand over their eldest son to be conscripted into the Russian Army for life?"

He didn't, but he did know that although anti-Semitism was outlawed by the Bolsheviks, it was still endemic throughout the Soviet Union.

"I didn't know that. I'm afraid that anti-Jewish sentiment is still alive in Britain. There was an unofficial ban on Jewish immigration to Britain in the 1930s, even when it was clear long before the war started that Jews were being persecuted in Germany."

To his surprise, Natasha turned to face him and grasped his hands in hers.

"You are a good, compassionate man, Major. But I understand the event you're thinking about happened some years ago, and millions of people have watched their loved ones die since then, unable to help them. If we all continue to blame ourselves, then society would grind to a halt through the weight of our collective guilt.

"We have a saying in Russia: *Nichevo*. It means 'Don't worry, let things take their course'. It sums up the spirit of the Russian people, although I believe people from the West find it fatalistic. But maybe you can learn something from us on this visit. You cannot change past events, so perhaps stop feeling guilty and embrace whatever comes your way."

At this point she released his hands and threw her arms around him in a crushing bear hug, shouting, "*Nichevo!!*"

In spite of himself, he burst out laughing, hugged her back and yelled out at the top of his voice, "*Nichevo!*"

They released each other, a little embarrassed, and walked on in silence.

After several minutes, she said, "Has there been anyone special in your life since then? A lover, girlfriend, wife?"

An hour ago he would have been astonished by such a personal question, but now it seemed a perfectly obvious thing to ask.

"There is someone I love who I hope to build a life with. We met many years ago and talked about a future together, but I couldn't give her what she really wanted at the time. I didn't realise then that I wanted that too; I was a fool and she married someone else. We have a child together and although her marriage is over her husband makes things difficult.

"Have you been close to anyone since Vladislav died?"

Natasha just kept on walking without saying anything. Eventually, she looked at him and said, "Not unless you count having a drunken encounter with a comrade over two months ago when we ended up staying overnight in an abandoned hotel when our vehicle broke down."

"These things happen in wartime. As long as no one gets hurt, then my philosophy is to enjoy the memory."

She looked at him knowingly and said, "This must remain between us, Major. I have more than just a memory from that night, if you understand me."

"Oh, I see. What will you do?"

"I'm determined to keep my child, but I know that I'll have to fight my superiors. The Red Army might treat women as equals in theory, but the thought of a pregnant woman marching around the place is too much for them to contemplate."

He gave her a broad smile.

"I wish you well, Colonel. Both of you."

There was little conversation between them during the evening meal. He was tired after four long interviews with increasingly despondent scientists in the afternoon, and excused himself early. But he found it difficult to get to sleep, dwelling on the difficult time that undoubtedly lay ahead for Natasha and musing on the morality of his role facilitating the transfer of unwilling scientists to the Soviet Union. He was glad to be going back.

They maintained a professional relationship for his last two days, meeting each morning to discuss his schedule for the day's interviews. As he was packing to leave, a corporal came to his room with a message from the colonel to *'please come to my office before you leave'.*

"I wanted to thank you before you left, Major. We have all benefited greatly from your work here during the last five days. I appreciated your expertise and discretion and would like you to accept this case of Russian vodka, with my gratitude. I have written an order on this note, saying you must be allowed to take it out of the Soviet sector!"

"That's very generous, Colonel. Thank you for taking such good care of me, I will take back happy memories of my time here. Please look after yourselves. I hope our two nations will continue in this spirit of co-operation."

As he walked into the mess and put the case on the bar, Freddy almost dropped the beer glass he was wiping.

"Don't say I don't deliver on my promises, Freddy. Compliments of Colonel Volkov, for services rendered. I'm handing it over to you to make the appropriate arrangements."

"Bloody hell, sir! That's the best stuff, too. Exactly what services did you render to get that?"

"That's strictly confidential, I'm afraid."

31

NOVEMBER 1945, THE LEAVING PARTY

By mid-November it was clear to everyone in John's group that their mission in Berlin was running out of German scientists to interview. Initially, those considered to be a potential security risk had to be weeded out. Some of the original group who had expressed a wish to emigrate to Britain had changed their minds and decided to stay in the Allied sector of Berlin which was going to be run by the Western powers for the foreseeable future. Order was slowly – very slowly – being re-established. Others had been accepted by the British and then poached by the Americans, causing a huge rift which threatened to destroy the trust between the two Allies until a high-level meeting was arranged to sort out the bad feeling. Although some interviewees kept coming forwards, John began to hope that he'd be returning to Britain within a month at most.

His buoyant mood at the prospect of getting back to his old job and seeing Sophie and Alice again was flattened one bleak mid-

November morning when he received a letter from the Red Cross. Heart pounding, he opened it.

Herr Samson,
It is with great sadness that I have to inform you that we've received confirmation that Ilse Donetz (née Lipsky), her husband and her mother, Frau Lipsky, were all transported to the Sobibor death camp in December 1944 and didn't survive. Her father had already perished from ill health in Westerbork. I'm so sorry to be the one to tell you this. I understand that the number of Jews deliberately murdered by the Nazis is thought to exceed six million; we may never know the final figure. The world must ensure that such horrors never happen again.
Our sincere condolences,
Red Cross Resettlement Centre

He'd tried to prepare himself for this news, of course. During the last two months rumours of the extent of the Nazis' programme for the mass extermination of Jews and other groups had been horrifyingly confirmed. He was a realist and a scientist and he knew the odds were stacked against finding Ilse alive. But he'd continued to hope.

He walked back to his room, poured a glass of Scotch and relived his memories of the remarkable human being he'd last seen walking out of his cell nineteen years ago.

Two days later, Colonel Smart gathered the scientists and their support team together, informed them that their mission was complete, thanked them for their dedicated work for their country and told them they'd be going home as soon as transport could be organised.

"I've arranged to give you all a leaving party in the mess this Friday. Enjoy yourselves, you deserve it. I've put ten quid behind the bar, after that it's buy your own drinks."

John and a few colleagues made an effort to decorate the mess. It took his mind off Ilse. With the help of two local women who'd formed 'liaisons' with colleagues who'd already gone home to their wives and families, the dining hall was turned into something slightly less austere. Freddy made sure Colonel Smart's tenner went a lot further than it should have and everyone got extremely drunk on a mixture of beer, vodka and schnapps. Everyone except for John, the officer on guard duty and Ursula, one of the local women, who'd had a liaison with one of his colleagues called Samuel.

At some point after midnight John forced himself to make a start clearing up the worst of the chaos. Relaxing in an armchair with a vodka and orange, Ursula got up and joined him.

"I never thought I'd see a British officer getting his hands dirty cleaning up other people's mess. Let me help."

"That's very good of you, Ursula, the more the merrier. I'm not really an officer, just a civilian currently employed by the army. You could start by clearing away the empty bottles, thank you."

"Would you mind if I put the rubbish in the bin and collected the uneaten food, please? I'd like to take it back to my family, if that's all right? We're luckier than most – my mother looks after my daughter when I go to work and queue for food. But we go hungry most days, and our rooms are freezing."

John looked at her, feeling ashamed. It hadn't crossed his mind to wonder what Ursula and her friend would think about the comfortable surroundings and the free food. Life in Berlin was going to remain very tough for families like hers in the foreseeable future, especially this coming winter. Only now did he notice the efforts she'd made to disguise her unwashed hair and frayed dress. She'd obviously come to grab any leftover food.

"Please take the food back, Ursula. Is there anything else you'd like?"

"Do you mean that? If you have any blankets you could spare, that would be wonderful. My daughter and mother get so cold at night."

"There are spare blankets in my quarters that I'm not using. You're welcome to have those. I'll get them when we've finished here. If the sentry stops you, say I gave them to you as your daughter is sick."

They carried on clearing the debris away, Ursula carefully separating the uneaten food from the rest and parcelling it up.

After they'd got the room into a condition that wouldn't cause a walk-out by the cleaners in the morning and thrown the last of the rubbish out, John said, "We've done more than enough now, Ursula, let's have a toast to our labours. What would you like?"

"That's very tempting, but I should get back or my mother will be worried. Do you mind?"

"Of course not. I wasn't thinking. Let's get the blankets."

Ursula collected her coat, which seemed to have more patches than original material. As they walked three hundred yards to his room in the freezing air, he made a decision.

"May I ask what happened to your daughter's father?"

Ursula looked suspicious, then decided to trust him.

"We don't know – an awful situation to be in. He's officially missing in action, presumed dead, or in a Soviet labour camp. For his sake, I hope it's not the last one. But until he's found alive or dead, I can't grieve for my husband properly, my daughter doesn't know if her papa is coming back and I can't collect my war widow's allowance."

"What's your daughter's name, Ursula?"

"Ilse."

John visibly flinched.

"Are you okay?"

"Twenty years ago, when I was working in Berlin, I fell in love with a young woman of that name. It didn't last, and just last week I learnt from the Red Cross that she was murdered in Sobibor."

Ursula looked stricken.

"We, all Germans, have to face the horror of what we did. The world shouldn't ever forgive us, and probably won't. You've probably heard some of my countrymen and women telling you they knew nothing about the mass murder. That's rubbish, we all knew that something was going on, me included. I just convinced myself I couldn't do anything to stop it. It was too dangerous, and I had my daughter and mother to think about."

John was impressed by Ursula's openness about her fellow citizens' culpability. It was unusual in his experience. She carried on. "And then came the Russians."

"I understand some Russian soldiers treated women horribly."

"My daughter was four when three of them burst into our flat. All of us had heard the stories about what these young men, fuelled by hatred and vodka, were doing to women and girls. I was terrified but I had to protect my daughter. They took turns with me, then two raped my mother. When one went for Ilse, I pushed him away and he held a knife to my throat. Ilse saw all this, of course. Luckily, the other two pulled him away and they left, wrenching my wedding ring off as they went."

Unable to think of anything to say except "I'm so sorry," John felt her tense as he put his arm around her as they walked to his room.

She followed him into his cosy room and looked enviously around at the washbasin, toiletries, mirror, armchairs, electric heater and kettle.

"The blankets are in this cupboard. Would you like a hot drink?"

He turned and saw Ursula sitting on his bed, removing her stockings. She looked sad and disappointed. Suddenly understanding, he said, "Stop, please, Ursula! I don't want that! Please, put your stockings back on while I get something out of the safe."

He went to a small safe in the corner of the room where records of his interviews with German scientists were kept and took ten black market dollars out.

"I want you to take this. Please, I can spare it, and it would mean a lot to me if you'd accept. If it helps, take it for Ilse, for her future."

Tears began to run down Ursula's cheeks, then she started to laugh.

"You don't know what this means to us, John. Thank you from my heart. I obviously chose the wrong Englishman to hook up with; Samuel's breath smells and he takes too long."

They burst out laughing, then she leapt off the bed and hugged him.

He walked her to the gate.

"Ilse and your mama are very lucky to have you. Goodbye, Ursula."

"Goodbye, John."

Three days later, John learnt that his group would be flown back in another three days on a Dakota which would otherwise be flying back empty. He was pondering how to spend his last days in Berlin when he received a message to go to Colonel Smart's office.

"Come in, John, please sit down. I'm sure you're looking forward to going home. I've just received a message from Colonel Volkov, who you liaised with recently. She's currently in the British sector, attending a meeting with representatives from all four Allies called to discuss tightening up security at the checkpoints into the Soviet sector. The message reads: *'If Major Samson is available, I would very much like to see him at 14.00 hours this afternoon before I return. I will be at the Russian Consulate and I've told the guards on duty to escort Major Samson into the building when he arrives.'*

"Such a request is almost unheard of, Major. Unless you can think of a reason why a colonel in the Red Army would wish to see you, there may be something of interest she wishes to communicate to us. Did you get any hint of that when you were there?"

"No, Colonel, not really."

"Well, have your wits about you and be prepared for the unexpected. You'd better get your skates on if you're going to get there by 14.00 hours."

Hurrying the half mile to the Russian Consulate, his imagination began to conjure a number of possible scenarios. None of them as far-fetched as the one he was about to hear.

John walked up to the friendlier-looking guard outside the Consulate, held out his ID and said in German, "I'm here to see Colonel Volkov. She said that you would be expecting me and to show me into the Consulate."

As the guard looked blank, his less friendly comrade shouted across, "He doesn't speak German. Or English. Come here and tell me what you want."

"German or English?"

"English."

"I'm here to see Colonel Volkov. She said that you would be expecting me and you're to show me into the Consulate."

The guard looked at his ID, then at John, and said, "Please follow me, Major Samson."

Natasha was waiting by the reception desk as they walked through the door and smiled discreetly when she saw him. Unfriendly Comrade marched up to her, saluted and said, "Major Samson to see you, Comrade Volkov."

"Thank you, Comrade. You can get back to your duties. Thank you for coming at such short notice, Major. Please, come this way."

He followed her up a short flight of stairs past portraits of Stalin, Zhukov and Rokossovsky and led him to an open, but discreet area with two sumptuous-looking sofas.

She beckoned him to sit on one, then sat on the other. Sweeping an arm around their surroundings, she smiled and said, "This used to be a residence for high-ranking Nazis and their mistresses. They looked after themselves, didn't they?"

"It's good to see you again, Natasha. You're looking well. Is everything okay?"

"Yes and no. We can't be overheard here, so we can talk candidly. Many of the rooms have recording devices."

"I was intrigued by your message. I hope this isn't a last-minute request for more interviews, as I'm flying back to Britain in three days' time."

"Nothing of that sort, although I told my superiors that I wanted to check some of the details from two of your interviews. I have a very big favour to ask of you. Since I last saw you I have discovered that it would be impossible for an officer of my rank to keep my baby. The army would insist I have an abortion. My first instinct was to request to be discharged. I've served my country since I joined thirteen years ago, and according to the rules I'm entitled to leave after twelve. So in theory, there should be no problem. In practice, I know it won't be as simple as that."

Increasingly puzzled, John was about to interrupt her, but she cut him off.

"Hear me out, please. I know you must be thinking, 'What has this got to do with me?'. Believe it or not, you are the only person I can completely trust in Berlin. As soon as I put in my request to be discharged from the army, two things will happen. My comrades will start spreading lies about my record in an attempt to discredit me. Much worse, the post-war paranoia in the Party is feeding a culture of searching for traitors and conspirators around every corner and under every desk. The NKVD may see my request as evidence of anti-Soviet tendencies and interrogate me. After that, anything could happen; I can't take the risk that I'll be imprisoned and my baby taken for adoption."

"Are you sure it's safe for us to talk here?"

"Yes, completely safe. Please listen carefully, we don't have much time and I can only say this once. I want to defect to the British, and I want you to persuade Colonel Smart to bring me across. I'm here for two days. I'll give you the time and place where I can be picked up and brought in. I hope you feel that you can vouch for me. I know I'm asking a huge favour, but you're really my only chance of becoming a mother. What do you say?"

Once he'd taken in her shocking proposal and the risk she was prepared to take, he realised he had to give her an answer now. He wanted to help her, but he would be stupid not to consider the risk to himself. Smart would want him to provide a cast-iron reference for her motives and character before her request stood a chance of being taken up. If John got it wrong, and she proved to be a Soviet plant, he'd be responsible for embedding a Soviet spy inside Army Intelligence. His heart and gut told him to trust and help her. His head urged caution.

"You must realise that I can't guarantee that Smart will agree to this. Presumably that will leave you terribly exposed. If you're prepared to take that risk, I will do what you ask."

Natasha's expression gave nothing away.

"When he hears what I've got to tell him I think he'll agree. I'll give you the pick-up details as we walk to the exit, so please make sure you memorise them. This means everything to me; I hope one day we'll meet again and I can thank you properly."

As soon as he returned, John went to see Smart, appraised him of Natasha's request and vouched for her. He thought the chances of him going for it were fifty-fifty at best, but Smart was enthused by the idea and told him he'd arrange for a member of MI6 to pick her up the following day.

Natasha's determination to risk everything for her unborn child had inspired and shamed him. Why hadn't he fought harder for Sophie and Alice? Of course, Sophie had felt bullied and unnerved by Tom's threats to get the Child Welfare Board to take Alice away from her if she tried to divorce him. But why hadn't he tried to take Tom on in court? Sophie would have had a good case on the grounds of his cruelty and adultery.

He went back to his room, wrote her a letter and just made the collection deadline for airmail to England.

> *Dearest Sophie,*
>
> *My job here in Berlin is now ending. I've been thinking very hard about you, me and Alice and our future together. I want to marry you, Sophie, and I'll fight Tom to the finish if he tries to prevent you getting divorced. He doesn't have all the best cards to play, and I'm sure once we threaten to expose his adultery and cruelty with a good lawyer he'll back down. Please think about what I'm saying; I'm coming home for good in three days and we can talk then. No more hiding! I've never stopped loving you and I don't want us to be apart ever again.*
>
> *All my love, darling,*
>
> *John xx*

He was sorting through his belongings the following day, deciding what to take back and what to leave for the German cleaner when there was a knock on his door.

"Sorry to disturb you, sir. Colonel Smart thought you'd want to know that the operation to pick up your contact today was successful. They've been taken to HQ for debriefing."

"Thank you, Corporal."

Grinning involuntarily with delight at the way everything had worked out for Natasha, he paused his packing. Her determination to risk everything to become a mother had touched something deep in him.

32

GOING HOME

The mood amongst his colleagues in the back of the 'three tonner' was upbeat as they drove to Tempelhof Airport, although with high winds and rain forecast all the way to Croydon, few of them were looking forward to the flight. John was longing to see Sophie again; over the last two days he'd kept imagining her reaction as she opened his letter. He had a sense – no, he knew – that Berlin had changed him fundamentally. He'd got to know some inspiring human beings who were coping incredibly well in desperate circumstances. He was thinking about Natasha and Ursula, but also the ordinary people of Berlin. Some had undoubtedly done appalling things. But others, flawed but fundamentally decent, were trying to do their best in a terrible situation. Not always succeeding, sometimes behaving badly. He'd come to accept that he was one of them.

At that moment, Sophie sat writing a letter she thought she'd never be able to write.

She'd only just had confirmation about the tragic event two

days ago, even though it was apparently the talk of the East End. Once over her shock, she'd felt a wave of elation and release. Only now, when she'd steadied her feelings and pardoned herself for her initial euphoria, could she put pen to paper.

Dearest John,

My head is still spinning as I write this. Earlier today I heard that Tom has been killed by the husband of the woman he's been messing around with for years, off and on. The guy has been with the British Army in Borneo and when he got back his mates had taken him to the pub and told him what she'd been up to with Tom. He waited for Tom outside his pub and attacked him repeatedly with a hammer, fracturing his skull in several places. Tom was rushed to hospital but died on the operating table.

I'm feeling very weird at the moment because I know I should put on a façade of the grieving widow, when all I feel inside is a giddy happiness. I've got to look sad for Alice, of course, so that helps me keep up the charade. She's very upset about Tom; he was her daddy as far as she was concerned, and we'll have to handle things between us carefully when you return.

I hope that last sentence wasn't too presumptuous, my darling. We can be together at last, and once a decent period has gone by then who knows what we might get up to?

Please write back as soon as you receive this, I'm longing to hear from you.

All my love.

Your adoring Sophie xx

33

THE END

The Douglas Dakota aeroplane was known as the workhorse of the war, flying millions of miles ferrying cargo, passengers and paratroopers to their destinations and destinies. The Douglas Corporation made thousands of them and they were well regarded by pilots as reliable and easy to fly. Flight Sergeants Ramage and McDuff, pilot and navigator for John's flight back to Croydon, were on their second trip of the day and were keen to get back before the weather closed in.

John strapped himself into his rudimentary seat as the first engine spluttered and fired, making such a shattering noise inside the metal fuselage that he temporarily lost his facility for coherent thought. He knew he'd be airsick, even with the medicine that the doctor at the base had given him, but such was his elation to be going back home he didn't care.

When Berlin was divided between the four Allied powers at the end of the war, it became a geographical island within Soviet East Germany. Planes flying west from Berlin towards Britain had to keep to an agreed air corridor as they flew over Soviet territory.

The arrangement had been respected by the Soviets and there'd been few incidents. If a plane strayed from the corridor as a result of a navigational error, it would be picked up on radar in Tempelhof and the pilot told to correct his course. Even if this system failed, as it could if radio communication was badly affected by a storm, there was a failsafe agreement with the Soviet air force. If an Allied plane unintentionally continued its journey into East German airspace, a fighter would be sent to intercept it. The Soviet pilot would make radio contact on an agreed frequency and instruct the Allied pilot to change course. If all else failed, the fighter pilot was allowed to fire a warning shot in front of the plane.

The outcome of the investigation into why a British Dakota had crashed into a field just east of the village of Gardelegen on the evening of 22nd November 1945, with the loss of everyone on board, was never made public. Neither side wished to create a diplomatic incident at an increasingly fractious time in Soviet-British relations. Sources close to the Air Ministry let it be known to their contacts in the press that pilot error was 'almost certainly' to blame. The bodies of passengers and crew, many burnt beyond recognition, were hastily buried in a communal grave to deter a forensic examination of the site.

On the anniversary of the crash in November 1990, after the border between East and West Germany had finally been taken down, a ninety-four-year-old woman made her way carefully along the gravel path to the site on the outskirts of Gardelegen, escorted by her daughter, Alice, and her husband and their son, John.

They slowly made their way towards a dark, discoloured marble slab, engraved with the names of those who'd perished on the flight.

Standing in front of the tombstone, remembering the handsome, confident young man walking up to her in the Golden

Slipper one night sixty-three years ago, Sophie took her daughter's hand and clearly read out the name of the only man she'd ever loved, smiling as tears ran down her cheeks.

"John Samson, British Scientist."

You were so much more, my darling man; a dearly loved companion, father, brother, uncle and son, and striver for a better world.

ACKNOWLEDGEMENTS

I would like to thank my wife Francesca for her amazing support. She's been my tireless reader, provider of perceptive feedback and 'on-call editor' throughout the time I was writing this novel. Thanks also to my close friends Philip, Farquhar, Alison and Neil for their invaluable help in reading and commenting frankly on early drafts. Finally, my thanks and appreciation to Rosie, Carolina and Emily from The Book Guild.